W9-CEC-967

THE HISTORY OF MAN

Siphiwe Gloria Ndlovu

AUTHOR OF *THE THEORY OF FLIGHT*

CATALYST PRESS
ANTHONY, TEXAS

Copyright © Siphiwe Gloria Ndlovu, 2022
All rights reserved.

No part of this book may be used or reproduced
in any manner whatsoever without written consent
from the publisher, except for brief quotations for reviews.

For further information, write Catalyst Press at
info@catalystpress.org

In North America, this book is distributed by
Consortium Book Sales & Distribution, a division of Ingram.
Phone: 612/746-2600
cbsdinfo@ingramcontent.com
www.cbsd.com

Originally published by Penguin Books,
an imprint of Penguin Random House South Africa,
in South Africa in 2020.

FIRST EDITION
10 9 8 7 6 5 4 3 2 1

Library of Congress Control Number: 2021940058

Cover design by Karen Vermeulen, Cape Town, South Africa

For my loving mother

and all her formidable grace

———◆———

PROLOGUE

————◆————

When news of the cease-fire arrived, on December 21, 1979, Emil Coetzee was washing blood off his hands. He watched the rust-colored water slosh up until it almost filled the white enamel basin and then he turned off the cold-water tap. It did not turn off entirely and water kept drip, drip, dripping into the basin, as though holding on to a memory. The water gurgled down the drain until it was a disappearing swirl. Next, Emil reached for the black plug that was, by some miracle, still attached to the sink. He pulled the plug up by its metal chain and pushed it in before turning on the hot-water tap and letting the scalding water rise halfway up the basin. Without having to look, he reached for the bottle of antiseptic liquid that was under the sink. As advertised, when he poured a capful of the liquid into the water it mushroomed into a cloud of purity. He submerged his hands into the water and his broken skin was thankful for all the many stings it felt. Emil was no Pontius Pilate, however, and so, next, he scrubbed his hands with a bar of lye soap until they were raw and red. As he dried them on the once-white cloth in the towel dispenser, he decided that this was to be his last day at the Organization of Domestic Affairs.

As always, he ignored the rarely used purple pump bottle of lavender-scented lanolin lotion that was stationed between the two taps. He had always felt that whoever had left it on the sink had meant it as a cruel joke. This was definitely not the place for sweet-smelling things.

Before he left the room, Emil peered at his reflection in the tarnished mirror above the water basin; his glance was brief as it always was now, and for the first time he noticed how tired he looked. He was weary, more weary of the world than any man in his fifties ought to be. After the bombastic hubris of youth and the blundering determination of adulthood, there was supposed to be blissful self-assuredness, was there not? Or was that self-assuredness only reserved for a particular kind of man, a man that he had not become?

He looked into his eyes to see what they carried within them. Nothing. Even on a day such as this, his eyes stared back blankly as though long unseeing.

Emil took one last look at the dark, gray, concrete room with its naked lightbulb that hung from the ceiling and bathed the room and its rudimentary furniture in a cold welcome. It was not much to gaze upon, to be sure, but this had been the crucible of his manhood. Emil tried to reconcile himself to this fact before he switched off the light and closed the door firmly behind him, shutting out the sound of the drip, drip, dripping tap.

Instead of taking the six flights of stairs to his office, he chose to take the elevator. He often avoided the lift and its proximity-induced forced camaraderie. However, with news of the cease-fire, he felt that the atmosphere in the lift would be somber and subdued enough to allow people to take complete notice of one another. Emil suddenly had the perverse desire to be seen—really seen. He wanted, just this once, for others to notice the oil-colored stains on his veldskoene and know, not just suspect, what he had been up to all these years.

When he entered the lift there were, in addition to the lift operator, two elderly ladies who were all rosewater and talcum powder, a tall man in a baby-blue safari suit, and a brunette with red-wine lipstick and Farrah Fawcetted hair.

Emil's supposition had been correct: the lift was filled with a stunned and solemn silence. The silence let Emil know that he was not alone—that he was not the only one who all of a sudden felt as if he was...hanging in the balance. The war had given them everything: an identity, a purpose, a state. It had made them feel a sense of belonging that had previously eluded them. The cease-fire had taken all that away and had done so without any hesitation.

Emil knew all the people in the lift. The two elderly ladies, Prudence and Prunella Pickford, were the spinster aunts of an ever-jolly man, Lars Pickford, who worked in the Processing department on the third floor; the man in the safari suit was Samuel Levi, who worked in the Accounts department on the fifth floor; the brunette, Cecelia Chatsworth, was engaged, perhaps even recently married, judging by the ring on her finger, to Claude McCloud, who worked in the Computer department on the second floor. Emil knew some of their histories: Prudence and Prunella had raised Lars since his parents had died in a road accident when he was a baby. They brought him freshly baked goods every day for his ten o'clock tea; Samuel Levi, who only wore pastel-colored polyester safari suits, had a penchant for being rather creative with the books and had been fired twice before being hired by The Organization of Domestic Affairs for this particular talent; Cecelia Chatsworth, or Mrs. Claude McCloud, as it were, believed that the country was surely going to the dogs and had recently resigned from her job as a teller at the CABS bank and now spent her time putting pressure on Claude to emigrate to South Africa.

Emil realized that the invitation to the McCloud wedding was probably lost in the pile of letters and correspondence that he had not bothered to open since Kuki had left him. She had always been the one to handle their considerably full social calendar and to arrange their very busy lives. Everyone in the lift, even the operator, knew that he and Kuki were separated; the City of Kings' size made it extremely difficult not to know your neighbor and his business. Feeling justifiably snubbed, Mrs. Claude McCloud was making a point of not catching Emil's eye. She, unfortunately, made the mistake of looking at his feet. Before she could stop herself, her eyes flew up at Emil's as she hastily got off on the second floor. He had expected his blood-stained shoes to elicit looks of horror, but Mrs. Claude McCloud had given him such a pitying glance that he found himself placing his hands in his pockets, as though to hide them.

As Emil got off on the sixth floor, he nodded stiffly to the operator who, once so acknowledged, smiled in relief. The smile made Emil try to recollect the young man's name; he had said it several times, at Emil's prompting, when they said good morning to each other, every morning before Emil took the stairs. The name would not come to Emil. It was one of those multisyllabic African names with more consonants than sense...a name like Sibonubuhle...no...no...no...that was not him but his tiredness talking. He managed to smile back at the operator before the doors closed, and that, at least, was something.

On this, his last day as The Head of The Organization of Domestic Affairs, Emil Coetzee entered his office and went to sit behind his desk. He picked up a black orb that had, embedded within it, a gorgeous multi-colored glittery twirl that created the sensation of looking into a vortex. He believed that he had received it as a present from his son, Everleigh. He could only believe this and not know it with certainty because he did not remember receiving it, but it was the sort of beautiful thing that his son would give, or, more precisely, would have given when he was younger. Emil had recently found the orb sitting on top of a forgotten pile of *National Geographic* magazines in his den at home and had decided to bring it to the office to use as a paperweight.

From under the paperweight that he believed, but no longer recalled with certainty, had been a gift from his son, Emil retrieved the only letter that Everleigh had ever written him. He knew the letter by heart and no longer had to physically read it, but he liked the materiality of the now flimsy and fragile paper in his hands—liked the weight, the burden of it. As Emil read the letter, he tried not to look at his hands.

You finally got your wish. You have always wanted me to kill something and now I have. I hope you are finally proud of me. I have become the son that you have always wanted.

He always read the ending aloud and let the words fill the silence of the office.

Although his hands were trembling when he finished reading the letter, he managed to carefully fold it and place it under the paperweight that may or may not have been a present from his son.

The reading of the letter from Everleigh was the first half of his morning ritual. For the second half of his morning ritual, Emil opened the top drawer of his desk and retrieved his wallet. He allowed his hands to become still before he opened it and took out five notes written in a left-leaning cursive on azure-colored paper. He placed the notes on top of his desk, in the order they had been received:

No. 1 Pioneer Road

There is a basin in the mind where words float around on

thought and thought on sound and sight. Then there is a depth of thought untouched by words and deeper still a gulf of formless feelings untouched by thought.
—Zora Neale Hurston

There are years that ask questions and years that answer.
—Zora Neale Hurston

Let's meet. We need to talk. H&S. Friday at 2 p.m.

When God had made The Man, he made him out of stuff that sung all the time and glittered all over. Then after that some angels got jealous and chopped him into millions of pieces, but still he glittered and hummed. So they beat him down to nothing but sparks but each little spark had a shine and a song. So they covered each one with mud. And the lonesomeness in the sparks make them hunt for one another.
—Zora Neale Hurston

The man that Emil truly was existed at a point somewhere between the letter from his son and the five notes from the woman that he loved. He wished that he could pinpoint the exact spot and know himself confidently and completely. He wanted to be assured, as other men in their fifties must be, but he was not. He imagined these men beholding their reflections in mirrors and feeling something specific like contentment, confidence, or resignation.

On the rare occasions that he looked at himself in the mirror, Emil never felt anything specific; his inner world was too unresolved for him to feel settled in it. All his life he had seemed only to be able to grasp at the edges of things, never to see or experience the whole, to find himself in the middle of something that had already begun. He could have very easily been another kind of man if he had known how to be anything else but himself.

Emil's thoughts were interrupted by a knock on the door. Before he could tell whoever it was to enter, a young woman let herself into his office. She wore an army jacket, khaki shorts, a white tank top with no bra underneath it, and hiking boots. A rucksack was carelessly slung over her right shoulder. It was a very calculated look that was meant to get the attention of men, Emil objectively observed.

She smiled at him and offered her hand for him to shake. One of her front teeth was discolored and Emil tried not to stare at its dull grayness as he shook her hand. He examined her entire face and noticed that she was not as young as she had at first appeared. There was a hardness about her that must have come with some of the necessary disappointments of age.

She carried with her a scent that was sickly sweet like the smell of decaying roses. The scent hung heavily in the air and soon filled the entire office.

"My name is Saskia Hargrave. I am a journalist with *The Chronicle*," she said, sitting herself down opposite Emil despite the fact that he had not asked her to. "I would like to write your story—a feature in *The Sunday News*."

That explained her aggressive behavior. She had commandeered the space around them because she meant to take charge of what came next, to corner him, to not take no for an answer.

"My story? I don't have a story," he said.

"You're Emil Coetzee, the head of The Organization," she retorted as though this was news to him. "Of course you have a story. You're one of the country's heroes."

"The country must be in a truly bad state if it has a man

like me for a hero."

Saskia appeared confused by this for a moment and then she blinked away her confusion. "Oh...I see. Humility. A nice touch."

She reached for her rucksack and retrieved her notebook and pen. She scribbled something hurriedly and then stared at him and smiled.

"Miss Hargrave," Emil said, as delicately as he could, "I really do not have a story for you."

"But you're the man of the hour," she said, her smile faltering slightly.

The smell of decaying roses soon overpowered Emil. He excused himself and went to open a bay window and stand by it for a moment. He gratefully breathed in the polluted air of the City of Kings.

"Emil?" Saskia said. "I was actually contemplating doing more than a feature...I would like to write your biography. Your life has just been so full, rich and exciting. Your story has to be told."

Emil clearly saw how it was with her. Saskia Hargrave believed that he was merely portraying false modesty and expecting to be flattered and so she was trying to flatter him. However, she was not particularly good at flattering people. Flattery was something newly acquired in her arsenal. Until recently, hubris had made her rely on the fact that she was young and attractive and could easily, therefore, invite the interest of men. She was young no longer and she was now at a loss because she had put all her power and sense of self in the most transient thing—youth.

Even so, she had been sure that she was still young and attractive enough to excite the interest of a middle-aged man, like him, who must be desperate to savor youth. That was why she had not worn a bra. She had wanted him to know, from the very first moment he saw her, that she was sexually available to him. Saskia Hargrave had been so sure that this tactic would work that she had not prepared herself for another outcome.

Emil was not a saint. The entire City of Kings knew this. Nevertheless, sinner though he was, he had long ago found the woman who would redeem him. He glanced over at the azure-colored notes on his desk and wondered how he could put them back in his wallet without bringing too much attention to them. Saskia Hargrave appeared to be a very inquisitive sort and so it was probably best for him to stay by the window and make her look at him and not the contents of his desk.

"Emil, things are changing in this country...rapidly. Men like you may very well be forgotten in a year or two. You want to be remembered, don't you?"

Did he want to be remembered? There had been a time when he had wanted nothing more than to make an impact and leave his mark—to be a man of history. But now that he had succeeded in realizing his dream, he felt almost certain that he should have wanted something else of his life.

"You want to be remembered, don't you?" Saskia Hargrave repeated, this time with uncertainty in her voice.

"Not particularly. At least not for the things that people know me for...the big events of my life. If I am to be remembered, I want to be remembered for the quieter...truer... moments of my life. I don't need a story for those...I need someone."

Saskia Hargrave smiled at him encouragingly, clearly misreading the situation.

"Luckily for me, I already have someone who retains those moments," Emil said, walking away from the window and making his way back to his desk.

"Your wife?" Saskia Hargrave asked, prying in order to mask her disappointment.

Emil merely smiled in response, aware that his smile did not encourage further inquiry.

As soon as Emil sat down at his desk, he noticed that one of the azure-colored notes was missing and that the folded letter was no longer under the paperweight and was now half-opened.

"Did you take one of the notes on my desk?" Emil asked as a courtesy. There was no other way to explain its disappearance. "Miss Hargrave?" Emil asked, making sure that she felt that those two words had been spoken not by the middle-aged man she had been trying, unsuccessfully, to flirt with and seduce, but by Emil Coetzee, The Head of The Organization of Domestic Affairs and one of the most powerful men in the country.

Saskia Hargrave tried to dissemble by smiling coquettishly as she retrieved an azure-colored piece of paper from her notebook.

"It is such a pretty color...I was just admiring it...forgot it was there. I was so absorbed by our conversation."

Emil made it a point to stare at her discolored tooth as she spoke. He did so until it became clear to her that there was nothing to be gained by not leaving immediately.

Once Saskia Hargrave was gone, Emil gazed down at the note.

There are years that ask questions and years that answer.
—Zora Neale Hurston

Emil put the note in its rightful place. He read all the notes over again and then placed them carefully, like perfect treasures, in his wallet.

He examined the half-opened letter and delicately folded it before placing it back under the paperweight.

His story, if it were ever told, would have to contain the lows of the letter and the highs of the notes. It would have to be told chronologically in a linear fashion, with a definite beginning, middle and end—none of that starting-in-the-middle-or-end modern nonsense. It would have to be told in this fashion because that was the only way to make any sense of the dark, gray, concrete room with its naked lightbulb, forever drip, drip, dripping tap and the man with blood on his hands.

PART ONE

———◆———

BOYHOOD -
A WALKING SHADOW

CHAPTER 1

———•———

Like most people who have truly loved, Emil Coetzee knew the exact moment that he fell in love for the first time and would remember it always. He was standing outside the government-issued, bungalow-style house with whitewashed walls and no veranda that he called home. His back was against the wall and his eyes were surveying the vast veld—this beautiful and golden great expanse—that lay before him.

It was a windy day that promised rain and the clouds were gathering gray in anticipation of the coming downpour. He peered up at the sky in time to see the clouds part and let the sun shine through brightly. God's visit. That was what his mother called this phenomenon. The sun had been there the entire time, hidden by the clouds. Emil marveled at this always-being-thereness of the sun and then reached his hand up to the sun as if to touch it. The sun disappeared behind the clouds again, but now Emil knew that it was there and felt comforted.

He gazed out at the veld and took in its vastness. The wild wind made the elephant grass sing and swoon before it came and kissed his face. Emil closed his eyes, placed the palms of both his hands against the whitewashed walls, took a deep breath and let the beauty of all that surrounded him enter his body. As that beauty traveled through his body, it turned into something else, and he knew that this thing that he felt in every fiber of his being, this wondrous and rarefied thing, this thing called love, was something that he would cherish all the days of his life.

Emil was six years old when he, at that moment master of all that he surveyed, beheld the veld and fell in love with it. This was to be his first concrete and complete memory. There would be other memories too, of the British South Africa Police outpost at the foot of the Matopos Hills, which was where the government-issued, bungalow-style house with whitewashed walls and no veranda that he called home was situated.

He remembered the sundowners that his parents, Johan and Gemma Coetzee, hosted every Friday evening and how his mother, in her black drop-waist dress and red cloche hat, would frenetically flap and flail the Charleston before his father joined her for a foxtrot promenade, while Emil, wrapped and rapt in admiration, happily sipped on lukewarm lime cordial.

He remembered walking into the singing elephant grass of the savannah, losing himself in it, all the while knowing that he had found his true self, that this was his natural habitat. He remembered his black shadow traveling the most beautiful land ever created as he explored the environs of the Matopos Hills. It was at this site that he could find all the heroes he had learned about in school: Cecil John Rhodes, Leander Starr Jameson, Charles Coghlan, Allan Wilson and the brave members of the Shanghai Patrol. It was here at "World's View" that they were buried or memorialized. The Matopos Hills was also the place where the god of the Matabele resided and where, accordingly, they came to ask for blessings, which for them always came in the form of rain. Proud men in loincloths and regal women in beads—rain dancers—would ascend the hills, then for hours there would be the sounds of drumming, stomping, ululating and shrieking, followed by an absolute silence that came before the rain dancers would descend the hills, looking, to Emil, as he watched in wonderment, as if they were carrying the solemn-looking clouds on their heads, shoulders, and backs.

But probably the most magnificent of all the things at the site were the San cave paintings that told the intricate story of the hunt, that is, the story of how man and animal moved toward and away from one another in a rhythm that became a dance of respect, honor, love and ultimately death. His father would take him to the Bambata, Nswatugi and Silozwane caves, hoist him on his broad shoulders and together they would decipher the paintings—writing, really— on the wall. The narratives were realistic and fair: sometimes man outmaneuvered animal, sometimes animal overpowered man. Emil always imagined himself to be part of the hunt; of all the things in the world, this was what he desired most, to test his might and mettle against that of an animal.

In his dreams, he was something beautifully wild and ferocious. He ran barefoot through the grasslands, carrying an assegai in his hand and knowing exactly when to strike at the heart of the dark, looming creature in his environment. He was a hero and the creature was something out of a fable. When he awoke his heart would be pounding with an excitement that made him jump out of bed and run around the small patch of land that constituted their front yard, yowling and brandishing an imagined weapon as he prepared himself to vanquish the creature of his dreams.

What Emil did not recollect of his childhood, his parents told him. According to them, he had been born, after a somewhat lengthy courtship and hasty marriage on their part, at the Sandhurst Private Hospital in Durban on 18 April 1927. Six months later he was baptized and christened Emil Coetzee. Possibly hoping to have the relationship with his son that he had not had with his father, Johan had proudly named his son Emil after his father. While this would prove to be a rather damning inheritance in many ways, none of those ways were apparent at the moment of christening.

Although his name was Afrikaans, and his father's name, Johan Coetzee, was also Afrikaans, Emil had in fact, for all intents and purposes, been born into an English family. This was because Johan was the product of a relatively short-lived and ill-fated union between a rambling ne'er-do-well called Emil Coetzee and a dancer named Bethany Miller. When he was still in his swaddling clothes, Johan's mother had taken him to a home for orphans, waifs, and strays that was run by the Pioneer Benevolence Society of the City of Kings. Her name was registered as Bethany Miller and her occupation listed as "dancer," which, as Johan grew older, he began to appreciate was a euphemism for something else entirely. Johan came to know of his father's name and lack of righteousness because his mother had had enough time to tell the ladies of the Pioneer Benevolence Society of the City of Kings both these things before leaving her newborn baby son in their care. Consequently, whenever the young Johan did anything that was construed as vaguely untoward, he was warned vehemently against becoming like his father, Emil Coetzee, and, as a result, all Johan had received from his father was his last name, Coetzee.

Bethany Miller had left Johan at the Pioneer Benevolence Society of the City of Kings without so much as a final glance. This last detail Johan always added to prevent himself from feeling overly sentimental and thus romanticizing the memory of the woman who had abandoned him. It was at the Pioneer Benevolence Society of the City of Kings that Johan received a very thorough and very proper English education. He later used this education to apply for a post in the British South

Africa Police and soon, by his nineteenth birthday, became a traffic controller.

This was a new position and both the BSAP and the young colony were extremely proud of having need of persons to conduct their traffic, because it showed not only that the country was growing, but that it was moving forward in a civilized fashion. Whereas in the early days the city fathers had been content to allow the barely manageable melee— the ox-drawn wagons whose span dictated the width of the city's avenues, the horse-drawn carriages driven by the affluent, the donkey-drawn scotch carts that were often unpredictable, the always-speeding Zeederberg mail and passenger coaches, the zigzagging joyous jinrickshas, the always-on-the-go Raleigh, Rover and Hercules bicycles, and the hundreds of constantly to-ing and fro-ing feet—to create its own rhyme and reason, now that that most modern invention, the automobile, was added to this commotion, they no longer felt safe leaving everything to chance. Man had long had mastery of himself and the animal, but the machine was something altogether different. Order would now have to be created out of the chaos and the BSAP happily provided the men that would do so.

And so, with a starched and ironed crisp khaki uniform, a polished silver whistle and a bleached pair of white gloves, Johan stood in the middle of the muddle and set it to rights. He did more than that, however—he performed his task with the grace, poise and mastery of not merely a conductor but a maestro, a virtuoso at his craft. It was pleasure in itself to watch him work.

The details of how well his father performed his job were contributed by Emil's mother. She did not tell her son these details solely because she was proud of how well the man who would become her husband did his job; she told her son these details because they helped usher in the part of the story that she loved to tell best of all: the part where she, Gemma Roberts, entered it, brought forward by a force of nature.

An overly enthusiastic gust of wind had blown off Gemma's straw hat just as she was crossing the intersection of Borrow Street and Selborne Avenue, and she had chased after it unaware of, absolutely oblivious to, the fact that she had stopped traffic on both streets as she ran, giggling, through the intersection.

The way she had laughed, her blonde hair blowing riotously in the wind, had made Johan instantly fall in love with her carefree spirit. Instead of doing his job as the traffic controller, Johan had selfishly stopped traffic on Borrow Street and Selborne Avenue and ignored the hooting, braying, and neighing. At that moment all he wanted in the world was to watch the girl with the golden hair and experience her for as long as possible.

When he next saw her, a few days later, Johan had asked her for her name and she had given it to him: Gemma Roberts. She gently rocked her body beautifully from side to side, blushed, and batted impossibly long eyelashes up at him as she also gave him her address, even though he had not asked for it. As Johan wrote down her details he was glad that she did not know that his palm itched with the desire to touch her. He feared that she could hear his thumping heartbeat and worried that the sweat collecting on his brow would give the game away.

If she noticed any of this, Gemma had not been much affected by it for she had long been aware of the traffic controller's maestro-like movements and matinee-idol good looks and in her mind he was as near to perfection as any man had any right to be.

Gemma gave Johan her name and her address in full view of those who were traveling on Borrow Street and Selborne Avenue, even though she had spent many a morning in Beit Hall with other girls in brown cotton dresses with Peter Pan collars whose straw-hatted heads were all turned at the same angle toward the headmistress, Miss Grace Milne Langdon, as she warned them about the inherent dangers of fraternizing with the male of the species and strictly forbade them to do so in public, for an Eveline girl had to live each moment of her life with grace, dignity, and decorum. Gemma took secret pleasure in the knowledge that her schoolmates from Eveline High School, who stood gawking at the intersection of Borrow Street and Selborne Avenue, were, at that very moment, eating their hearts out.

As Johan frowned down at the address that Gemma had given him, she explained to him that, as she was seventeen, this was to be her last year at Eveline High School and that he would have to write to her when she got home to Durban. In fact, it was the very last day of her last term at the school. Gemma thought, but did not say, how serendipitous she felt their meeting like this at the eleventh hour was. And she felt certain that this man, Johan Coetzee, was to be her destiny.

Gemma received her first letter from Johan on 5 January 1921 and although it was written on BSAP official stationery and written with a pen whose ink tended to bleed and run, she chose to overlook these facts because the words themselves practically amounted to a declaration of Johan Coetzee's undying love for her and made her heart sing and soar. Gemma found the idea of a courtship conducted solely via correspondence utterly romantic; this was very much like being a Victorian heroine and she could barely bear it. It occurred to her that, in entering her life, Johan had removed it from its trajectory of continued ordinariness and elevated it to a higher plane. As all great love stories with magical beginnings and happily-ever-after endings bloomed from the same bud that their own story had, Gemma had no choice but to feel very optimistic about her future.

She responded promptly, unabashedly protesting her own feelings of love on baby-pink writing paper decorated with silver and gold curlicues woven together to look like butterflies dancing at the margins. She wrote delicately and deliberately, with more care than she had ever written any- thing in her life, because she wanted Johan to make out every word and fully comprehend its meaning. After which she care- fully folded the letter into four equal quarters and placed it in the waiting pink envelope. Just as she was about to seal the envelope she realized that she had forgotten something and gently removed the folded letter. She cautiously sprinkled a few drops of rosewater onto it, making sure not to interfere with the ink, and then placed the letter in the envelope that was already addressed to Constable Johan Coetzee of the BSAP.

Two weeks after Gemma had sent her letter, she, at this point breathless with anticipation, received another from Johan. His second letter was also written on BSAP stationery, but this time the ink did not bleed and run. Gemma noted this with great satisfaction. Thus began the love story of Gemma and Johan. Letters were sent back and forth containing words that brought their bearers to a fever pitch of passion and on several occasions made both the writer and the recipient blush profusely.

And so their courtship continued until a fateful day late in July when the letter written on BSAP stationery was inter- cepted by Mrs. Williams.

Mrs. Williams was Gemma's maternal grandmother,

whom she lived with because her own mother had married Anthony Simons, and he did not much take to the idea of children—his own or anyone else's. Gemma's mother had, six months before her marriage to Anthony Simons, been widowed by Gemma's father, Philip Roberts, who had never been quite the same after his service during the Great War. Gemma's mother had been planning to divorce him before he was mercifully taken by the Spanish flu while recuperating in a sanatorium.

When Gemma's mother had remarried, she—believing that absence would make the heart grow fonder—was glad that Gemma attended a school that was as far away from Durban as it was possible to be. But when Gemma finished school a year later, Anthony Simons still proved intransigent when it came to children, and so Gemma found herself living with her grandmother, Mrs. Williams, which was what she had done every school holiday since the strain in her parents' marriage had first appeared.

This arrangement perfectly suited almost all involved as Mrs. Williams ran a boarding house, The Williams Arms, and, although elderly and often infirm, preferred to have a hand in the running of her establishment. Given that Mrs. Williams's idea of "having a hand in" consisted of barking orders from the comfort of her armchair, Gemma served as her much-needed eyes, ears, hands and feet.

On that fateful day in July when Mrs. Williams (and that was what Gemma called her grandmother, not "grandmother," not "Grandma," not "Nana," not anything affectionate, but Mrs. Williams—and this at the behest of her grandmother) intercepted the BSAP letter, she had come upon Gemma smiling to herself by the Welcome Dover stove in the kitchen while a meal she was preparing was burning to a charred crisp right in front of her.

Mrs. Williams had immediately deduced that something was afoot and, when the mail arrived, fetched it herself. She opened the letter from the BSAP clumsily with her stubby and arthritic fingers and in the process tore the envelope, not knowing or caring that previously all envelopes received from the BSAP had been opened with great care by a silver letter opener with a fleur-de-lis handle. Mrs. Williams had read the letter...well, not much of it, actually, she only read the name Johan Coetzee, and could read no more because all she could see was red. She had lost her two sons in the Anglo–Boer War, one on the battlefield and the other to dysentery, but she laid both their deaths at the door of the Afrikaners. After these deaths she had been left with only one child, and that child had grown up to give birth to a child who would, in turn, grow up to have something to do with an Afrikaner. This could not be borne. Grabbing Gemma by the hair and parading her through The Williams Arms, Mrs. Williams told her just as much.

All appeared to be doomed. Gemma allowed her heart to break. She let herself cry and mope...and to feel "blue," as the music from America suggested she should when dealing with disappointed hopes. Blue...she liked the color of the emotion, liked that she could feel it because her heart was broken, liked that her heart was broken not because she had been jilted but because Mrs. Williams, after everything the Boers had taken from her, would not countenance (her word) an Afrikaner for a grandson-in-law, liked that there was something wonderfully tragic about the whole affair.

Gemma's mother had done right by her, probably for the first time in her life, when, on one of the rare occasions she visited her daughter, she spirited away a letter addressed to the BSAP and two weeks later clandestinely gave Gemma a letter written on BSAP stationery. Gemma was ecstatic that in his letter Johan said that he would wait for her no matter how long it took, till his dying breath if need be. Ooohhh...it was all just too romantic for words. Gemma, like Bessie Smith, had the Downhearted Blues, but also the satisfaction of knowing that her man still loved her.

Luckily for Johan, he did not have to wait until his dying breath because a few years after the clandestine letter arrived, Mrs. Williams suffered a massive stroke that left her speechless and even more dependent on Gemma. Gemma happily nursed her grandmother and, while caring for her, chiseled away incessantly at Mrs. Williams's prejudice, at least where Johan Coetzee was concerned.

Johan was truly the best of men. Both his parents had died and left him to be raised by the exceptionally English ladies of the Pioneer Benevolence Society of the City of Kings. His mother—yes, she believed Johan had mentioned this in one of his letters—had been very English before her death.

So you see, apart from the name, which Gemma agreed was rather unfortunate, Johan Coetzee was as English as they came. And truly there was nothing else to be done because he had captured her heart as no other man ever could or would.

Gemma was relentless in her pursuit of her grandmother's blessings and after almost three years had passed, Mrs. Williams made a sound in the back of her throat before resignedly nodding her head. Gemma chose to interpret this as her grandmother's resounding consent to her union with Johan Coetzee.

An elated Gemma wrote to Johan immediately, but in place of a letter arriving within the fortnight, Johan Coetzee himself appeared and did so just in time because Gemma was on the verge of feeling truly blue. She was happy to see that he was even more dashing and handsome than she had remembered him to be and so, quite naturally, she fell in love with him all over again.

Weakened and suffering the humiliation of defeat, Mrs. Williams had no choice but to welcome into her home something she had never thought she would in her long-living life—an Afrikaner. And perhaps she made Johan feel too welcome because...well, because events transpired that made it necessary for Johan Coetzee and Gemma Roberts to be married on 18 December 1926, exactly four months before Emil was born.

Emil would live the first five years of his life with his mother and Mrs. Williams and the several tenants who had rooms at The Williams Arms. He would recall nothing of this time: of the frequent trips to the nearby Indian Ocean; of the waiting patiently with his mother for his father to arrive at the train station on one of his many visits; of the tropical vegetation that his mother loved and would always long for after Mrs. Williams had peacefully died in her sleep and Johan had come to take his wife and son away from the life that had been theirs.

Before Mrs. Williams died there had been talk of Johan moving to Durban to help take care of the boarding house, but Anthony Simons, whose fortunes, like the fortunes of many, had drastically changed in 1929, made his wife take over the running of The Williams Arms after Mrs. Williams died and let it be known that he still had not changed his mind about having children about him.

By the time Johan came to take Gemma and Emil to what they would all, from then on, call their home and what the BSAP accommodation listings described as a government-issued, bungalow-style house with whitewashed walls and no veranda, he was no longer a traffic controller. He had been promoted up the ranks to first sergeant and been assigned to man a BSAP outpost at the foot of the Matopos Hills.

It was here, at the foot of the Matopos Hills, that Emil would have his first memory and fall in love so effortlessly with the veld. It was here that his mother, missing the humidity of Durban and suffering through the dryness of the savannah, would tell him stories, all of which began with a girl wearing an Eveline High School uniform who, in chasing her straw hat across the intersection of Borrow Street and Selborne Avenue, captured the heart of Johan Coetzee, a truly remarkable man.

To illustrate the highlights of her story, his mother often produced photographs of the moments she described and this is how Emil knew that he had walked into the Indian Ocean for the first time holding his mother's and father's hands, that he had once stood in a cloud of smoke tearfully waving goodbye to his father at a train station, that he had sat on his mother's lap playing with her string of pearls while she wore a black dress and mourned the grandmother she had only been allowed to call Mrs. Williams. His mother told these stories with such great detail that he could see images, even those that had not been captured on celluloid clearly in his mind's eye.

Yet, try as he might, Emil could not feel a real connection to these memories; though they formed a part of his life, the images they conjured did not move with the pace of real life. The people contained in these memories—his younger self, his in-love parents, his formidable-but-frail great-grandmother, his twice-married grandmother, his shell-shocked grandfather, his paedophobic step-grandfather, his dancing paternal grandmother, his never-doing-well paternal grandfather and namesake, the very English ladies of the Pioneer Benevolence Society of the City of Kings, the tenants of The Williams Arms, the people traveling on Borrow Street and

Selborne Avenue, the rows upon rows of Eveline girls with their straw-hatted heads turned at the same angle toward Miss Langdon, the soldiers fighting the Anglo–Boer War and the Great War—all lived in a black-and-white world in which their movements seemed slightly speeded up so that everything they did appeared somewhat awkward, hesitant, and haphazard. Their rare smiles, which were bashful, seemed to have been coerced, and all around them was a silence so profound that one felt afraid of breaking it. Their inhabited world was so pristine that all Emil could feel for it was a deep-seated nostalgia that would not allow him to connect further for fear of contaminating its bygoneness.

CHAPTER 2

In the beginning of the Coetzees' life together at the foot of the Matopos Hills, there was a happiness that made itself most manifest during the sundowners that Gemma and Johan hosted at their government-issued, bungalow-style house with whitewashed walls and no veranda, where they held captive an audience of their son, Emil, and Johan's deputies, Scott Fitzgerald and Walter Musgrave.

When they had first arrived at the outpost that was but a stone's throw from the Rhodes Matopos National Park, Gemma had been worried because Johan had honestly told her that they and his two deputies were the only Europeans within a ten-kilometer radius. The only other Europeans they would occasionally see were tourists, the day trippers and sightseers that came to visit the national park. Even if Johan did not say it, they both thought it—Gemma was the only white woman for miles around. It was 1933, so by then they had both, separately, read or heard about the Black Peril, and they had both, separately, been frightened by it. Keeping a brave front, neither of them voiced their fears to the other. They chose, instead, to focus on finally being able to live together and start a life together.

As it turned out, there had been nothing to fear. The natives in the nearby village paid very little attention to Gemma except when she did something that amused them, like hiding from the sun, standing in the rain, having her servants transport water from the river so that they could do the laundry in the yard (when it could far more conveniently be washed in the river), having cold, raw vegetables served to her family as part of supper, painting her face even when there was no special occasion or ceremony and buying feeding bottles as presents for the pregnant women in the village, bottles she was always upset to see put to other, more practical uses.

On second thoughts, maybe the natives did pay Gemma a lot of attention, but that was because she did much to amuse them. She gave the distinct impression of having things upside down and back to front. She was cock-eyed or rather kokayi, as their tongues had transmogrified the word. It was a word that the villagers who worked in the industries of the City of Kings had brought back with them to the village in the same way that they had brought back mirrors, tins of that greatest creation of all, condensed milk, and the knowledge that the Europeans, using a highly esoteric system, had deemed them to be an inferior species of human. "Cock-eyed" had fast become a familiar term as it was used often by their baas to chastise them and make them feel inadequate, small or lacking. Like most of the things that they brought back from the city, the word was part of a shift in the order of things. Perhaps in an effort to make things right again, "kokayi" was used often by the natives whenever Gemma Coetzee did something out of the ordinary. But if any of them intended to make her feel inadequate, small or lacking, they found that they did not have the power to humiliate her.

Since there was genuinely nothing to fear from the natives save the occasional giggle or shake of the head, Gemma relaxed and became happy. She was, after all, the only white woman within a ten-kilometer radius, and therefore something quite exotic, like a rare bird with exquisite plumage that attracted ornithologists from far and wide. During those

Friday sundowners she held three European men and one European boy in her sway. They loved her and she loved to be loved by them. Scott Fitzgerald said that she resembled Janet Gaynor; Walter Musgrave swore she resembled Carole Lombard; and, for her part, Gemma was happy to be anywhere between these two points—angel or vixen—because it meant that her beauty was of a screen-siren quality. She found it comforting to be considered so beautiful that the entire world would want to gaze upon her.

Scott Fitzgerald, who had absolutely no desire to be a policeman all his life, made no secret of the fact that he was using Gemma as his muse for what was to be his first novel. Gemma happily allowed him to find inspiration in her because she could readily see that there was poetry in his soul and that, because of this, they were kindred. Walter Musgrave, after he had met Gemma, would spend his days off no longer painting watercolor landscapes of the veld around them or the Matopos Hills, but would, instead, have her sit for him so that he could immortalize her on canvas because she was, according to him, the ideal of beauty and femininity. Gemma contentedly basked in the warm glow of both men's adoration and felt that life on the BSAP outpost would never be anything but good.

Johan did not mind the unguarded attention that his wife received from his two deputies because he loved his wife and knew that she genuinely loved him too. Several years of fevered and fervored correspondence had made him confident in their love for each other. Besides, Scott Fitzgerald and Walter Musgrave could not have known of the nights when Gemma, while performing a tantalizing striptease, would sing with persuasive breathlessness about how much she wanted to be loved by Johan and nobody else but Johan.

Yes, Gemma was happy because she was the jewel in the crown, the apple of every European eye that fell upon her in the outpost. She did not mind that her days were usually taken over by an easy ennui because it happily unshackled itself on Fridays and gave way to a frenzied furor as Gemma reinvented herself as something she had fantasized being, but had, in reality, been too busy to be: a flapper girl.

In their collective imagination, Gemma became the quintessential 1920s carefree, daring, and modern woman. And this image that they had of her was true...to an extent. She had danced the Charleston in wild abandon at Durban's Kenilworth Tea Rooms on more than one occasion, and because one could not dance the Charleston in wild abandon at the Kenilworth Tea Rooms and expect to be taken seriously without the proper attire, Gemma had bought herself, for her twentieth birthday, a bright red cloche hat and, to complete the look, her mother, during a rare act of motherliness, had bought her a black chiffon and lace drop-waist dress that came to her knees. So, despite the fact that she had spent most of the 1920s in a long courtship with Johan and helping Mrs. Williams cater to her tenants' needs, Gemma had felt herself to have been carefree, daring and very modern through it all. She felt in her heart of hearts that she still possessed these qualities at the foot of the Matopos Hills and proved this by donning her red cloche hat and black chiffon and lace drop-waist dress and dancing with abandon at every sundowner on the patch of grass that masqueraded as a lawn and stood where a veranda should have been. The 1930s were not like the 1920s—1929 had seen to that and sobered the world—but those on the outpost did not have to let go of the heavenly 1920s, not as long as they had Gemma to play the happy, wild, and enticing flapper girl.

Gemma's gesticulations amused the natives to no end because they knew that she considered the enthusiastic flailing of her arms and legs dancing, which it most certainly was not. Nevertheless, as she danced to "You're the Cream in My Coffee," Gemma's European audience was enthralled. Sometimes Johan, not much of a dancer himself, became so enraptured by the thrill in Gemma's movements that he would join her in a foxtrot promenade, a dance that Emil would always remember in beautiful and brilliant Technicolor.

Life on the outpost would have continued uninterrupted on this steady path that showed every sign of leading to only more happiness...if a native girl had not arrived on the patch of grass that masqueraded as a lawn and stood where a veranda should have been. But the native girl had arrived carrying a baby boy with skin the color of tea with milk in it and a generous spray of curly sand-colored hair and their arrival changed everything.

The native girl had asked for Walter and this—not the presence of the native girl or the existence of the light-brown baby in her arms, but the fact that she had simply asked for Walter—was what struck Gemma the most. She had not asked for baas, or Mr. Musgrave, or Mr. Walter—just Walter. The native girl had not cast her eyes down as she spoke to Gemma, as the short history lived together with the Europeans had taught most natives to do. Uncharacteristically, and rather defiantly, the native girl had looked Gemma in the eye, shifted the baby on her hip, and said, "I ask to see Walter."

Instead of responding, Gemma clutched at her throat, which made a gurgling sound as she stifled a primitive and primal scream. The omnipresent heat had, at that moment, become unexpectedly oppressive. Gemma felt the back of her neck grow very hot before she suddenly became light-headed. In the confusion of her light-headedness, she became determined. She had been born in Africa; there was no way the unforgiving heat would affect her. She raised her chin rebelliously and tilted it against the heat before falling on her kitchen floor in a fainted heap.

Gemma must have hit her head on the concrete floor because she woke up with a bump on her forehead and a migraine. The now oppressive heat was still there. The native girl and the baby boy were also still there. The only thing new was Walter Musgrave walking toward her carrying a glass of water in one hand and gesturing toward the native girl and the baby boy with the other. "I see you have met Lili and my son," Walter Musgrave said casually, without the slightest hint of the mortification he surely must have felt on such an occasion and at having been thus discovered. "Somewhat incorrigible is our Lili," Walter Musgrave went on, offering Gemma the glass of water. The water in the glass was steady, suspiciously so. Gemma examined the hand that carried the glass of water and noticed that it did not tremble. The hand was as steady as the heartbeat of a saint. "She does not think that the rules of propriety apply to her," Walter Musgrave said with something very much like indulgent affection in his voice. Gemma stared at the mouth that had uttered these words, the very mouth that had told her that she was the epitome of beauty and femininity, and finally understood its treachery.

"Get out!" Gemma snarled before hitting the glass of water out of Walter Musgrave's hand and onto the wall. With a little satisfaction, he watched the glass shatter and then litter the floor with tiny, dangerous pieces that gleamed like diamonds in the dust. That was all she had energy for before she crumpled back into a forlorn heap.

Gemma had been too distraught throughout this entire scene to notice her son watching it unfold from within the shadows of his room. Maybe she would have acted better had she known that she had an audience.

Nothing was the same after that. Walter Musgrave was

sent to another outpost and evidently had taken the native girl, Lili, and the light-brown baby boy, his son, with him.

"While he just refuses to do the proper thing, he says he knows that he is doing the right thing," Johan explained to a still dejected Gemma.

"Somewhat incorrigible is our Walter," Gemma replied, trying to sound as nonchalant as she could not feel. "He does not think that the rules of propriety apply to him." To her deep dismay, she noticed that her hands were trembling uncontrollably as she said this.

Just like that, the roaring sundowners became a thing of the past. Gemma spent most of her days in bed feeling blue and complaining about the oppressive heat, which just would not abate. There goes madam, hiding from the sun again, the natives said, amused, after not having seen Gemma for days on end. She will be out when the rain falls, they collectively conjectured and then carried on with their lives. So, when the rain finally fell and Gemma hid from it too, the natives were not amused. The natives were worried. They had heard stories of madams who had been driven mad or been killed by the very climate that had nurtured them for centuries.

Their madam had appeared to be made of sterner stuff than these storied madams but perhaps she was not and perhaps they should have been wary of the easy way in which she had immediately appeared to be at home amongst them. They began to appreciate that, quite possibly, there was more to the ways of Europeans than there appeared to be on the surface.

For his part, Johan was eager to make Gemma happy again, but all his efforts were in vain because he could not successfully do anything about the heat that she now found stifling. He bought a fan and a refrigerator, both at great expense to himself, but neither ameliorated the situation. He made a request to the BSAP to have extra windows added to the house. Predictably, the request was denied because government-issued homes could not be modified.

Since nothing could be done about the fact that she was baking herself mad in a government-issued oven, Gemma wanted to live elsewhere. She wanted to live in a house that belonged not to the government but to Johan Coetzee, a house that she could modify to suit her needs and tastes, a house that she could make herself comfortable in. The house that belonged to Johan began to take shape in Gemma's mind. It was a colonial-style house with French windows, a red wraparound veranda and an English rose garden. Gemma spent most afternoons in bed furnishing this imagined house with the best ball-and-claw furniture, the finest delicate china and the most modern kitchen appliances that money could buy. The house was so perfect and so very much theirs that Gemma began to yearn to live in it. She was convinced that the happiness and love they would feel in this house would be everlasting because they would not be government-issued emotions but, rather, the proud property of the Coetzees.

The house of Gemma's imagination became such a concrete thing that Johan began to see it and long to live in it as well. Still, even in his dreaming, Johan was practical enough to know that they could only live in such a house if he got a promotion, and so he applied for one, a year before he was eligible. Unfortunately, the BSAP, at this particular moment in its history, was being audited and investigated for corruption and thus, having to be seen doing everything by the book, had no choice but to soundly reject Johan's application.

At the end of his tether, Johan suggested to Gemma that she take Emil to Durban until such a time as he could provide her with the life she so desperately wanted. However, since The Williams Arms was now being run by her mother and

Anthony Simons, and Gemma did not relish spending time with people who had not only cheated her of her rightful inheritance but had also always made her feel as unwanted as an unwelcome guest, Johan's suggestion was not taken up.

Gemma stopped listening to the jazz that had made her so happy and returned to her roots, the blues. The somber tones of Bessie Smith's voice traveled through the Master's Voice gramophone and enveloped Gemma in a melancholic sadness that gave her purpose. She spent entire days exploring the many byways of her heavy moods and emotions. She did not have to do anything but feel blue and she did so wholeheartedly, minutely examining every emotion for sufficient blueness and heaviness. The byways that she traveled inevitably led back to that first letter she had received, seemingly a lifetime ago now, the letter that had arrived on BSAP stationery, the letter that had been written with a bleeding pen. Gemma saw now what she had not seen then—that the letter had not been written with much care, and that there was something she desperately needed that the letter writer could not provide. She was not altogether sure what that something was but she was sure that the missing of it was making her blue.

She did not stop loving Johan, though—he looked too much like Douglas Fairbanks Jr. for any woman in her right mind not to love him. She just saw him with clarity now and that clarity made it near impossible for her to get out of bed every morning.

Not knowing the inner workings of his mother's mind, Emil, at eight, believed that the reason his parents no longer danced to "You're the green in my coffee; you're the salt in my shoe" at sundown on the patch of grass that masqueraded as a lawn and stood where a veranda should have been while he sipped on lukewarm lime cordial had everything to do with the fact that he had "gone native" as his mother now often screamed to him that he had.

Although he kept this to himself, Emil knew that he had grown a little wild because of a recurring dream... a nightmare, really. This nightmare of a dream had regrettably taken the place of his favorite dream, the one about the hunt. In the nightmare he would come home, from the government school for natives that he attended, to find the government-issued, bungalow-style house with whitewashed walls and no veranda empty. Emil would put his rucksack on the kitchen table and the eerie emptiness of the rest of the house would fill his body with apprehension. He would enter and thoroughly check all the rooms of the house and in each room his parents would not be there. When the apprehension turned to fear, he would return to the kitchen to find the native girl and the baby boy with light-brown skin sitting at the very table where his rucksack lay, and the native girl would ask him what he was doing in her house. When he opened his mouth to tell her that he lived in the house with his mother and father, instead of words coming out, the howl of a wounded animal would escape from his throat. The native girl, seeming to perfectly understand the animal sound, would respond and tell him that she and her baby had always lived there. Emil, not knowing what else to do, would howl an apology and run out of the house, instantly regretting that he had left his rucksack behind. He would loiter outside the house waiting for Walter Musgrave to arrive so that he could explain the situation to him. No longer trusting that he would reliably find his voice, he would repeat his name over and over again—Emil...Coetzee...Emil...Coetzee...Emil...Coetzee—until he felt assured that he was still capable of language. But then a question would rudely present itself: what made him so sure that the house belonged to Walter Musgrave?

When Emil woke up from this dream, he struggled to breathe. He was afraid of both the emptiness that his parents created by not being there and the presence that the native girl and baby boy with light-brown skin created by being there. His situation became so dire that sometimes he did not have to dream that emptiness or that presence; he just had to conjure it up and his throat would tighten up and he would start to wheeze.

This recurring dream unsettled Emil and made him feel disconnected, as if he did not belong. It threatened to rob him of that deep love, so much like reverence, that he had breathed in through his first memory. Before, he had gone exploring because of the beauty of the land that lay all around him, but now he did so because he only felt at peace when he glanced down at the black shadow that he cast over the veld and felt it connect him to all that surrounded him. And so he spent more time in the veld than he did in the government-issued, bungalow-style house with whitewashed walls and no veranda. After all, it was there, in the middle of the yellow, green, red and brown savannah grasslands, that he truly belonged. It was there that he was at home.

CHAPTER 3

———— ✦ ————

By choosing a post that would settle the Coetzees in the City of Kings, Johan was eventually able to make Gemma happy again. Sadly, this solution came at a great cost to Johan, as he had to accept something of a demotion within the BSAP when he left the outpost two years earlier than initially agreed upon. As a result, he could not buy the colonial-style house with French windows, a red wraparound veranda and an English rose garden that had long existed vividly in Gemma's imagination. What he could do was rent a flat—Flat 2A to be exact—at the Prince's Mansions, which were located on the corner of Borrow Street and Selborne Avenue, opposite Eveline High School, overlooking the very intersection where Johan had first laid eyes on Gemma and fallen in love with her blowing blonde hair and giggling pink lips.

When Gemma saw the flat and gazed out of their bedroom window to see the very spot where her very own Douglas Fairbanks Jr. had first approached her, she felt the romance of it all, and the house of her dreams was immediately forgotten and Johan was forever forgiven. The man that she had married might not have been able to give her her own home, but he was able to give her a testament to his deep awareness of her romantic nature. Why would Gemma ever need her own English rose garden to tend when she could forever gaze on the place where her true love had first blossomed?

Not only was the intersection of Borrow Street and Selborne Avenue the location of their first meeting, it was also the heart of the city, and Gemma was soon determined to be part of its heartbeat. If the City of Kings had an oppressive heat, Gemma did not feel it. She was too busy to feel anything but happiness. Besides, if a day in the city did present itself with any heat worth feeling, she could always go to the Municipal Bathing Pools on Borrow Street with Johan, Emil, or by herself. Of an evening, if Gemma found that she needed cooling down, all she had to do was put on her best dress, accept Johan's arm, and walk a short distance down Selborne Avenue to the theatre. All of life's pleasures were suddenly within easy reach.

Gemma was so contented that she finally said goodbye to the halcyon days of the Roaring Twenties and accepted the more sober joys of the 1930s by becoming a member of the Women's Institute. Soon enough she began to take a genuine pleasure in making her own tea cozies, embroidering and crocheting her own tablecloths, baking Victoria sandwiches for cake sales and baking competitions, and painstakingly embossing the linen with the words *Mr. and Mrs. J. Coetzee.*

To top off this new-found contentedness, Gemma's mind was finally at peace again when Emil started attending Milton School on Selborne Avenue. On the BSAP outpost, he had attended the only school available in the vicinity, which was the government school that had been begrudgingly built for the natives. He attended the school because it had been suggested to his father, by the governor, that this would be the best way to encourage education in the region. Native education, as long as it was not of a very high standard or to a very high degree, was instrumental to the successful running of a self-governing colony. Gemma, who felt certain that Emil was receiving a negligible education at the school, agreed to this arrangement with the understanding that when he was nine, before any real damage had been done, Emil would attend Milton School in the City of Kings. She had imagined that he would attend the school as a boarder and this had filled her with guilt and apprehension, and so she was ever so pleased when the move to the Prince's Mansions meant that she could walk him to and from school.

For his part, Emil could not bring himself to love the City of Kings—its wide avenues lined with jacarandas, flamboyants and acacias, its concrete buildings, its rail-line arteries, its noisy motor cars, its parks manicured to unnaturalness, its factories constantly exhaling smoke into the air, its traffic robots that had made the jobs of traffic controllers almost obsolete. When he surveyed the city, all he saw was a miasma and all he heard was a cacophony and he was convinced that he could never be at home in such a place.

Emil blamed himself for the move away from the BSAP outpost at the foot of the Matopos Hills. How could he not? He assumed that the move was all because he had gone native. Being in the city did not help matters; the nightmare of the native girl who had a light-brown baby persisted, more frequently now that he was away from his natural environment. The nightmare took on more ominous and terrifying details. Whenever he tried to scream his name into the veld, all that came out was the howl of the wounded animal, and when he glanced at the black shadow he cast, it was no longer his shadow but that of an animal-like thing walking on all fours. In the dream he would put his hands out in front of him and expect to see a pair of paws or hooves, but the expectation was never fulfiled because he could never bring himself to discover what existed at the end of his outstretched arms.

Inevitably, Emil's wheezing chest worsened in the City of Kings. It was all because of the pollution from the motor vehicles, trains, and smoke-stacks, Dr. Stromberg explained to Gemma before letting her know that, while there was no cure for asthma, there was a palliative. The result of all this was that after the visit to Dr. Stromberg, Gemma religiously took Emil to Galen House every Wednesday morning. Together they would descend the stairs to the basement and while his mother flipped, a bit absent-mindedly, through the latest home or fashion magazine, Emil would sit by a giant machine that churned out foul-tasting vapor, put a pipe to his lips, and suck in the vapor. This large machine was the only thing in the basement, save two chairs and a coffee table stacked high with back issues of magazines. It was an eerie, gray and cold place. Emil hated that basement.

He hated the weekly Wednesday visits. He hated the perceived weakness in his chest. He stopped just short of hating the nonchalance of his mother as she flipped through the magazines. Hatred was a new and powerful emotion for the young Emil. While living at the outpost, he had loved everything that his eyes beheld—the veld, the hills, the cave paintings, the rain dancers...even the government-issued, bungalow-style house with whitewashed walls and no veranda that he called home. He had loved best his black shadow walking on the ground, connecting him to the soil and the history that was all around him.

When he saw how much pleasure his parents, especially his mother, derived from the city, he tried to love the things she loved—the public park, the theatre, the Municipal Bathing Pools—but all he could do was appreciate them. The park with its neatly manicured lawns and landscaped gardens set amidst serene walking paths could not even come close to comparing to the wide open veld. The theatre put on plays that could not capture his imagination the way the San stories of the hunt painted on cave walls could. The Municipal Bathing Pools did not have the depths and possible dangers of the Mtshelele Dam. The City of Kings was just not where he belonged. But, however much he wished it, Emil knew in his heart that there was no going back to the BSAP outpost at the foot of the Matopos Hills.

Having an entirely different frame of reference to the boys at Milton School, Emil did not make friends because he did not try to. The boys at Milton School tended to love the City of Kings and the delights it had to offer. As they played with or exchanged marbles, compared plastic model cars, set off stink bombs or spun yo-yos, they talked ad nauseam about the hero of the latest Western at the bioscope; about the delights of traveling by rail to Salisbury, Gwelo, Umtali and Fort Victoria to visit relatives; about how they had personally witnessed a potentially fatal car accident that was avoided because the city's avenues were so wisely wide. These boys loved and took pride in the very things that Emil found fault with.

As a substitute for the incomparable adventures of the veld, Emil found some solace in the books available in the school and public libraries. He, perhaps too wholeheartedly and unreservedly, dived into the imaginations of H. Rider Haggard, Edgar Rice Burroughs and Rudyard Kipling and found an approximation of the excitement that was now sorely lacking in his life. He would escape into the wild worlds that the authors created and wish that the stories would never come to an end. "I, Allan Quatermain, of Durban, Natal, Gentleman..." In a month, he would read those lines at least twice, eagerly opening *King Solomon's Mines* and beginning the adventure anew. Emil particularly liked that he shared his birthplace, the place that he no longer remembered having lived in, with the man who had fast become his hero, Allan Quatermain. "I, Emil Coetzee, of Durban, Natal, Gentleman..." He would write over and over again in the margins of his exercise books as he watched the city's life pass him by and daydreamed about being in the bush again. While this writing in the margins never did make him feel that he was "of" Durban, it did, nevertheless, make him feel that he could perhaps be the hero of a story.

His schoolmaster, Mr. Bartleby, was quite a perceptive and sensitive man and noticed that Emil's transition to city life was not a happy one. When he saw Emil devouring book after book in the library, he supposed that what he was witnessing was a very studious young man. A studious young man whose life had to be filled with adventures—the kind of adventures not found in the city. The kind of adventures found in the savannah of the country they lived in.

Mr. Bartleby took the boy's many scribbles of "I, Emil Coetzee, of Durban, Natal, Gentleman..." as cries for help and set about searching for a way to save him. Once he found it, he called in the boy's parents. As they sat before him looking like beautiful movie stars straight out of a picture show at the bioscope, Mr. Bartleby understood that some people just had serendipitous lives and found their perfect other, and, simultaneously, that he had had no such great fortune visit upon his life.

"The Selous School for Boys," Mr. Bartleby said, as he pushed the pamphlet across his desk toward them.

The wife picked up the pamphlet and frowned at it slightly.

"Best school in the country," he explained to her frown as he watched her peruse the pamphlet and deepen her frown before passing it to her husband, whose turn it was to frown.

"That is where the boy should go," Mr. Bartleby explained, realizing that there was an order in which he should have done things and that it was now too late to try to establish it.

The perfect couple exchanged confused expressions before she said, "The boy? You mean our boy, Emil?"

"Yes. Yes. Emil. That's the chap. Yes."

The husband chortled charmingly. "I'm afraid we don't understand."

We don't understand, not *I* don't understand. *Such uniformity of mind must be a wonderful thing to have*, Mr. Bartleby conjectured.

"The boy has already secured himself a place and a full bursary."

They exchanged their perfectly confused expressions again.

"He wrote an essay in my class about casting his shadow over Rhodes' grave up at World's View. Very affecting stuff. I sent the essay to the headmaster of the Selous School for Boys. He read it and was rightly impressed by it. We both agree that the best thing for the boy is for him to leave Milton School at term's end."

"Leave Milton at term's end?" the husband mumbled beneath a beautifully trimmed moustache.

"Yes."

"But I have always dreamed of Emil attending Milton. And besides, we live just up the road, the Prince's Mansions at the corner of Borrow and Selborne. It is so convenient and I do so enjoy walking him to and from school every day," the wife said, her mouth beginning to pout becomingly.

Mr. Bartleby so hated to go against her desires, but he was afraid that there was nothing else to be done. "The boy is not entirely happy here."

This had evidently come as news to the perfect couple because they looked at each other questioningly.

"He has the call of the wild, that one, and will never be truly happy or at home in the city."

"Oh," they said in unison.

"Where exactly is this school?" she asked, reaching for the

pamphlet that her husband still held in his hands.

"The Midlands."

"The Midlands!" they exclaimed in unison again.

"I cannot stress this enough. It is the best school in the country. The very best."

"A boarding school? But he is only nine years old," she said.

They exchanged yet another look. Mr. Bartleby understood the look of dread that passed between them. Their own, probably not so happy, boarding-school memories were flashing before them.

"The school itself is situated within hectares and hectares of untamed savannah. He will be able to explore, hunt, fish, camp...all while getting the best education that a young man can get in this country."

"The best?" she asked, still a little wary.

"The *very* best. The Selous School for Boys turns boys into the men of history," Mr. Bartleby said, hoping that this would impress upon them how much they were supposed to be impressed.

At dinner that evening, Gemma's natural flair for detail deserted her. She could not quite capture the essence of the meeting when she announced, as she placed more cucumber salad onto his plate than Emil could ever possibly eat, "Poppet, we have met with Mr. Bartleby and it has been decided that you shall attend the Selous School for Boys at the beginning of the coming year. Is that not a wonderful thing?" she concluded with a weak smile.

Johan scrutinized his son's face. The first thing to register on it was confusion.

"It is in the Midlands," Johan added cautiously.

"The Midlands?"

The second thing to register on Emil's face was panic.

"It is the best school in the entire country," Gemma said.

"The very best," Johan corrected.

"You're a lucky duck for getting in," Gemma said, her smile weaker still.

The third thing to register on Emil's face was fear.

"Have I done something wrong?"

"Wrong? What could you possibly ever do wrong, poppet?" Gemma said, giving Emil's cheek a gentle squeeze. "This is a good thing, darling. A wonderful thing."

Emil stared at his father, his eyes pleading with him to, for once, take a view contrary to his mother's.

"Lots of hunting and shooting to be had, so we're told, our boy. Just your sort of thing," Johan said, as he reached over and ruffled his son's hair.

"It will be just like living on the outpost, but this time you will be receiving the best education in the country," Gemma said as her fingers gently righted Emil's ruffled hair. "The *very* best."

"They turn boys into the men of history."

"Or some such thing."

"In the Midlands?"

"Yes. In the Midlands," Gemma and Johan said in unison, both also trying to reconcile themselves to this fact.

Things moved along with frightening alacrity after that. Term's end came. Mr. Bartleby told Emil that his life was just about to change for the better, that he was very fortunate to have this rare opportunity afforded him and that he had every confidence that Emil would prove worthy of it. As Mr. Bartleby said all this, Emil tried not to cast his eye on a postcard of the gargoyles at Sanssouci Palace on the schoolmaster's desk. After Emil whispered a confused, "Thank you, sir," Mr. Bartleby gave him a cowboy hat as a parting present. Neither Mr. Bartleby nor Emil could have known at that moment that a cowboy hat would one day become a permanent fixture on Emil Coetzee's head.

Gemma stoically went to the Meikles Department Store to buy Emil's trunk; this was an extravagance, given Johan's meager civil-service salary, but she felt that the boy deserved the best. Once it came home from the store, Johan meticulously stenciled EMIL COETZEE onto the trunk. As the Coetzees were trying to decide what next to do, a letter came from the Selous School for Boys congratulating Emil on his acceptance and providing a very extensive list of required items. Gemma and Johan divided the list into two and set about buying the items on it. Johan wished that they had more than one holiday break and, consequently, more than one pay check to prepare for Emil's departure for boarding school. Emil might have received a full bursary, but school uniforms for both summer and winter needed to be purchased, along with a cadet uniform, several sports kits and a litany of sundry items that included a rifle and a pistol (which were to be the first in a series of firearms that the boy would need to acquire over the years at the school). Emil was a growing boy and chances were that the start of every academic year would see the need for such expenditure. Luckily, Gemma had long learned how to stretch a civil servant's salary and had developed an eagle eye for bargains and sales. She managed to successfully stretch Johan's one pay check to afford all that was needed by the Selous School for Boys and graciously accepted Scott Fitzgerald's Christmas and New Year's invitations so that the Coetzees could have a wonderfully festive season before Emil left for school. Scott Fitzgerald had followed close on the heels of the Coetzees when they left the BSAP outpost and, like them, had resettled in the City of Kings. At Scott Fitzgerald's parties, Gemma hoped that no one noticed that her stockings were darned.

With nothing much required of him, Emil watched as his trunk gradually filled up and he wished with all his heart that he could have found it in himself to have loved the City of Kings better, because that love would have saved him from the fate that had now befallen him.

The trunk, filled to capacity, was finally shut the day before he was to depart for the Selous School for Boys.

"Wouldn't it be lovely if we went out to Centenary Park?" Gemma said suddenly, as she latched the locks of the trunk. "You could ride the train there. You'd like that, wouldn't you?"

Emil nodded. Was it too late now to pretend to love all the things the city had to offer?

"We could go to the natural history museum afterwards... or...or the theatre for the matinée. There's a wonderful production of *Anything Goes*, I gather," Gemma said, searching for her hat. Just like that, she had decided on a day out. "It has a lot of musical numbers. You would like that, I dare say, and we could also get some ice cream. We'll make an entire day of it. I'll leave a note for your pa and instructions on how best to warm up the cottage pie. I don't want him to worry when he finds us not here for lunch." Gemma breathlessly inspected her reflection in the hallway mirror. "I know you'd like your father to be there for this last hurrah....We can all go to the bioscope in the evening. You would love that, wouldn't you?"

Emil nodded slowly as his mother set his appearance to rights.

"Yes. We will make an entire day of it and it will all be lovely ...very, very lovely indeed," Gemma said, as she wrote a note for Johan.

Gemma, determined to have the best day with her son, crossed Borrow Street with Emil held safely and firmly in hand. The day started out promisingly enough. They rode along on the train through Centenary Park and Gemma, occasionally stroking her son's blond hair as it was ruffled by the breeze, made herself smile at nothing in particular. When they hopped off the train, she bought them ice cream, which they ate as they made their way to the National Museum of Natural History. They spent a little too much time for Gemma's liking poring over lithographs, letters, pottery, tools, weapons, fossils, menageries and trophies that represented some aspect of the country's past. Emil was evidently enjoying himself and so Gemma let him peruse at his leisure...until she heard him wheeze as he stood before a miniature bungalow that looked very much like the government-issued house that had been their home at the foot of the Matopos Hills. Probably all the dust in the place, Gemma supposed as she led Emil out of the museum. Hopefully he would feel better at the theatre and they could carry on enjoying the day.

They did not even make it to the intermission of *Anything Goes*. Emil's wheezing had at first attracted sympathetic glances that became a few glares here and there and finally a united voice that loudly whispered, "I judge that it is best you take the poor fellow home."

Gemma obeyed the wishes of the many, held Emil by the hand, walked him back up Selborne Avenue to the Prince's Mansions and led him up the stairs. She opened the door to the flat, immediately stopped short, let out a scream and was very surprised when no sound came out.

When Emil saw his father in his mother's red cloche hat, black chiffon and lace drop-waist dress, string of pearls, rouge and lipstick, he assumed it was a joke, something funny his father had prepared for his departure, and he was just about to laugh when he saw the look of absolute horror on his mother's face. When he glanced over at his father and saw the guilt, humiliation, and shame on his face, Emil was filled with dread and knew that, whatever this was, it was not supposed to be happening.

Gemma let go of Emil's hand and went to the medicine cabinet in the bathroom. She left father and son staring at each other. With the comforting aroma of cottage pie wafting between them, Johan's eyes traveled to a spot just above Emil's head and settled there, and there his gaze would remain whenever he looked at his son. Gemma returned with Emil's medication and gave it to him. She then went to her bedroom and shut the door behind her.

The quiet that surrounded them was absolute.

After what Johan had done, both he and Gemma were afraid of what the other would say, so they stopped speaking to each other altogether. In this way she never had to ask him about what she had witnessed and he, therefore, thankfully, never had to explain himself to her or to himself.

Emil was left alone in the confusion of the peace.

CHAPTER 4

———◆———

Emil had seen the Selous School for Boys in his mind's eye every day since he had learned that he was to attend it. At night, he created dreamscapes in which the school was a sprawling and rambling gray Gothic building, complete with gargoyles as grotesque and ghastly as the ones he had seen on the picture postcard of Sanssouci in Potsdam, Germany, that was on Mr. Bartleby's desk. To heighten his trepidation, the school was, for whatever reason, situated in the middle of a moat that had a healthy population of piranhas living in it. As a result, Emil's impression of the place was that there was no prospect of his ever being happy there.

Not a word was spoken during the long journey to the Midlands in the car his father had borrowed from Scott Fitzgerald, which did not help matters because what Emil needed more than anything else at that moment was the gentle cushion that his parents' voices would have provided. His mother, sitting beside him in the back seat, had simply put her white-gloved right hand over his bare hands, smiled feebly at him and then stared out of the window. His father, sitting in the driver's seat, would, by peering at the rear-view mirror, periodically steal glances at the space above Emil's head and satisfy himself that all was well enough with his son.

As he sat there, as silent as a sphynx, Emil wondered what it was exactly that had been witnessed by his mother and him the day before and why it could not be spoken of. But, in lieu of asking this question, Emil gazed out of the window and attempted to console himself with the changing landscape: city, suburbs, smallholdings, farms, villages and, finally and refreshingly, wide open spaces with singing elephant grass.

As their journey carried them closer and closer to the gray Gothic castle with gargoyles, Emil gradually grasped that, whether he was ready to or not, he was growing up. He came to understand that this was his first step away from his parents and this terrified him more than the nightmares he had had of the Selous School for Boys. The momentousness of the occasion having dawned on him, Emil's stomach, long queasy, lurched and he quickly squeezed his mother's hand twice, which was his new way of communicating to her that he needed to relieve himself in a nearby bush. She, in turn, tapped the back of the driver's seat and his father promptly parked the car on the side of the road.

Emil walked into the singing elephant grass by himself and had not walked far when he vomited all the three meals that the Coetzees had stopped to eat in silence at lay-by stations along the way. Although he felt physically better afterwards, he was not yet ready to go back to the car and join the silence of his parents. Thankfully, he heard voices in the distance and walked toward them until he saw an African homestead. A celebration. Women cooking on open fires. Men drinking from shared calabashes. Children chasing a tire. Much conversation and lots of laughter. For a brief, mad moment, Emil contemplated joining them and partaking in their joy and happiness. But of course he could not.

He was about to turn back when he saw them—a hen and a chick straying dangerously far away from the homestead and toward the unknown environs around it. The chick seemed to apprehend the danger better than its mother, for it showed every sign of being anxious; it stayed close to her and wove itself between her legs even though on more than one occasion it had been pushed aside by her scratching feet. Frantic, the chick flew and landed on its mother's back. It could not stay there for long, though, and soon fell down, only to play at her feet again.

Emil could not save himself from the fate that lay in wait for him but he could definitely save the chick, and so he moved abruptly in the elephant grass, making a sound that the chicken sensibly ran away from. The chick ran gratefully after its mother and away from danger, but, sadly, not away from its mother's indifference.

Emil could not help but cry and, as he cried, he vowed to himself that this would be the last time that he would ever cry because, in that moment, he realized that tears did not change the workings of the world.

The Selous School for Boys, founded in the Midlands in 1918, was not the Gothic castle of Emil's dreams but a series of red-roofed, white colonial-style buildings of varying size and stature that stood immaculately in a tranquil, lush, and verdant valley. The school's proud motto, "It is here that boys become the men of history," was the banner that one drove under as one entered the school's premises. Emil read the school's motto and was glad and relieved that it was not written in Latin. The school had the appearance of being welcoming enough, but Emil was not fooled; he had recently learned that things were not always what they appeared to be on the surface.

Besides, Emil was only nine years old. What business did he have becoming a man?

Johan parked Scott Fitzgerald's car in the parking berth, where there was much ado as various families lumbered out of cars, struggled with trunks and made both gregarious and polite conversation. There were boys as young as six who seemed to have been swallowed whole by their uniforms, there were boys of about Emil's age who were all knobby knees and wide eyes, there were boys of about thirteen and fourteen who were determined to help their fathers carry their trunks, there were boys of sixteen and seventeen whose malicious eyes searched the crowd for newcomers. All these boys were to spend the next years of their lives together, becoming men. Emil felt sick to his stomach and was rather glad that he had already expelled its contents, otherwise this would have been a very unfortunate beginning indeed.

Once in the dormitory, Johan found Emil's bed and put his trunk, which he had labored with up the staircase, next to it. Gemma made up the bed with the linen they found folded at the foot of the bed. Emil removed select things (there was a list provided on his headboard) from his trunk and put them in the bedside cabinet. The Coetzees did these things in silence and afterwards sat awkwardly on the bed until the matron came in and smiled before telling the parents that they needed to leave.

Emil, with a heavy heart and wishing that he had the courage to break the silence, walked his parents back to Scott Fitzgerald's car. His mother kissed him on both cheeks as she smiled back tears. Someone, unseen, made a whistling sound as Emil's mother hugged him briefly before quickly getting in the back seat of the car. His father, gazing at the space above Emil's head, offered him his hand, which Emil shook, hoping for so much more.

Emil stood on the tarred road as he watched the car drive away. He thought of the quiet that existed in that car and could not bring himself to wave goodbye to it because, even though it was new, he understood that it would be with them for some time.

Long after Scott Fitzgerald's car had disappeared from

sight, Emil found his way back to the dormitory that contained what was now his bed. He sat at the very edge of the bed and tried to stop his knees from knocking as he scanned the bare white walls, fluorescent strips of light affixed to the ceiling, rows of iron-rail beds with chipped and peeling cream-colored paint, and made a failed attempt to feel welcomed by the room. When a bell finally rang, Emil made his way, as did all the boys, to the dining hall where Sunday Lunch, as the menu on the long table heralded, consisted of roast beef, boiled potatoes with parsley, and mushy peas for the main course, and Black Forest trifle for dessert. Emil ate but did not taste any of the meal that he was sure he would have enjoyed under different circumstances.

As leaden feet carried him up the stairs that led back to his dormitory, a group of older boys passed him and said that they could still smell his mother's milk on him. Emil, understanding full well what they meant by that, regretted having promised himself, only earlier that day, never to cry again.

The silver lining was that at no point in all his imaginings had he thought that his first day at the school would be anything but a misery, so at least his first day at the Selous School for Boys was meeting, if not exceeding, his expectations.

As he made his way up the stairs, the weight of the day suddenly exhausted Emil and when he arrived at his dormitory, he collapsed on his bed and, briefly comforted by his mother's rosewater scent on the bed linen, fell fast and deeply asleep and dreamt that the chick he had seen earlier that day had flown onto his shoulder and walked along the veld with him.

Emil awoke to hands rudely and roughly pulling him off the bed and shoving his face toward gray and grimy unpolished boots.

"Lick my boots!" a pompous voice instructed.

Emil was too shocked and scared to cry.

"Lick my boots, I say!" the pompous voice repeated and this time the words were followed by a thump in the small of Emil's back, flattening him to the ground.

An unpolished boot pushed itself against Emil's lips.

"What? Too high and mighty to lick my boots, are you?"

There was another thump on Emil's back.

Emil knew that this torture would only end when he licked the boot. So he closed his eyes, stuck out his tongue, and licked the boot.

"You're a bootlicker," the pompous voice said triumphantly.

There were guffaws and snickers.

Emil, expecting that the worst was over, chose to lie there with his eyes tightly shut until they were all gone.

But, of course, the worst was not over.

"What are you?" another voice asked, clearly second in command.

Someone grabbed him by the hair and lifted his head. "Not only a bootlicker, but you also still smell of your mother's milk."

"What are you?" the pompous voice asked.

It would have been the easiest thing for Emil to say the words "I am a bootlicker," but something within him railed against the idea. He knew, deep within himself, that he would never say those words and that gave him the courage to do what he did next. He collected a gob of saliva in his mouth and blindly spat it out, not caring much where it landed as long as it made contact with someone's skin.

Everything happened quickly after that. There were several hands all over his body stripping his clothes off, leaving him only in his underdrawers, carrying him away from the dormitory ward, down the stairs, out the door, and throwing him onto the ground. Emil was certain that the worst was yet to come and prepared himself for it, but all he heard was the sound of feet moving away...and then a sniffle. The sniffle did not belong to him and so he opened his eyes to see who it belonged to.

He was surprised to find that night had fallen. He had slept through supper and no one had bothered to wake him up. *This* was the best school in the country?

Emil heard the sniffle again and squinted through the darkness until he made out a figure: a boy, standing about a meter away from him. He was about to speak to the figure when another sound got his attention. Several voices carrying lights were traveling toward him and the figure of the boy.

Soon the voices manifested in the form of several men, European and African, carrying on their shoulders a magnificent beast, and holding in their hands lamps that looked like luminous, nocturnal flying creatures. The arrival of these men was the most marvelous sight that Emil had ever witnessed; it was the stuff of legend. These men seemed to have been born of the night itself. Speaking in low voices, some began to make a fire while others began to skin and disembowel the animal. The lamps made the pooling crimson blood glisten in the dark. The figure a meter away from Emil made a gagging sound and then coughed.

The men instinctively and immediately stopped what they were doing and listened to the darkness. One man, carrying a hurricane lamp above his head, broke away from the hunters and made his way toward Emil and the figure beside him.

Even though he did not know what would happen next, Emil was grateful when he was illuminated by the light of the hurricane lamp. He basked in its glow and almost forgot that he was near naked.

The man carrying the lamp peered down at him, his expression difficult to read because of the shadow falling over his face. The man's eyes traveled to the figure standing a meter from Emil. Emil turned to observe the figure as well. The silhouette was of a slightly plump boy who was about Emil's age and who looked every bit like a cherub that had lost its wings. Emil was not surprised that the boy had been targeted with a face like that.

"Ah! You must be the Two Unfortunates," the man carrying the hurricane lamp said. "Every year they pick the two boys that they deem to be the weakest and ostracize them. It is all very predictably Darwinian." The man blinked at the two boys. "You are not weak, are you, boys?" Emil felt himself shake his head, not because he believed that he was not weak, but because he felt that the man standing before him truly believed that he was not weak and Emil did not want to disabuse him of this notion.

"We are supposed to be creating men, but sometimes, I could swear, we are creating little horrors," the man continued, more to himself than to Emil and the cherub beside him. "So, Unfortunates, what are your names?"

The two boys eyeballed each other, both willing the other to give his name first.

The man smiled briefly. "I am Archibald Bertrand Fortesque the Third. Unfortunate, I know. Luckily, you can call me Master Archie."

"Courteney Smythe-Sinclair," the cherub next to Emil volunteered.

"Your misfortune is almost as severe as mine," Master Archie said, shaking Courteney's hand.

When he introduced himself simply as "Emil Coetzee," while shaking Master Archie's hand, Emil deeply regretted that his parents had never thought to give him a middle name.

"Not so difficult that, now was it?" Master Archie said before adding, "Gentlemen, I am honored to make your acquaintance."

There was a genuine sincerity in Master Archie's voice that made Emil smile, a smile that was long and lasting.

"Would you like to help us skin him?" Master Archie asked, inclining his head toward the campfire.

To finally be part of the hunt! Emil eagerly nodded. He glanced over at Courteney, who, even with the warm glow of the hurricane lamp on him, still looked green in the face. Feeling sorry for him, Emil walked up to Courteney, stood next to him, and stared at him until they both sort of nodded at each other. Courteney looked at Master Archie with new-found courage and nodded his head but not as enthusiastically as Emil had.

There. Just like that. Emil had made a friend, as easy as you please.

By the campfire an African man was cutting the animal's heart into pieces. Emil watched, absolutely enthralled, while Courteney ran to a nearby bush and retched. The man speared through the pieces of the animal's heart with his assegai and offered each man there a piece. Each man accepted the piece and popped it into his mouth. Master Archie did likewise when a piece was proffered to him.

Emil had not been expecting to receive the piece of the heart that he now held in his hands and so was surprised by the warmth of it...the texture of it...the weight of it. He found that he loved the reality of the thing that, until that moment, had existed for him mostly as metaphor.

"You have to eat it while it is still warm," Master Archie said.

Emil focused on the piece of the heart in his hand and was suddenly overcome with sorrow that its beauty was so ephemeral.

Mistaking the reason for Emil's hesitation, Master Archie

said, "Quite naturally, you do not have to eat it if you do not want to. No one is expecting you to. It is not every man that can eat the heart of an animal."

Emil carefully put the still-warm substance in his mouth and slowly chewed it. It tasted like...the heart of something. It was neither delicious nor dreadful. He chewed for quite some time as he broke it down. Once he had swallowed the masticated heart, Emil looked at Master Archie and smiled a bloody smile.

The other men laughed and some patted Emil on the back until he felt like he had passed some secret test.

For his part, Master Archie studied Emil but did not laugh or pat him on the back. Instead, he said to him, "To kill something is a very serious business, never to be taken lightly because life itself is so precious. We eat the heart while it is still warm so that the animal does not die in vain. We metabolize it so that it continues to live within us. You are now carrying that animal within you and shall continue to do so for the rest of your days."

CHAPTER 5

————— ✦ —————

As hard as it was for him to accept it, in time, Emil had to admit to himself that he preferred to be at school rather than at home. He felt guilty about this, to be sure, but even with the sporadic bullying that he received at the hands of the boys that he collectively called "The Bootlickers," he was never alone at the Selous School for Boys. At the Selous School for Boys, Emil always had Courteney.

It was with Courteney that he sought the sanctuary of the library before supper and after the gruelling sessions of compulsory sports and cadet training. Together, Emil and Courteney consumed the entire oeuvre of the school's namesake, Frederick Courteney Selous. Within the pages of such books as *A Hunter's Wanderings in Africa*, *Twenty Years in Zambesia* and *Sunshine and Storm*, Selous captured the imagination of Emil Coetzee and soon became his second hero.

In all honesty, Emil did not actually read the works of Selous, Courteney did. Emil began well enough with *A Hunter's Wanderings in Africa*:

On the 4th of September 1871, I set foot for the first time upon the sandy shores of Algoa Bay, with 400 pounds in my pocket, and the weight of only nineteen years upon my shoulders. Having carefully read all the works that had been written on sport and travel in South Africa, I had long ago determined to make my way into the interior of the country as soon as ever circumstances would enable me to do so; for the free-and-easy gipsy sort of life described by Gordon, Cumming, Baldwin, and other authors, had quite captivated my imagination, and done much to determine me to adopt the life of ever-varying scenes and constant excitement, which I have never since regretted, and for which an inborn love of all branches of natural history, and that desire so common amongst our countrymen of penetrating to regions where no one else has been, in some way fitted me.

In spite of this awe-inspiring beginning, Selous's dense and dry prose soon started to drift away from Emil and so, as a result, it was Courteney who, in summary, would tell Emil all that he needed to know about the man who had been the inspiration for H. Rider Haggard's *Allan Quatermain*, Emil's first hero.

Emil often imagined himself, at nineteen, setting off on a great quest—an adventure that would be the making of him, and he could hardly wait for this future to come into being. While he waited for this future, he sat next to Courteney in the school library and reread the works of Haggard, Burroughs, and Kipling. He would occasionally gaze up at the portrait of Frederick Courteney Selous that hung in the library and admire the quintessential outdoorsman with requisite hat, boots and rifle. Some day that will be me, Emil would think with pride.

Courteney was not as taken with Selous as Emil was and actually read him only in order to provide Emil with summaries and to improve their collective vocabulary. An uninspired Courteney wondered if his parents had named him after Selous, but never remembered to ask them this in the biweekly letters that he sent home.

They were not exactly cut from the same cloth, Emil and

Courteney, but the friendship of the Two Unfortunates of 1937 had taken root fast and held strong.

It was with Courteney that Emil enjoyed Master Archie's English class, struggled through Master Findlay's science class, and suffered through Master Duthie's history class. In truth, Courteney was too intelligent to struggle or suffer through anything academic. Preferring to challenge himself mentally and not exert himself physically, where Courteney truly suffered and struggled was on the sports field, where he was expected to participate in rugby and cricket, and in the wide open veld where he was expected to build a fire, pitch a tent, and shoot a moving target with equal degrees of determination. Yet he made every effort to enjoy these pursuits because of Emil, who was happily in training to be an outdoorsman. In return, Emil understood and appreciated the particularity of Courteney's friendship and made every effort to love poetry and enjoy plays the way that not only Courteney but Master Archie would wish him to.

By the time Emil returned home after his first term away, his parents had already grown accustomed to their quiet existence. In flat 2A, notes were delicately written back and forth on pastel-colored paper. Collars were now starched and shoes were now laced without a word being spoken or a song being sung. Meals were eaten at the kitchen table and Emil used as an emissary to pass the salt, the butter, the gravy and the vegetables. For most of the day, the only voices to be heard within their flat came from his mother's His Master's Voice gramophone and his father's Philips wireless radio.

During Emil's absence, it had been Gemma who had written the first note and put it on the kitchen table. Johan had responded to the note and left his response on the kitchen table and thus had begun something that was not quite new between them, a relationship that was lived out through correspondence.

Gemma and Johan struggled at first, jotting down only a few hesitant and halting lines, but with the passing of time the notes became longer, more elaborate, containing much more than just what was deliberately not being said. Eventually they began to enjoy the silence. Gemma would take trips to Haddon & Sly to buy reams of paper in pretty pastel colors. She particularly agonized over the type of pen to be used and often bought more than one for them to try out. He was the first to sign the note "with love," to which she responded with a "Dear Johan."

"Dear Johan, just back from H&S. I trust that I have found the perfect pen. Try it out and let me know what you think."

"Dear Gemma, it writes like a dream. I believe this is the one."

"Remember that first letter that you sent with the bleeding ink?"

"I was too excited and nervous to notice what the ink did."

"Oh...Dear Johan..."

It was this particular correspondence that Emil found on the kitchen table when he returned home from his first term at the Selous School for Boys.

His parents spoke to him, of course. His mother had pointedly superficial conversations with him: he appeared thinner; was he being well fed at school? He was getting positively brown; was he spending too much time in the sun? He was growing taller; did he need new uniforms already? He was getting handsomer by the day, was it not such a pity that there were no girls at the school? Did he know that blushing became him? His father, still unable to meet Emil's eyes, asked more or less the same questions about school to the space above Emil's head: The schoolmasters were all right, were they? He had since heard something of a Master Duthie; not causing any problems, was he? He understood how older boys could be toward newcomers; how were things on that score? This friend that he had made, this Courteney Smythe-Sinclair, was proving to be a good friend, was he? And this Master Archie, was he the proper sort? And the animal's warm heart; he really had had to eat it, had he?

The fact that his parents broke their silence for him must have seemed to them to be an act of kindness. Emil wished that he could have felt it as such, but he could not. The little that they said to him made him feel as if they had brought him into the world only to have very little interest in him.

He knew that this was unfair, but he felt the cruelty of his situation keenly because he remembered the days on the BSAP outpost—days that were filled with laughter, love, and lukewarm lime cordial. Days lived together with his mother, and not his father, wearing the red cloche hat.

His father's wearing of the red cloche hat had created a crisis within the Coetzee household and it had taken only a term at the Selous School for Boys to teach Emil why. In his religious studies class, Emil had been taught that God created man to have dominion over all the other living things of the land and sea and that it was man's mandate, as the superior being, to not only name all living things but also to categorize them and thus create an order of things from the seeming chaos. The primary pursuit of man, therefore, was to make the world not only habitable but knowable, and known as well, which was why the voyages of discovery and imperial expansion had been so important; they fulfiled the sacred covenant between God and man. God had chosen the European man to spread the light of Christianity and civilization to the rest of the world. As a result, men, real men, men like Frederick Courteney Selous, held sacred their covenant with God. They wore it as a badge of honor and made it a point of pride. Emil understood that no European man working in the service of God and King would willingly give up this destined and privileged position, even for a brief moment, and in that same view, Emil understood that his father, in choosing to appear feminine, had, for a brief moment, given up his position and irredeemably and irreparably upset the natural order of things. There was no hope of return from such a sorry state of affairs.

Due to the many silences that the flat contained, Emil always felt that he had to escape it. He found refuge in the places that he had struggled to love before: the Centenary Park, the Municipal Bathing Pools, the theatre. He tended to go to the theatre whenever he acutely missed Courteney, who spent his holidays in Essexvale being fattened, pampered and cossetted by a mother and six sisters who were hell-bent on restoring his cherubic state.

As the years went on Emil found himself, during his school holidays, seeking solace in the peaceful jacaranda, flamboyant and acacia-lined avenues of the suburbs that he could get to within five minutes of walking down the perfect straightness of Selborne Avenue. Here in the suburbs, Emil would listen for sounds, any sounds, of family life—children playing and laughing; dogs barking and being told to voetsek; wives screaming and demanding that their husbands tell them why they liked dancing with Victoria so much; husbands saying that they had had enough; the sound of a slap and the slam of a door— in an attempt to experience, albeit vicariously and briefly, the lives of others. Emil welcomed all of the sounds but they were few and far between in the serenity of the suburbs and he often wondered if the silence that had taken hold in his family existed in other families as well.

Emil's walk through the suburbs would usually end at a colonial-style house with French windows, a red wraparound veranda and an English rose garden that was so much like the house that his mother had dreamed of living in once upon a time, not so long ago. Emil would stand outside this house and stare at it for a moment and wonder...just wonder if things would have been different if...

The house had been built by and belonged to Scott Fitzgerald and even though he called it home, it seemed to need more than one person to make it so.

Scott Fitzgerald, who was no longer a policeman and was now an advertising agent, was more often found at home than at work because, while he had a comfortable office in the city center, he rarely used it. Since he still harbored dreams of becoming an author, he preferred to be at home, where he could labor over his manuscript on his Remington Noiseless Portable Typewriter whenever inspiration struck. Although that was the idea, what he usually did with his time at home was dash off memorable phrases of preferably less than six and definitely not more than twelve words, and he did this so easily and wonderfully that he was permitted to work from home.

He was the best in the country at writing advertisements. A housewife would, while comparing prices (as housewives always do), recollect one of Scott Fitzgerald's six-word jingles that she had heard on her 1940 HMV New Yorker Smart Wireless and make what she believed to be a highly informed decision. A retired engineer knew that by providing for all his needs through Morrison's Mail Order Catalog, he could best stretch his pension funds because a carefully placed advert in the Railway Review had told him so. A young man, wanting to impress his sweetheart and his boss alike, went to buy his first Rolex watch at T. Forbes & Son, Ltd, on Abercorn Street because, according to the intertitle he had read at the bioscope the night before, the watches sold there were for men who meant business. The newly engaged young lady who wanted the best honeymoon that money could buy knew to subtly suggest the new Woodholme Hotel in east London to her fiancé because it was said by *The Chronicle* to be modern, situated on a golden beach and overlooking the sparkling Indian Ocean. The frugal housewife, the retired engineer, the impressive young man and the aspirational fiancée acted individually without knowing that they had all been spurred to action by one man, Scott Fitzgerald, such was the amorphous nature of his power.

Ever since he had arrived in the City of Kings, Scott Fitzgerald had encouraged Emil to call him Uncle Scott. When Emil visited him, Uncle Scott would, as soon as Emil arrived, gratefully stand up, move away from the typewriter and the bottle of whiskey (a sad cliché if ever there was one, he often lamented), grab his overcoat, regardless of what the weather was like outside and say, over his shoulder, "Ah...the prodigal returns. Let us go forth and be men," before leading Emil out of the house and back onto the tree-lined avenues of the suburbs.

"Being men" according to Uncle Scott consisted of going to Scobie's on Selborne Avenue where he ordered a whiskey on the rocks for himself and an ice-cold lime cordial for Emil. Uncle Scott's frequent patronage of Scobie's, and the six words—*The place with a pioneering spirit*—that he had written that made Scobie's the favorite haunt of a particular type of man, brought with it such privileges as bringing his underage "nephew" into the bar with him.

Emil scrutinized the men sitting at Scobie's. They were a constant at any hour of the productive day and he strongly suspected that they were what Master Duthie called "the rejects of empire"—men who, with all the superiority of their European race, had not been able to amount to much because their dashed prospects had rendered them men too disappointed to do anything other than feel sorry for themselves. Master Duthie would constantly caution, "I never want to hear that any of you sitting here before me today grew up to be the rejects of empire. The imperial project is the greatest event in the world's history. It takes men, real men, to carry it out. And we here at the Selous School for Boys are in the business of making men, real men."

After a few years at the Selous School for Boys, the last thing in the world Emil wanted was to be a reject of empire. He wanted to be a man, a real man, a man like Frederick Courteney Selous.

In spite of the fact that he spent a lot of time at Scobie's, Uncle Scott was, most certainly, not a reject of empire. He spent his days writing words that would transact in the necessary exchange of goods and services for money. As Master Duthie often pointed out, commerce was the hallmark of a civilization and capitalism the hallmark of a superior civilization. Uncle Scott was the oil that made the entire imperial machine run smoothly. He wrote words that made people *want* to buy things. In a fledgling capitalist country, there was a lot to be admired in that.

Uncle Scott's own thoughts, on the other hand, were often far from imperialism, capitalism, or civilization. "How is your mother?" he would ask after his first sip of whiskey. "Still as lovely as ever, I'd wager. Still sweetness and light. I have almost captured her in the novel...tell her that. This time...this time she will love the portrayal. I can almost guarantee it." Uncle Scott would take another sip of whiskey and then say the words Emil had been waiting for all along, "Remember the outpost? Remember the wonderful time we had there?"

"Yes."

"Remember how she danced the Charleston and the fox-trot? She made us fall in love with her, didn't she?"

"Yes."

"So, it is really not our fault that we are in this sorry state now, is it?"

"No."

Even at a young age, Emil understood that Uncle Scott's frustration lay in being able to persuade everyone but the woman he loved with his words.

CHAPTER 6

———◆———

It was through Uncle Scott that Emil made his first great discovery. When Emil first received the ticket printed on flimsy pink manila paper, good for three entries at the La Grange Skating Rink, he felt sure that he would not use it. The La Grange Skating Rink, constructed in 1911, had, even before it officially opened, been threatened with closure, a threat that hung over its head for almost twenty years. Having an ice-skating rink in the City of Kings was to have something exotic, and under the ownership of anyone other than La Grange, its novelty and the respite it offered from the dry heat of the city would have been exploited to great advantage. However, La Grange, probably understanding too acutely the uniqueness of the thing he held in his possession, had decided to use it to perpetually vex the European population by erecting the skating rink in a virtual no man's land on the outskirts of the European part of the city and also just outside the Native Location. The colony was still relatively young then and the various governing bodies of the city had not, as yet, found their way to having jurisdiction over that particular patch of land, and it was this quality that La Grange chose to exploit. He let the city fathers know that he intended to make the skating rink available and accessible to all races.

The very unsavory idea of having Europeans, Africans, Coloureds and Asians twirling, pirouetting, figure-eighting, swishing and gliding in such proximity, with the ever-present danger of potentially bumping into one another, had created such an uproar in certain quarters of the city that as soon as they got wind of La Grange's plan, the upright women of the Pioneer Benevolence Society of the City of Kings wrote a righteously scathing letter to both the mayor and the town clerk and had it, for good measure, printed in *The Chronicle*. The letter questioned the propriety of such a scheme and threatened not only to boycott the skating rink but also to hold a candlelight vigil for the death of morals in the City of Kings. Within a few days other civic organizations joined in the outcry and the town clerk had no choice but to write to La Grange and strongly advise him against opening the skating rink to "all and sundry." Even though he privately joked with the town clerk that the wonderful ladies of the Pioneer Benevolence Society of the City of Kings were less concerned with the commingling of the races than they were with being seen by the natives wobbling on their skates and falling ungraciously on their behinds, the mayor, a few days later, sent the exact same letter that the town clerk had sent, only this time the words "strongly advise against" had been replaced with the words "strictly prohibit."

La Grange gave the impression of appreciating the collective wisdom of the European community by publicly proclaiming, via *The Chronicle*, that his establishment was for Europeans only. On the day that the skating rink first opened, the charitable ladies of the Pioneer Benevolence Society of the City of Kings were the first to wobble and waddle over the ice. When they fell, which they often did, they laughed, comfortable in the knowledge that no eyes but theirs had seen their petticoats. The skating rink was an instant phenomenon, soon attracting Europeans from all over the country and all walks of life.

And then the rumors began to spread of multiracial carousing and rabble-rousing taking place at the skating rink after hours. The town clerk received many letters and complaints. The mayor and the location superintendent pushed for legislation to be passed declaring the no man's land on which the skating rink was situated part of the European section of the city. The BSAP was deployed to conduct sporadic raids on the skating rink—sometimes they broke up parties, sometimes they found evidence of revelries that had come and gone, sometimes they found nothing but La Grange and some Coloured men in various stages of inebriation—and reported the miscellaneous misdemeanors they came across to the town clerk. La Grange was deemed too friendly with the Coloureds and the natives to be trustworthy and the skating rink was thus constantly under threat of closure.

The skating rink's tribulations made it such an infamous place that, over time, only a certain caliber of citizen would patronize it. In 1935, La Grange was charged with contravening the country's anti-miscegenation laws by encouraging racial mixing and was imprisoned for five years. During his incarceration, the City Council oversaw the running of the skating rink. They made a great show of "cleaning up" the property, which amounted to the removal of all Coloured men and natives who lived on the property, and opening it up for what they called 'respectable business.'

So, when Uncle Scott (who had visited the rink several times during its more infamous days) bought the pink ticket valid for three entries for Emil's thirteenth birthday, he was confident that there was nothing that the boy would see and experience that was beyond his years.

Equally because of its reputation and its location, the skating rink had never had much attraction for Emil when he moved to the City of Kings, but then again, to be fair, nothing had. The stories whispered in the dormitories of the

Selous School for Boys of the seedy goings-on at the skating rink had done nothing to arouse his interest in the place, so when he received the ticket, he had thanked Uncle Scott and lied to him for the first time by promising that he would use it, when he knew he would not.

However, on 18 April 1940, the day of his birthday, as Emil sat silently at the kitchen table with his mother and father, waiting to blow out the thirteen blue candles his mother had carefully arranged on the surface of a homemade Victoria sandwich that had the four letters of his name dusted with icing sugar on its top layer, he felt that the birthday that marked the end of boyhood—as his father kept on reminding the space above his head—deserved a better commemoration than what was honestly a paltry affair. With a somewhat shaky hand, his father used a cigarette lighter to set flame to the thirteen candle wicks and, before anyone could ask him to, Emil blew out all thirteen candles in one puff. His mother reminded him to make a wish and since all he could wish for was a better thirteenth birthday, that was what he wished for. With no other recourse left, he promised himself that he would use Uncle Scott's birthday present and add some excitement to his day. He briefly entertained the idea of taking his parents along, but then instinctively felt that the upcoming adventure was one he needed to experience on his own.

It did not take Emil as long as he had gauged it would to arrive at the edges of the European section of the city. As he walked down Lobengula Street for the first time, he marveled at how everything was so murky and gray compared to the heart of the city. Here it was as if the city knew that it could give up trying and had happily done so. But, while the look of the place was drab and lackluster, its mood was anything but. There was music in the air. It sounded like the jazz his mother had danced to on the BSAP outpost, but this music was different: it was at home in its present environment, and the people he passed on the street—mostly black, sometimes brown, and rarely white—appeared to be moving to its tempo; even the trains at the nearby railway station sounded as if they were choo-chooing to its rhythm. The music was in everything the people did—in the way men bowed their heads in greeting, in the way women lifted babies and bags onto their backs and heads, in the way they threw their heads back in easy laughter, in the way they waved their hands to known but distant passers-by, in the way store proprietors beckoned would-be customers into their shops, in the way they stopped to glance this way and that before crossing the street, in the way their feet stepped on and off the dusty pavement. Their movements were not dancing, as such, but the promise of a dance.

Feeling a happiness that seemed almost forgotten, Emil wondered as he moved like a foreign thing in their midst, if his movements too were beginning to take on the rhythm of his surroundings. Was he now suddenly less gangly and awkward and more proud and sure-footed? As he felt for the pink ticket in his trouser pocket, he ignored the sweatiness of his palms and allowed himself to believe he was on the verge of dancing, which was a very titillating and scintillating place to be.

The rhythm that made Emil believe he was capable of dance was the beginning of a sound that would capture the City of Kings for the next three decades and come to be known as "township jazz." The next time Emil would hear the sound was when he heard August Musarurwa's song about the illegal African brew "skokiaan" (a brew that coincidentally helped create some memorable moments during the skating rink's more infamous years) many years later at a party hosted by Courteney. The tune would be blown from Louis

Armstrong's trumpet, and Emil, no longer remembering all the details of his thirteenth birthday, would not marvel as he ought to upon hearing the song, at how a tune born in the City of Kings and first played by August Musarurwa and the African Dance Band of the Cold Storage Commission had managed to travel over land and ocean until it reached the ears of the man who was undoubtedly the greatest musician of his time.

When he found it, the skating rink was a splash of color in an otherwise gray world. Everywhere Emil looked, there was something to dazzle the eye: pink tufts of cotton candy, yellow cones of Italian ice cream, mountains of buttery popcorn, red glossy orbs of toffee apples, orange fountains of squash, brown pillars of fudge and caramel, oodles and oodles of pastel-colored taffy. His mouth watering, he looked at the ice-cream men in blue-, gray-and-white starched uniforms, at the carousel with ivory and gold horses that had crimson saddles and bridles, and at the red mouth of the tunnel of love and wished that he had had the foresight to ask his parents for pocket money.

The place itself was organized chaos and cacophony. There was so much movement: children running and screaming everywhere, frantic parents rushing here and there, teenage girls jumping up and down in anticipation as they watched teenage boys take aim and shoot at sitting ducks. Because he could not afford to do anything else, Emil became interested in what was happening on the skating rink. He watched as a group of Lutheran missionaries from Sweden allowed their stern faces to crack with smiles as they glided over the icy surface.

It was because Emil was staring at the missionaries that he saw her—a girl of about fourteen who wore a blue-and-white scarf around her head, standing next to the skating rink. When his eyes fell upon her, it was as if Emil had discovered a whole new world. In all of Emil's thirteen years, girls had never featured in any aspect of his life, and for this reason he had just assumed that they were unimportant.

Indeed, when he considered them collectively, even now, they did not seem to make any contribution to life in general and to his in particular, but somehow this girl standing outside the skating rink was different. He watched her as she unwrapped the blue-and-white scarf from her head and felt that this simple act, in itself, was making a contribution to his life. When an unruly golden-brown mass of curls, freed by the removal of the scarf, fell all over the girl's face, Emil found himself transfixed and more aware of her than he was of his own self at that moment.

She was considerably tall for a girl and had a rectangular body, spindly legs and arms and knobby knees, and as Emil watched her climb onto the skating rink, he was certain that she was as light as air. Her first few steps on the ice were a little shaky, but then she bent over slightly, created fists out of both hands, tilted her chin up as though preparing for a starter's pistol on a running track...and quite simply, thereafter, became a graceful thing. She skated effortlessly on the ice, her majestic hair trailing behind her. Emil watched her until all he could hear was his heart beating. That was when he became aware of the fact that he was probably falling in love. This was most inconvenient, as he had intended to fall in love for the first time at some point after he had set out on the great adventure of his life.

Once, when the girl skated past him, she focused on him with big gray eyes that triggered something in him. Without knowing how he had come to be standing where he was, he found himself holding, in his slightly trembling hands, the blue-and-white scarf she had unraveled from her hair. The idea struck him then and he acted on it impulsively. As he stuffed as much of the scarf as he could into his trouser pocket, he decided that he would put the scarf on a chipped rail of the footboard of his bed at the Selous School for Boys, and, in this way, always remember the girl.

After he had completed the act of putting away the scarf, he suddenly felt afraid and decided to leave the skating rink. At that moment the girl was gliding away from him and it saddened him to know that this would be his last image of her.

He was safely out of the skating rink building when a giant hand that smelled of cotton candy, toffee apples, and popcorn seized him by the shoulder. Emil turned around to see a dark, looming figure towering over him. The figure skewered him with bespectacled blue eyes and demanded that he return what was not his. The sun was in his eyes and fear was in his heart and so he could not see the sinister figure clearly. "The scarf!" the figure barked. "You have my granddaughter's scarf in your pocket. I saw you take it. You're a little thief!" it brayed. Emil was mortified when the figure yanked the scarf out of his pocket. In all the time he had been watching the girl, it never occurred to him that he was also being watched. He hoped and prayed that the girl would not come out and witness his humiliation. He could not bear to think of her thinking of him as a thief for the rest of her life. The figure stomped off without waiting for Emil's apology.

As Emil ran along Lobengula Street, the rhythm he had become so attuned to only an hour before now seemed discordant. He was not a thief, but he sincerely wished that he had been able to take the blue-and-white scarf away with him.

As he turned onto Selborne Avenue, Emil was aware that he was fighting back tears. Even though he would always have the memory of the girl gliding gracefully over the ice, he knew that something had been gained and something had been lost.

Emil comforted himself with the fact that he could salvage enough from the day to make for a very compelling story he would tell Courteney. Yet, when the school term began in May, Emil found himself keeping the story of the girl a secret. He did not fully understand why; he just knew, then, that some things were sacred.

CHAPTER 7

When Emil, in that May of his fourteenth year, peeked at a sepia-colored photograph that Clement Rutherford proudly displayed, it was not the first time he had seen the body of a naked woman. He had already done so, a few weeks earlier, in Mistress Findlay's art class. A nude, she had called the painting as he, along with the rest of the class, gawked and sniggered at the alabaster-white flesh reclining on a divan and the pinkish hand placed languidly on a thigh. He had dared himself to glance at what Master Findlay, in an earlier science class, very objectively and dispassionately had called the mons pubis. Emil also tried to examine the pinkish brown areola with a scientific eye, but, for whatever reason, it made him blush deeply and he took comfort in the fact that, without looking at them, he knew that all the other boys were blushing as well.

"The female form is nothing to laugh at, boys. The female form is something to be appreciated...celebrated even," Mistress Findlay had said, smacking a few easels with a paintbrush in that somewhat detached and permanently preoccupied way of hers, as her swan-like neck pivoted this way and that so that her eye fell on every boy in the room.

So, having already seen a female nude in Mistress Findlay's class, Emil was not too shocked when Clement Rutherford produced the sepia-colored photograph of another naked woman. But while Emil had seen the body of a naked woman before, he had to admit that there was something about the experience of seeing this body that was...not the same. The pose was very much the same—pinkish flesh (because of the sepia tone) lying on a settee, a hand on the thigh, mons pubis and brownish pink areola. The only real difference was that the photograph had become creased over the years of much handling and as a result the woman's body looked like a puzzle that had been pieced together. Emil responded to the image, but not in the way he had in Mistress Findlay's class. His body responded in a physical and noticeable way that immediately made him feel deeply ashamed.

"My father has an entire collection of these," Rutherford said proudly. Clement Rutherford, known by his last name as all boys at the school were known by their last name, was the son of a prominent businessman and aspiring politician.

Did his own father, Johan Coetzee, also have such a collection of photographs? Emil wondered. The notion briefly filled him with horror until he recalled the red cloche hat and relaxed. Of course his father would not have any such collection.

Emil and Rutherford were huddled in the sports pavilion with the rest of the under-14 rugby team. At thirteen, Emil, who was the vice-captain of the team, was the tallest and broadest of them all and that, more than his position, gave him the most revered stature within the group. So he was not surprised when Rutherford, the captain of the team, stared pointedly at him to gauge his reaction. To cover his mortification, Emil attempted an assured smile. It was weak and barely perceptible and apparently all the encouragement that Rutherford needed.

"She's just gasping for it, isn't she?" Rutherford said, his voice no longer sounding like his own.

Gasping for what? Emil would have liked to know. He strongly suspected that whatever it was, it had something to do with what Master Findlay objectively and dispassionately called the "biology of humans," which, in turn, had everything to do with the way his body had just responded to the photograph and with the way Rutherford's timbre had changed.

Emil peeked at the hand on the thigh, at the dip of the waist, at the areola, and felt, amidst all the shame, an excitement that traveled throughout his whole body, electrifying him...until he saw the dead expression in the woman's gray eyes. Those eyes filled him with so much guilt that he immediately walked away from the huddle.

"As soon as you saw what it was, why didn't you just walk away?" Courteney asked a few hours later.

"I couldn't."

"Why not?" Courteney's cherubic face frowned.

Whereas puberty had already visited Emil, it had yet to appear to Courteney.

"You wouldn't understand."

"What is there to understand? You knew that it was wrong to look at her so you should have walked away."

Emil had not expected this reaction from Courteney. Curiosity, yes. Envy, maybe. But not this...this...unrelenting righteousness.

"You did know that it was wrong to look at her, didn't you?" Courteney persisted. "Didn't you?"

"Yes. Of course I did."

"Then you should have walked away," Courteney said before walking away from Emil and thus demonstrating how easy a thing it was to do.

Courteney did not appreciate what it was like to be caught up in the camaraderie of a team. How could he? After his first two years at the school, Courteney's mother had written a very long letter to the headmaster. The letter was accompanied by a doctor's note so detailed that it fell just short of proclaiming that Courteney was at death's door and thus had the desired effect of exempting him from all compulsory sports and most outdoor activities. This allowed Courteney to spend most of his time outside of class in the library or in Master Archie's rooms, reading and discussing all manner of literature. After four years at the Selous School for Boys, Courteney was still very much the nine-year-old boy that he had been when he first arrived.

Emil had, on the other hand, changed in those same four years. Possibly shocked away by the reality of the Selous School for Boys, the memory of the native girl and the light-brown baby boy who lived in the government-issued, bungalow-style house with whitewashed walls and no veranda that had been Emil's childhood home did not visit Emil in his dreams and, for that reason, Emil's wheezing attacks had left him and never returned, allowing him to give full and free rein to his love for the outdoors and sports. As a result, he increasingly spent most of his time with the other boys at the school, boys that he called by their last names, boys he grew more and more like with each passing year, boys who in previous years he had called "The Bootlickers."

Emil continued to hold on to his tenuous relationship with Courteney, even as it was becoming more and more difficult because of all the differences that were manifesting between them. He got the distinct impression that Courteney was also beginning to let go of him, having found, over the years, other Unfortunates to befriend. So even though they were now technically connected by a thread as thin as gossamer, there continued to be a something between them that they both felt was worth saving.

That night, Emil dreamt of the woman in Rutherford's photograph. It was a confused dream that could very well have been a nightmare. The sepia woman, facing away from him, lifted her hand from her thigh and beckoned to him. As he approached her, he stretched out his hand, wanting to touch the dip of her waist. Just as he was about to touch her, she turned to him and looked at him with her dead gray eyes.

Emil woke with a start to find his breath caught in his chest. As he waited to exhale, he felt a sticky wetness between his thighs. He knew that it was what Rutherford, who boasted of having had many, called a wet dream. He got out of bed to change his nightclothes and sheets. Unfortunately, in so doing, he woke up one of the Unfortunates whose bed was opposite his. The Unfortunate called Emil a deviant and jeered at him loudly enough to wake up some of the other boys.

Before Emil could fully register what he was doing, he had leapt onto the Unfortunate's bed and, his fists landing indiscriminately on the boy's body, pummeled the laughter out of him. Anyone else who had been entertaining the idea of laughing at Emil as well was effectively silenced.

Emil would have probably beaten the Unfortunate to a pulp if Master Duthie had not come to pull him off the boy.

Shortly afterwards, standing in front of a very disappointed Master Archie and a slightly impressed Master Duthie, Emil had no choice but to tell them about the soiled sheets. He did not choose to tell them about the photograph Rutherford had or how the woman in it had visited him in his dreams.

The two masters glanced at each other uncomfortably. They never agreed on anything so it was a surprise when they nodded to each other briefly before Master Duthie said, "You're becoming a man."

"What is happening to you is natural...normal...something all adolescent boys go through," Master Archie said, attempting to make things clearer.

Emil, who had supposed that the Unfortunate was right in

thinking that only deviants had wet dreams, was just about to smile with relief when Master Archie said, "This does not excuse your behavior. This is not how a true gentleman behaves."

"Gentleman! I know not of gentlemen, wot, but I'd say that a man, a real man—" Master Duthie burst out before Master Archie's eyes could stop him from continuing.

"This is your first infraction of the rules," Master Archie said. "We will let you go with a strong warning this time. There will not be a repeat of this. Have we made ourselves perfectly clear?"

"Yes, sir!"

When Emil returned to the dormitory ward, he found that Courteney had been woken up by the commotion and was apparently awaiting his return. He was sitting on the bed of the Unfortunate whom Emil had pummeled. He did not say anything to Emil; he just observed him with an expression of worry. As Emil approached the bed and prepared his apology, the matron came in with her first-aid kit and Emil realized then that Courteney had not been waiting for him at all.

That realization finally broke the thin thread that connected them and brought about the end of the something between them.

All endings have their beginnings, as we all know, and the end of the something between Emil and Courteney began months before, on that early September morning in 1939 when Master Archie received the message that interrupted his lesson on Joseph Conrad's *Heart of Darkness*. Even though Master Archie was trying to encourage Emil to read Conrad with a more critical eye, *Heart of Darkness* was a new favorite of his because it had elements of Haggard, Burroughs, and Kipling.

When Master Archie returned to class after having left abruptly, he was a grave and changed man. Instead of having the boys continue with the Conrad lesson, he had them read Wilfred Owen's *"Dulce et Decorum Est."* Master Archie assigned Emil to read the last four lines:

> *My friend, you would not tell with such high zest*
> *To children ardent for some desperate glory,*
> *The old* Lie: Dulce et decorum est
> Pro patria mori.

After Emil had read the last stanza, breathing in all the right places, using the punctuation to help him build a rhythm, and enunciating and articulating the diction with care as he had been taught, Master Archie informed the class that Germany had, hours before, invaded Poland and that Britain and France had declared war on Germany.

"This is the business of empire, make no mistake," Master Archie said. "What else could possibly come of a few countries carving out the rest of the world for themselves? It was inevitable that their rapacious greed would turn inward on itself...I want you to ask yourselves, gentlemen, where the real heart of darkness lies."

Emil could not follow much of what Master Archie was saying—he was disappointed that the lesson on Conrad had been dropped and kept hoping all of this was leading back to it. He was also somewhat disappointed in himself because he felt that he had not done the four lines of the poem sufficient justice. He strongly suspected that he had mangled the Latin. If only Master Archie had given him other lines to read. What he could have done, for instance, with lines as rich in alliteration and assonance as:

If you could hear, at every jolt, the blood
Come gargling from the froth-corrupted lungs,
Obscene as cancer, bitter as the cud
Of vile, incurable sores on innocent tongues, –

Rutherford had hurried over those lines without any thought or care.

While Emil was thus lost in his own reflections, Courteney, by contrast, listened avidly to what Master Archie was saying and nodded slowly as if things long up in the air were finally beginning to settle in his head. Of the entire class, he was the only boy nodding; the others listlessly shifted in their seats.

When they arrived in Master Duthie's class, Courteney, still pondering what Master Archie had said, asked Master Duthie, "Do you agree with Master Archie, sir, that Germany's invasion of Poland was inevitable given that Europe has been colonizing the rest of the world for centuries now?"

Master Duthie glared at Courteney as if he had, in front of his very eyes, sprouted a second head, before barking out, "Wot? Wot? Master Archie, wot?"

Courteney was about to repeat the question when Master Duthie put up his hand and stopped him. He took off his pince nez and rubbed the bridge of his nose before resigning himself to a certain reality and saying, "Master Archibald is too much of a gentleman to realize that empire-building is not the business of gentlemen but the business of men."

Not satisfied, Courteney pressed his point, whatever it was, by asking, "What do you think of Germany's invasion of Poland, sir?"

This kind of tenacity in Master Duthie's class was a first for Courteney, who was generally known more for his retreats than for his advances.

Exasperated, Master Duthie explained to Courteney,

and, by extension, the rest of the class, a point he had made previously and that he had never imagined he would have to make again, which was that most of the world had been in darkness and needed the light of European civilization. "History alone can tell us why Germany has invaded Poland. From history we *know* that when the Europeans first arrived here, not a century ago, all was darkness. *All* was darkness, wot. There was no civilization. There was no history—"

"That is not true, sir," Courteney interrupted.

The class was shocked into silence. In the history of the History class at the Selous School for Boys, this was probably the first time that a student had ever interrupted Master Duthie.

Master Duthie's face was florid when he spat out, "I beg your pardon!"

"Not true, sir," Courteney repeated. Whatever he had heard in Master Archie's class had truly emboldened him. "The Africans have civilization. There are great examples of civilizations throughout the continent, some even more ancient than our own. Just in this country alone—"

Apoplectic, Master Duthie struck his palm down hard on the top of Courteney's desk. "We'll see about civilizations throughout the continent, wot!" Master Duthie spat. "Hands out in front of you, my boy!" he growled, before the ruler came down with a loud thwack ten times on Courteney's knuckles.

After that brief act of violence, Master Duthie was subdued and pacified when he said, "Anyone who says that we did not bring civilization to this part of the world is a liar... and an enemy of the empire."

The subject was closed.

Emil felt sorry for Courteney, who had been so soundly and roundly reprimanded in front of the whole class. Emil had not understood enough of the gist of what Master Archie had said to judge whether Courteney had been justified in tenaciously holding on to his point. He did know, all the same, that Courteney had gone about the entire business with Master Duthie the wrong way. The best way to have a confrontation with a man like Master Duthie was privately in his rooms, where he could suffer the unexpectedness of a challenge without an audience.

"You didn't have to say anything," Emil had said, by way of comfort, to Courteney after the class had ended.

"Yes, I did," Courteney said as he walked past Emil, who had waited for him.

Emil decided to let Courteney walk alone. That had been the beginning of the end of the something between them.

Separately, they walked to Science class, where Master Findlay gave an intentionally complicated and convoluted lecture on the importance of Reason in Man's life. Master Findlay took a not-so-secret delight in confounding rather than elucidating, but for all that, Emil picked up enough from the lecture to comprehend that Reason seemed to have replaced the "command of God" that he had learned of in his earlier Religious Studies classes. Where it had been God who gave Man his dominion over all the things he had created, now it was Reason that gave Man his supremacy and mastery. "To think is Man's distinct privilege. Cogito, ergo sum. Other species rely on instinct and not on reason and that is why we have the hierarchy we see all around us," Master Findlay said, rocking on his heels, thumbs hooked into his suspenders, enjoying what Master Archie called "obfuscating."

From the corner of his eye, Emil saw Courteney raise his hand. The entire class groaned in response.

Emil knew what Courteney would ask: "How do we know, for certain, that other species do not have Reason?" It was something that Emil and Courteney had discussed before and something Emil was wondering too. But when Master Findlay called on Courteney, he surprisingly asked, "What makes us so sure that Man is rational? What if he is without Reason... irrational?"

It was Master Findlay's turn to be confounded. He blinked several times, removed his glasses and cleaned them, inspected them, and then put them back on the bridge of his nose before saying to Courteney, "I am aware that today's news has come as a shock to us all. Smythe-Sinclair, you are excused. Please make your way to the sick bay."

Courteney did not argue, he quietly placed his books in his desk and left the classroom. The rest of the class cheered once he was gone. It occurred to Emil that there was something fundamentally different about Courteney. It was this something that still made him an Unfortunate. It was this something that made wide and unnavigable the rift that was growing between them, despite every thwarted attempt to salvage what they had once had.

CHAPTER 8

———◆———

By the time they were fifteen years old, Emil and Courteney were barely acquaintances, which was why the plagiarism incident that occurred mystified everyone.

As a response to a prompt that asked the students to compare and contrast the use of tone, voice, point of view and imagery in John McCrae's "In Flanders Fields" and Laurence Binyon's "For the Fallen,"' Master Archie had received almost identical essays from Emil and Courteney. Given that Courteney was the stronger student of the two, Master Archie charged Emil with cheating. Emil vehemently denied the charge and hinted that Master Archie was guilty of favoritism. According to Emil, if there was any similarity between the two essays, it was simply a coincidence. In defense of both of them, Courteney said that there was no conceivable way that Emil could have copied his essay because he had locked it away in his desk drawer soon after he had written it.

The matter should have ended there, but it did not. Master Archie would not let it; he was like a dog that had lost his favorite bone. With rabid zeal, he investigated the matter until Stuardts was standing in a puddle of his own urine in front of him, Master Duthie and the school headmaster. With knees knocking, eyes streaming, nose leaking, Stuardts explained that he had brought one of his father's skeleton keys to school and that Emil had borrowed it from him. He swore on his grandmother's grave that he had no idea what

Emil intended to do with the key.

Cheating was an actionable offense at the Selous School for Boys and so Emil could and should have been suspended for it. Be that as it may, Emil had become a vital part of the school's competitive sports teams, as Master Duthie purposefully and pointedly reminded Master Archie before he asked Emil to join them in the headmaster's office.

"Why did you do it?" Master Archie asked Emil, hypocritically looking crestfallen, as if he were not the one who had hounded out the truth.

Emil decided, in that moment, that he did not much care for hypocrites.

"Because my extracurricular activities and commitments take up all my time and I have no hours left in the day to dedicate to my homework," Emil honestly responded.

"That is a poor excuse."

It was not an excuse, poor or otherwise; it was a reality. Ever since Emil had proved that he was good at sports, he had been expected to excel at them. His coaches were always telling him that they relied on him to bring home wins and trophies. Master Archie knew this. Everybody knew this. Sitting there as imperious as a judge, pretending not to be aware of the strain the school put on its students with its unrelenting expectation that boys should excel at *everything*, Master Archie was being a hypocrite.

Again, Emil determined that he did not like hypocrites.

"Why did you do it?" Master Archie repeated.

"I did it because I did not want to fail," Emil truthfully replied.

"But you did fail!" Master Archie said incredulously. "You failed yourself. Can you not see that?"

Emil wanted to laugh at this. How could he possibly fail by cheating so that he could pass?

Perhaps he had, indeed, laughed, because Master Archie shook his head in sad resignation. With that shake of the head, Emil realized that Master Duthie was right; Master Archie was too much of a gentleman to understand the business of men.

Emil felt sorry for him.

Master Archie felt sorry enough for Emil to not seek his suspension. But his disappointment in him meant that things between them would never go back to what they had been before.

The rift between Emil, Courteney, and Master Archie grew even wider after the production of the Selous Springtime Follies, a revue the students put together toward the end of the school year. Most of the acts were well-worn lampoons of aspects of life at the Selous School for Boys. Emil and Rutherford's act, for instance, caricaturing the relationship between Master Archie and Master Duthie, had been part of the show in one form or another for over ten years. Other permanent fixtures were some eleven-year-old boy trying his luck with "Ave Maria," Master Duthie trying to be stiff upper-lipped during his rendition of "Danny Boy," and the entire school trying valiantly not to make faces during "Auld Lang Syne."

The acts were so unoriginal that, even though the show did not consist of a set list, Mistress Findlay usually wrote up the playbill in advance and the students filled in their names where appropriate. Therefore, even before he performed it on stage, Courteney's *The Tragedy of Adam Renders* had already caused quite a disturbance because Mistress Findlay had had to write up the playbill anew.

Adam Renders was a name that Master Duthie often mentioned in his History class as an example of a reject of empire. "The man was the first to set eyes on the ancient ruins of the Great City and instead of sharing what he had discovered with the world, he pitiably chose to give himself over to alcohol and to go native. He became almost as savage as the African, wot. They say he was truly wild by the end of it. Damn shame, that. He could have been a great man of history—instead he gave that honor to Karl Mauch, to whom he showed the ruins. Some men have a weakness within them...an inborn failing that does not allow them to fulfil their true potential. That is their tragedy. That was Adam Renders's tragedy."

Courteney's *The Tragedy of Adam Renders* was rehearsed by the Unfortunates in Master Archie's rooms, under his guidance, which was probably why no one thought to suspect anything. After sufficiently raucous laughter greeted Emil and Rutherford's act and modest applause followed Matthew Follett's shaky but heartfelt 'Ave Maria,' the stage was set for Courteney's production.

It soon became apparent that the Unfortunates had really outdone themselves. They had constructed a movable stage comprising a canopy of an ox-drawn wagon in the background and a campfire in the foreground. They, thanks to the tirelessly productive hands of the Smythe-Sinclair women, were dressed in realistic pioneer attire and their faces were made up to look like men. At first all sixteen of them sat around the campfire as they turned the carcass of some cardboard creature on the spit. Then Courteney, like the storyteller of yore, stood up and started his soliloquy. As he performed it the other Unfortunates reenacted what he was saying:

"My name is Adam Renders. I was born in Germany in 1822 but emigrated to the United States of America at a young age. That first voyage across the Atlantic gave me a taste for adventure that would be with me all the days of my life.

The times were full of the seduction of adventure. The world was all of a sudden a wide open and accessible thing that a man...any man...could reach. A man born into poverty and obscurity could suddenly remove the shackles of generations-long misfortune and make something of the family name. The very idea of it...the prospect of it...was heady, intoxicating. The very air we breathed was excitement itself. Some of us went mad with it. Manifest destiny! Go west, young man! I could have chosen to venture forth into the American West, but I chose South Africa in its place. Africa! Dark...wild... unknown. A man could come across a thing already extant— a genus of a flower, a waterfall that had raged since time immemorial—name it after himself or his queen and find himself, suddenly respectable, back in a European city, addressing some society or other. One could shoot species of exotic animals with abandon, knowing that the grand palaces and homes of Europe would gladly collect one's menagerie. If you placed your foot on some uncharted terri-tory and were lucky enough not to be killed by a virulent and pugnacious tropical disease, then you would almost certainly find your way into the history books. Suddenly an ordinary man could enter history and become a part of it. His name, his family name, would be recorded for posterity. You ventured forth for all the men in your family who had come before you and had labored on other men's lands, sailed on other men's ships and fought in other men's wars...men whose names had been easily forgotten soon after their final death knell had rung. You did it for yourself as well. As you walked through the treacherous tranquillity of the savannah grasslands, the sun overhead unrelentingly beating down on you, the sick-ness that had left your entire body weak and aching threaten-ing to finally stop you in your tracks and consume you whole... you used the meager energy reserve you had left to turn your head and glance over your shoulder to see the peasants, the sailors, the soldiers who had been so easy to forget following close behind...and you found the strength to carry on. At least that is how it was with me. I came for the fame. Others came for the fortune. The song was different but the siren was the same.

"Once in South Africa, I joined the Voortrekkers and married Elsje Pretorius, the daughter of Andries Pretorius, their leader. I loved to trade, hunt, and explore the country and it was during one of my many expeditions that, in 1867, I came across the ancient ruins of the Great City. They were truly a sight to behold. I attempted to annex the land for the Transvaal Republic and, in exchange, promised the local chief weapons to defend his people against marauding tribes in the region. I was so taken with the ruins that in 1868 I brought my family to this country and showed them where I wanted them to settle. My wife Elsje, for her part, was opposed to living so far away from civilization and amongst the native population. I took my family back to the Transvaal but visited the ruins every year. On one such trek I was shot by a native's poisoned arrow and died."

Apparently that had been the end of the first act, because the Unfortunates started rearranging themselves on the stage. There was scattered, hesitant applause and more than one boy stole a glance in Master Duthie's direction to assess how he was responding to the show so as to respond likewise. He sat with a straight back and a furrowed brow; there had been nothing, as yet, to offend. He did, nonetheless, say for good measure, loud enough for everyone in the hall to hear, "Wot? Is there more? How much of this utter nonsense should decent people be expected to sit through?" Most of the boys laughed at this and Master Duthie was pleased with himself.

The second act began with Courteney, as Adam Renders,

addressing the audience directly. As he did so, the other Unfortunates dismantled the canopy of the ox-drawn carriage and reconstructed it as a rudimentary map of Africa.

"Makes for a great story, does it not?" Courteney said. "Not surprisingly, there is as much fiction in it as there is fact. It is true that I was married to Elsje Pretorius. It is true that together we had four children, Helena Barendina Norbetha, Jan Adam, Willem Andries Pretorius and Hendrik Jacobus. It is also true that I left my family in 1869 and settled in the vicinity of the ancient ruins of the Great City. It is also true that I lived there with Chief Bika's daughter. It is also true that I was the father of another child, a child with light-brown skin. It was said of me that I had gone native—I suppose that was a thing that was easier to say than the truth. The truth is that I had rejected empire. My tragedy is that I did not discover anything because there was nothing to discover.

"Those who built the ancient ruins of the Great City knew of their existence, those who used it knew of their existence. Conceivably, I could have gone down in history as the first European man to see them—but I was not. The Portuguese have been in this region since the fifteenth century. Then there were the Arab slave traders—"

"Wot! Wot! Arabs wot!" Master Duthie interjected from the audience. If Courteney had had more to say, he never got a chance to because Master Duthie barked, "Smythe-Sinclair, off that stage, now!" Not waiting to be heeded, he leapt onto the stage and dragged Courteney off it. "I will make you sorry for this, my boy," he snarled. The rest of the hall sat in scandalized silence.

Master Duthie wanted Courtney and the Unfortunates expelled. Master Archie threatened to resign if such were the case. Master Duthie charged Master Archie with penning the show himself and using the Unfortunates as his mouthpiece.

What fifteen-year-old boy could write such a play, wot? The Smythe-Sinclairs were called to the school. All of them came: the father, the mother, and the six sisters. They could find nothing wrong with the play and were actually quite proud of it and of Courteney for having written it. Master Duthie came to the conclusion that the entire family was made up of imbeciles.

Mister Smythe-Sinclair, with great delicacy and diplomacy, reminded the headmaster that he was both on the board of trustees and an open-palmed donor to the school. At which point the headmaster stressed that he was happy to let the situation go unpunished. Boys will be boys. What was youth without its flights of fancy and all that?

For Emil the episode proved something that he had come to suspect during and after the plagiarism case: Master Archie, who almost had Emil suspended and who fought against Courteney's expulsion, had found in Courteney something that was lacking in Emil. Emil convinced himself that this situation was not something to be saddened by because it simply meant that he was a man and Master Archie... and Courteney...and the Unfortunates were not. But still, he remembered the warm glow of the hurricane lamp on that night when they had first met, he remembered eating the animal's still-warm heart, he remembered that brief moment when they had been gentlemen together and he allowed himself an equally brief moment to regret the loss of that warmth.

CHAPTER 9

————◆————

Emil did not know what to call it. He would never know what to call it.

Whatever it was, it did not last long and for that he was forever grateful.

During the thing that he could not give a name to, they met perhaps six times in all. She had offered to give him extra lessons. He was not doing particularly well in any subject and needed all the help he could get to avoid being put on academic probation and possibly even expelled. He might have been indispensable on the sports field, but the school also prided itself on its stellar national-exam performance, and so there was a need for him to show what the headmaster called 'a marked improvement' in his schoolwork. He was, therefore, initially very much obliged to her when she offered to help him.

True to her word, the first three meetings had consisted of lessons. He did a series of charcoal portraits that he was rather proud of and had began a watercolor painting that he was eager to finish. To be sure, she had touched him on the shoulder and on the knee, but it had all seemed to be in passing. She had also brushed his hair from his brow when he came in with the wind having untidied it, but she had seemed to be her usual somewhat detached and permanently preoccupied self, so Emil had not thought much of any of it.

On that fourth visit when she had said, almost as soon as he entered the room, "You have absolutely no idea how beautiful you are. You will devastatingly break a lot of hearts someday," he thought, briefly, that she wanted to paint him. But she had not. She had, instead, taken both his hands in hers and then placed them on her breasts. "Don't be shy," she said. "You need to appreciate the female form. No man in this godforsaken place does." She then instructed him to feel the shape and weight of her breasts. He did as he was told and comprehended only too late, when she threw her swan-like neck back and moaned, that there was no painting to be done that day.

He had not gone for the extra lesson the following week and she had made no mention of it. But then, two weeks later, in front of the class, she said, "Coetzee, do not forget you have an extra lesson with me here today at 2:30."

Whatever that was that had happened before would not happen again, Emil was certain, not after she had announced their meeting in front of the entire class.

He was right. It did not happen again.

"You'll be a love and forgive me for my madness, won't you?" she had said, laughing lightly. "We are friends, you and I, and friends have to forgive each other, don't they? I will paint you someday and you will see how absolutely breathtakingly beautiful you are. Then maybe you'll understand...friends?" she said, offering him her hand.

Emil had shaken it, relieved.

The lesson had gone well. Though she had stood a little too close to him, she never touched him.

But the sixth meeting was something very different. She must have undressed while he daubed at the canvas, absorbed in trying to get the right shading on his still life of a bowl of fruit, because when he turned to her she was reclining on a chaise lounge, her pinkish hand resting on her milk-white thigh. She was completely naked. When her hand began to stray to her mons pubis, Emil averted his eyes and stood up quickly, upsetting his easel and his canvas.

"It's all part of the lesson...don't be afraid. The madness has left me, I assure you. But you cannot draw, paint or sculpt the human form without touching it...without knowing it sensually," she said as she got up from the chaise lounge and walked toward him. The next thing he felt was her hot breath against his right ear as she whispered, "Touch me, Emil...touch me, My Own Little One. You have to feel me...art is very tactile ...sensory...physical...carnal even."

She took his paint-stained right hand and guided it over her lips, over the flesh of her throat, breasts, stomach and thighs. When she placed his hand in the space between her thighs, she gasped. In a frenzy, she smothered him with kisses, pushed him to the floor where he landed on the canvas of his still life painting, unbuttoned his trousers, held him in her hands, straddled his hips and placed her left breast in his mouth. Emil instinctively sucked on her areola and immediately regretted it. She screamed and rocked herself on top of him, all the while calling him "My Own Little One."

Soon it was over, but it was not over soon enough.

Shortly after he staggered out of the Art room, Emil vomited and vomited and vomited as though his body was trying to rid itself of all the sustenance he had received at the Selous School for Boys. Even when he had thrown up everything, he still felt sick to his stomach.

As he fumbled to put his clothes to rights outside the Art room door, he felt tears sting his eyes. He had promised himself, a long time ago, to never cry again. But he could not help it. Something precious had been lost. Something he needed to cry over, to mourn.

Emil only became aware of Master Archie regarding him

with an expression of horror as he was fastening the last button of his shirt. Master Archie's expression of horror turned to one of pity as his eye traveled repeatedly from Emil to the Art room door. Finally, Master Archie seemed to have decided on the right words to say, but just as he was about to say them, Courteney joined him with a smile on his face, ready to tell him something interesting.

It was all too much for Emil to bear. He ran off. Away from them. Trying not to think of that first night when they had met under the warm glow of friendship. The night, a lifetime ago, it seemed now, when his smile had been long and lasting.

That night Emil dreamt of the sepia-colored woman with the dead gray eyes. She gazed at him for a long time without saying or doing anything. When she eventually opened her mouth to speak, he realized that he was terrified of what she would say and woke up with a start.

Once he was awake, he remembered the blue-and-white scarf that had been snatched away from him outside the La Grange skating rink and he was glad that he had not been allowed to take it with him to the Selous School for Boys, as he had intended, because what kind of home would that have possibly been for such a beautiful and delicate thing?

The matron came to check on Emil, told him that Master Archie had excused him from class and activities, and took him to the sick bay. By midday a group of boys was gathered around Emil because they had heard that Mistress and Master Findlay had packed their belongings and left the school in the dead of night. There were rumors as to why that had happened and they all led to Emil. Emil was filled with dread. The last thing he wanted from his peers was sympathy. He did not want to be seen and thought of as a victim. He soon understood, however, that the boys around him were not offering him their sympathy but something entirely different.

They were offering him their...respect.

"I reckon she was just gasping for it. She was, wasn't she?" Rutherford asked with awe and envy in his voice. "Wasn't she?"

"Yes...yes, she was," Emil stammered.

"I knew it. She looks like the type that is always in heat. A right proper bitch."

Emil flinched at the words and decided not to respond.

"And I reckon you gave it to her good and proper, didn't you?" Rutherford sounded too assured to need reassurance but demanded it nonetheless. "Didn't you?"

"Yes...yes, I did."

"Did what?"

"I gave it to her good and proper."

There were whistles, hoots, and howls of appreciation.

Emil found himself the hero of his peers. Not only had he lost his virginity at fifteen, he had done so by seducing an older woman, his teacher at that, and when he had tired of her not only had he ended things with her, he had also got her fired along with her cuckold husband.

Emil took great comfort in this version of events because it was so very far from the awful truth.

Master Archie and Courteney tried to talk to him on several and separate occasions but he resolutely refused to talk to them. He knew that if he talked to them, he would tell them of how, over the years, she had invited him to the Art room and encouraged him to tell her about his parents and his life at home. How she had teared up when he told her of their silence. How she had told him about the stillborn baby she had had. How she had taken to calling him "My Own Little One." How she had started giving him birthday presents when he turned thirteen: a set of paintbrushes; a box of handkerchiefs that had his initials embroidered on them; a book of classical female nudes. How she had come to him in the guise of a mother and then turned into something that was the very opposite of a mother.

Emil chose, instead, to talk to the boys who had made a hero out of him. He repeated the story that they had created as though it was his own. The story of how he had conquered (he chose the word deliberately) Mrs. Findlay became more elaborate and sensational with each retelling and became the most requested story at bedtime.

At night, when all the other boys in the dormitory were peacefully asleep, the sepia-colored woman with the dead gray eyes would visit Emil trying to tell him something, but he always made sure to wake up before she could.

PART TWO

---•---

ADULTHOOD - A POOR PLAYER

CHAPTER 10

———◆———

There was still enough of the cherub about the face for Emil to know that it belonged to Courteney. Emil knew that he could never be pleased with a face like that, but judging by the way Courteney was assuredly and animatedly using it to express whatever it was that he was saying, Courteney liked his face well enough.

The last time they had seen each other had been five years earlier. One had been the Head Boy with a stellar academic record and the other the Sports Captain with a not-so-stellar academic record. As he silently helped his father put his trunk into the car, Emil glanced over at Courteney as he stood amidst a gaggle of seven women who were all fussing over him. He and Courteney had spoken to each other only when absolutely necessary during their last two years at the Selous School for Boys, but this was their last day at the school and they both felt that something should mark the occasion. They were now eighteen and the school had kept true to part of its motto and turned them from boys to men. Whether or not they would become the men of history, only the future could tell. As though having agreed on the gesture beforehand, they nodded to each other before the cossetted Courteney was ushered into a car and driven away.

Now, sitting at a corner table at Scobie's, Courteney looked as if he belonged to the set that patronized the most dignified and distinguished place in the City of Kings, the Gentleman's Club. The common currency of conversation at the Gentleman's Club was prosperity and the order of the day was polite diplomacy. Courteney looked decidedly out of place at Scobie's, where conversations about women, sports, dashed dreams and disappointed hopes could swiftly turn violent and ugly.

Even though Scobie's, no longer a haunt for the rejects of empire, was the place for a man like Emil, he had not patronized the establishment for over six years. The last time he had been to Scobie's was when he was seventeen. He had come, as always, with Uncle Scott on the eve of Uncle Scott's departure to go and fight the good fight. Uncle Scott, never a happy drunk, turned unexpectedly malicious when he yelled into Emil's face, "Your grandmother was a whore." At Emil's confused expression, he explained, "Your father's mother was a dancer. She may have started as a chorus girl, but she definitely did not end as one." Uncle Scott had conspiratorially put his arm around Emil. "Your father is literally a son of a bitch...and that is who your mother chooses to remain married to." Reasonably feeling insulted, Emil had stood up to leave, which instantly sobered up Uncle Scott. "I'm sorry," he slurred. "None of it is your fault, my boy...you and I have always had a good relationship, haven't we? The genuine article. No stringing along here."

Emil reluctantly sat back down on the bar stool.

"You're a right good-looking bastard...are you sure you're not mine?"

Emil smiled at Uncle Scott's bungled attempt at reconciliation.

"Son I never had," Uncle Scott mumbled into his whiskey glass. "When I come back I will take you to the third floor of the Cecil Hotel. Things happen there that will make you a man...I promise." Uncle Scott had hugged Emil to him with the desperation of a drunkard and tearfully whispered, "You are the only son-like thing I will ever know and hold."

Those were the last words that Uncle Scott, who did not return from the good fight, had ever said to Emil.

When news of Uncle Scott's non-return reached Emil via a surprisingly to-the-point letter from his father, he and Rutherford, who had forged a note from his father, had obtained a weekend pass and driven all night to the City of Kings, where they had gone straight to the third floor of the Cecil Hotel and done things there that had made them men.

"Emil?" a voice said now, interrupting his reverie. "It is you—I would know the back of that head anywhere," Courteney said, beaming and sitting down on the barstool next to Emil.

"Saw you earlier...didn't want to disturb," Emil said, his head indicating the seat that Courteney had just vacated.

"Chap was telling me about this new organization, the Capricorn Africa Society. Heard of it?"

Emil shook his head.

"Sounds interesting. Been invited. Will pop in and see," Courteney said, indicating to the bartender that he wanted to have his Collins glass refilled. Emil suspiciously eyed the lemon slice floating on the dregs of the cocktail and feared that at one point the drink had contained a cherry. He wouldn't be caught dead drinking something like that.

"You should come along," Courteney said as he happily welcomed another Tom Collins.

Courteney's curly hair flopped untidily over his brow, his cheeks still had their perpetual pinkish hue and his eyelashes had been bleached by the sun. He had long lost the chubbiness of his youth, but there was still something very boyish... no...something almost feminine about him. *God had been extremely cruel in making him male,* Emil thought. The Smythe-Sinclairs should have had seven girls.

"Would you like to?" Courteney asked, interrupting Emil's thoughts again.

"Like to what?"

"Come to the meeting of the Capricorn Africa Society?"

"Yes...I suppose."

"Good!" Courteney said, grinning as he patted Emil on the back.

What would you call a personality like this, Emil wondered. *Affable?* The girl that Emil was seeing...well, one of them... was into psychology and personalities. She was constantly trying to decipher his personality. "You seem so distant. You are so closed off. You refuse to connect on any meaningful level... I just cannot make you out," she would say as she scrutinized his face for something she seemed afraid to find. That was what he got for getting involved with a university student. The sex was good, though. But then again, with him the sex was always good. He made sure of it. His many lessons under the capable tutelage of the third floor of the Cecil Hotel had made sure of it. He had left her, the university student, in South Africa. He had left them all in South Africa. Just as four years earlier he had left them all here at home, in the City of Kings.

"You will devastatingly break a lot of hearts someday..."

Emil downed his beer and nodded to the bartender. It was time for the harder stuff.

"So what have you been up to?" Courteney asked with another pat on the back.

"Been in South Africa for the past four years."

"You don't say? Me too. Which university?"

Of course Courteney had attended university.

"At Wits myself. Studying Theatre Arts. Just finished my honors. Met a girl. She was studying English. Brightest spark I know. Married her. Almost two years ago now. Lovely, lovely girl. The best."

Of course Courteney had graduated with an honors. Of course Courteney had married the first girl he met. Of course the girl was a lovely girl. Of course Courteney thought that she was the best. Probably had not slept with the girl before marrying her. No sampling of the goods before purchasing them for our Courteney. He had respected and honored her virtue, until their wedding night when he had done his duty by her and to himself, all the while being very much the gentleman.

Married at twenty-one! God forbid! Only Courteney would believe that that was something to be proud of.

"So where did you attend?"

"The Williams Arms."

Courteney looked puzzled.

"My great-grandmother's boarding house in Durban. I helped my grandmother run it."

"Oh, I see...sounds like a bit of fun, that." To make his words sound true enough, Courteney smiled at Emil.

Seeing his smile, Emil wondered how many times Courteney had been punched in the face by someone who was just not in the mood for affable.

Courteney kept smiling encouragingly, waiting for more of the story. But there really was no more to tell of Emil's story— not to Courteney anyway.

Emil had scraped through enough of his final national examinations to qualify for a position in the BSAP, so he had taken the necessary steps toward joining its ranks. While in school, he had hoped to join the army and fight the good fight, but the war had ended just when he was eligible and ready to join up, and so he had not been able to avenge Uncle Scott's death. Regretting that the war had just ended, and tormenting himself with the knowledge that, at nineteen, Frederick Courteney Selous had already made his way to Algoa Bay and was poised to become a man of history, Emil, in the end, could not reconcile himself to simply following in his father's footsteps. Where was the adventure in that? If he wanted to be a man of history, and, at nineteen, he felt more than certain that he did, he could not go down the well-beaten track. He would have to chart his own course, and so, with very little regret, he had stopped training for the BSAP.

The opportunity to do something different with his life came from a rather unlikely source. His grandmother's husband, Anthony Simons, had died of a heart attack quite suddenly and his grandmother, never having learned how to exist without the help of a man, had urgently requested that Emil come to Durban. Still feeling wounded by her mother's and stepfather's treatment of her, his mother pouted her protestation, but Emil went anyway. He was nineteen and it was time for his own voyage of discovery to begin.

His decision to leave was not without its consequences; he left behind him a trail of hearts in varied stages and states of brokenness and disrepair. Emil had been a popular fixture on the social scene of the City of Kings ever since, at seventeen, he had stood on the diving board at the Municipal Bathing Pools and noticed that ladies of all ages were watching him appraisingly, approvingly, and admiringly. He had smiled uncertainly and the younger ladies had giggled. Emil dived into the pool, swam to the other side, and emerged a natural flirt.

He began to appreciate and enjoy the City of Kings after that: Centenary Park, the theatre and the Municipal Bathing Pools all became places where he could meet girls and...go through the paces...as he liked to call it. For all that, by the time he made his way to Durban, Emil had needed something new to happen in his life for quite some time. The pleasures of the City of Kings had begun to blanch and fade under the constant glare of the sun. The girls had been fun until he started to feel restless and they started to feel that he was somehow necessary to their happiness. Even though they were physically varied, they all appeared to have the same ambition, which was to be married...to him.

A nostalgic Emil recollected, and perhaps idealized, the adventures of his childhood on the BSAP outpost at the foot of the Matopos Hills. He had felt so free and alive then and he wanted that element of freedom back again. He wanted to be in the wide open veld and to be master of all he surveyed. As he went through the paces with different girls, he longed for that unadulterated sense of belonging that he had once felt, but it never came.

Truth be told, he had accepted his grandmother's offer because it was the only one that held the promise of a lost self that he might find again.

Once Emil arrived in Durban, he tried to love the city and failed miserably. The weather was too humid for him. The tropical vegetation was too foreign and exotic for a man who had breathed in the dry expanse of the savannah and made it a part of him.

He liked the girls in Durban well enough and, happily for him, they liked him well enough too. They were refreshingly less provincial than the girls back home, which made Emil happy. But that kind of happiness could only be fleeting and, inevitably, as seemed to be the wont of women everywhere, the Durban ladies, with all their worldliness, began to desire a permanence from him that he was not willing to give.

Soon enough, Emil was feeling cornered and trapped and, once again, in desperate need of a way out. So when Rutherford told Emil that he had used his father's connections to secure an entry-level position for him with the Department of Native Affairs, a position that would involve exploring and trekking the savannah, Emil had left Durban without a moment's hesitation.

Courteney did not need to, or deserve to, know any of this, Emil firmly concluded as he took a sip of his whiskey.

A slap on the back of the head that made Emil choke on his drink let him know that Rutherford had joined them.

"Coetzee."

"Rutherford."

"And what have we here?" Rutherford said, squeezing himself between Emil and Courteney. "Courteney 'The Sucker' Smythe-Sinclair." Rutherford giggled as he reached for a barstool to make himself more comfortable. "Are you finally going to tell us the truth about you and Master Archie?" he asked Courteney.

Courteney sent a pitying glance in Emil's direction. Emil did not understand why Courteney should be the one to feel sorry for him when Rutherford was teasing *him* about Master Archie. Besides, Emil did not want Courteney's sympathy— then, now or ever.

Courteney stood up and took a long drink from his Collins glass before patting Emil on the back, saying, "Right...I will see you Saturday at the Gentleman's Club. Meeting starts at six, but I suspect it will be well-attended so best to be there at 5:30 just to be on the safe side." He slammed his hand on top of the counter and said, rather theatrically, "And that will be me off, then."

Emil and Rutherford watched as Courteney, standing by the coat rack near the door, put on his coat and hat and transformed in front of their very eyes. Suddenly there was nothing even remotely boyish or feminine about Courteney Smythe-Sinclair because he came across as every bit the gentleman that he was.

"The Sucker still thinks he is better than the rest of us," Rutherford said.

Emil shrugged and asked, "Would you like to go to the Cecil Hotel?"

"Does a dog do it standing on its hind legs?" Rutherford asked, draining his glass. "It is so good to have you back. The City of Kings is just not the same without you. You really know how to thoroughly and rightly enjoy this place."

Emil stood up to go, aware that his glass was not the only thing that was empty.

There had been a time when the Cecil Hotel had brought Emil untold joy, but that time had come and gone without his being aware of its ending. Emil had relied on the third floor of the hotel to teach him about the relationship between men and women, and he had indeed learned much, but now that he had put that education to good use, he could not help but feel the...transactional quality...the reduction...the degradation of the very relationship that he had come to learn about. So, that night, before anything could actually happen, Emil found himself excusing himself, paying the lady and going to walk the streets of the City of Kings alone.

It might have been comforting for Emil to feel that he had outgrown the need for such a place, but he knew that he had not. Seeing it for what it truly was would not deter him from returning to it. He knew himself well enough to know that much at least. It was just that, at this very moment, what he sincerely missed, what he truthfully wanted, was the chase. How he loved the chase and how women loved to be chased. There was no chase on the third floor of the Cecil Hotel, just the barest necessities of life.

The chase worked best, without a doubt, if there was a pack of them. A party, a dance, a picnic, any gathering really, was where he did his best work. Emil would single one out —preferably not the prettiest one because she would be expecting it—and zero in on her and then move in for the kill. He would approach her while she was still there amongst the pack and talk to her exclusively as though, for him, in that moment, she was the only thing that existed. His plan of attack never failed. He always got the girl.

Emil had also discovered that, more than being chased, the weaker sex loved to be chosen. They liked knowing that of all the gems in the world, their particular way of glinting, gleaming and glittering was the one that attracted him.

The chase and the choice became Emil's modus operandi. While he always, inevitably, tired of the choice, he never tired of the chase.

In his heart, Emil knew that there was another way of going about things, and he knew this because of the young woman he had met on the beach in Durban. From the very first moment he set eyes on her, he sensed that she was different. Instead of waiting to be chosen, she self-selected out of her pack. While the rest of her party tested the blue-green waters of the Indian Ocean, she sat alone on the almost-white beach sand and showed every sign of being contented.

Yet, when Emil had first seen her from within the safe confines of his own party of friends, it was not her contentment or her aloneness that first caught his attention. What first caught his attention was the blue-and-white scarf she had tied around her waist. It fluttered in the wind invitingly, daring one to approach it.

It could not be. Not all the way here. But what if it was... her?

Emil had found himself walking away from his party and walking toward the blue-and-white scarf. It had been then, as he walked toward the young woman, that he had begun to notice the other things that made her: the wild golden-brown hair barely tamed under a large straw hat, the ivory swimming costume that emphasized her tanned skin, the long legs and arms that glowed in the sun. She had been like a beacon in a sea of navy and black as she sat there on a large baby-blue beach towel that she shared with a hardcover novel and a wicker basket. Smiling and squinting at the ocean, she had leaned back and planted her hands in the warmth of the sand.

Emil had pictured himself sitting close beside her, feeling the heat of her sun-kissed skin and leaning over to casually bury his face in the crook of her warm neck. He pictured her turning her head to kiss whichever part of his head her lips touched. He knew that the intimacy would not seem new because there would already be a knowing of each other.

When he was about three meters away from her, she turned to look at him with eyes that were the same green as the ocean. She smiled up at him and, transfixed, Emil found that he could not walk any further and so he sat down where he stood, which seemed close enough but felt so very far away from her.

He must have planned something to say to her, but he no longer recollected what it was. All he could think to talk about was the scarf. But what could he possibly have said? "Six years ago, on the eighteenth of April, did you ice skate at the La Grange skating rink in the City of Kings?" If she said no, what then?

"The day is an absolute delight, is it not?" the young woman had said and all Emil had been able to do, in response, was nod and smile. She had turned away from him and Emil felt that, in that short instant, the light of the world had been offered and then taken away from him.

Luckily for him, just then her straw hat flew off her head

and landed on his lap. She stood up, apologizing as she reached for the straw hat that he held out in his hands. When he saw the full glory of her riot of curls, he felt certain that it must be her, that this young woman standing before him under the sun had once been the girl who could glide over ice with grace.

As Emil gazed up at her, a name that he did not quite catch was called out from the ocean, swept up by the breeze, and came to carry the young woman away as she ran toward it, trailing the blue-and-white-scarf behind her. Emil had noticed then how the scarf accentuated the narrowness of her waist and the fullness of her hips. He watched her toss her straw hat to a matronly woman and then run laughing into the Indian Ocean. He watched her for a long time, until it was time for him to leave with his party.

Although he visited the beach often thereafter, he never saw her again. If only he had heard the name that the wind had carried! A name was something that he could have held on to, borne with him everywhere without feeling its weight. A name was something that could accompany him now as he walked the streets of the City of Kings alone.

CHAPTER 11

———— ◦ ————

As soon as Emil arrived at the Great Hall of the Gentleman's Club, he saw that Courteney had forgotten to mention several details, the most personally embarrassing for Emil being the dress code, so here he was looking like a cowboy trying to rustle a waddle of penguins. It did not help that he had arrived late, when almost everyone was already seated at various tables. He had had one drink and perhaps one woman too many over the past few days and he was yet to fully recover from his escapades. That would teach him to know when enough was enough.

Emil removed his cowboy hat and held it in his hands, uncertain of what to do next. Thankfully, just then he saw a hand waving at him from a table near the front of the hall. Courteney. Relieved, Emil started making his way to the waving hand. That was when he noticed the most striking detail that Courteney had forgotten to mention: the crowd that was gathered was multiracial. The room contained within it Europeans, Africans, Coloureds and Indians. Since his days in the village government school, Emil did not think that he had ever been in the same room with Africans without them serving him in some way. His step faltered. This was not only... out of the ordinary, was it not also...wrong...illegal...to mix the races like this? What exactly was Courteney getting him into? What was he allowing himself to be involved in? Emil turned to leave but before he could make it to the door, Courteney was by his side.

"Interesting choice of attire," Courteney said as he led him to the table near the front.

It struck Emil then that Courteney had not mentioned the dress code because he had expected Emil to know what was expected of him. In the circles that Courteney moved in, this sort of thing was a given. In Emil's world such things had to be clearly stated because men like him did not have a quality tuxedo lying conveniently about and would thus have to be told in advance so that arrangements could be made to rent one.

The occupants of Courteney's table were another European, an Indian, two Coloureds and two Africans.

"Emil has always marched to the beat of his own drum," Courteney charmingly lied with a smile, explaining away Emil's difference in dress.

"None of us would be here if we didn't do likewise," the Indian man said, nodding his understanding.

"I am glad you could make it," Courteney said with a squeeze to Emil's shoulder.

Was Courteney aware of how much he touched people... other men, Emil wondered.

Just as Courteney was about to make introductions, a bell rang and the din of conversation gave way to a respectful hush.

A man made his way to the podium. He was impressive in much the same way that Master Archie had been impressive the first time Emil had seen him: tall, handsome, eyes sparkling with intelligence and wit, back straight with integrity. Courteney gazed at the man the way he had gazed at Master Archie...as though he had seen the Second Coming.

The man said that the future was now; that the races had to coexist and govern the country together; that racism and segregation had no business in a post-war world; that the time

of the native was no more and the time of the African had arrived; that all civilized men should have the right to vote; that
the country could not go forward without every man's hand
at the helm.

There were murmurs of approval throughout the man's
speech. Some, Courteney amongst them, were so moved by
what the man said as to intermittently shout, "Hear! Hear!"
Every so often the man spoke of policies that had to be imple-
mented, acts that had to be amended or done away with, and
legislative decisions that had to be reversed. When his speech
was finished, the man received a standing ovation. Emil stood
up, mostly because he already stood out and he had no desire
to bring more attention to himself. Because he was not quite
as carried away as some of the others, Emil observed a group
of Africans sitting at the back. They did not stand up or clap
and Emil wondered what part of what the man had said had
displeased them.

During refreshments, Emil overheard snippets of conversations that confirmed for him what he already knew: this
was not his type of crowd. These men read books and jour-
nals and had engaged conversations about policies, acts and
legislature. He promised himself that after this he was going
to make a night of it at Scobie's.

Emil noticed one of the Africans who had not been part of
the standing ovation make his way toward him and, as best he
could, he prepared himself for his first real conversation with
an African.

Before Emil could ask the African man what he had
thought of it all, the man asked him, "What did you think of
the speech?"

Emil had been expecting a 'sir' at the end of the question.
He waited for it for a second or two before responding, "I liked
it well enough."

The man smiled broadly, the way, Emil was certain, only Africans could. It was a generous smile that dominated the face and caricatured it.

"Do you believe it is possible?" the man asked Emil.

Emil kept on expecting to hear the 'sir' that never came; hence his responses were somewhat delayed.

"Do I believe what is possible?"

"That this country of ours can have a multiracial government?"

"To be honest, it is not something that I have given much thought to...but I think in time, yes, a multiracial government can be achieved."

"In time...always...in time," the African man said, and then smiled broadly again. He stared at Emil for what felt like an uncomfortably long time before asking, "Did you fight in the war?"

"No, too young."

"Well, I did," the African man said. "I fought to protect the interests of the British Empire." The smile on the man's face no longer struck Emil as being generous. "That war taught me a very valuable lesson."

"Which was?"

"That every man has to know what is worth fighting for."

Emil was disappointed. He had hoped that the valuable lesson was one that he did not already know.

"I beg your pardon," Courteney interrupted. "Sorry to cut short what is evidently a very engaged tête-à-tête, but we need to leave now."

His first meaningful conversation with an African having proved disappointing and anticlimactic, Emil did not mind Courteney's interruption.

"Marion is here," Courteney explained as they headed out the front door.

Who is Marion? Emil wondered as he followed Courteney out of the confines of the well-lit Gentleman's Club and onto the dimly lit street.

As Emil stepped into the night, he placed his cowboy hat firmly back on his head, and that was when he saw her. Her, her. She created the impression of having been made for this very moment as she stood there smoking a cigarette and casually leaning against a car, an old-fashioned Aster.

Red dress. Red scarf. Red gloves. Red shoes. Red lips. Bold.

Even without the blue-and-white scarf, Emil was almost certain that it was her. That riot of golden-brown curls had been tamed by a hairdresser, but still...

Emil was trying to find a way to prudently and politely extricate himself from Courteney's company and make his way to her when Courteney exclaimed, "Ah! There she is," as he led Emil toward the woman.

No...she could not possibly be...

"Emil, I would like you to meet my wife, Marion Hartley. Marion, Emil Coetzee. He is the friend I told you about from the Selous School for Boys."

Emil did not remember having pictured Courteney's wife, but if he had, she certainly had not looked like this in his imagination. This time, though, he could not fault Courteney for leaving out a detail; after all, he *had* said that his wife was lovely. But when Courteney had said that his wife was lovely, Emil had supposed that he meant lovely in a sweet, slightly chubby and somewhat frumpy way—*that* kind of lovely. Not the kind of lovely that now stood before him.

Marion flicked her cigarette to the ground and trampled the ashes underfoot. She blew smoke in Emil's face as she extended a red-gloved right hand in greeting. Everything she did seemed sensual...inviting...like a prelude to something else.

"Charmed, I'm sure," Marion said with a smile. Her voice

was husky.

He had absolutely no idea what to say or how to say it. At least he had the presence of mind to shake her hand.

She never took her eyes off his, not even when she offered her cheek for Courteney to kiss. Was she trying to conjure up where she had seen him before?

When Emil smiled at her, the light dancing in her twinkling blue eyes let him know that she was not altogether immune to his dimples.

He was stammering Lord knew what when she abruptly removed her hand from his and turned to Courteney to say, "We are going to be late and we cannot afford to be late. No, more accurately, make that I cannot afford to be late. Your mother and sisters hate me enough as it is. You know I always invite them to join me for tea on Tuesdays at the Haddon & Sly Tea Rooms and they never do. The only time they suffer my company is when you are there."

"They don't hate you," Courteney said, heading to the passenger side of the car. "They are still trying to get accustomed to having another woman in my life."

"Potato...potahto," she said, turning her back on Emil. She entered the car without glancing back at him.

"I want to hear your thoughts on the Capricorn Africa Society and the speech," Courteney said to Emil before ducking his head into the car.

"How progressive can a group that holds its first meeting at the Gentleman's Club be, I wonder? It would all be so laughable if it wasn't all so awfully tragic," Marion said before starting the car.

They drove off. Courteney waved farewell through the car window. Marion did not acknowledge Emil's presence in any way. The entire exchange had, too soon, been relegated to memory.

It was her, was it not? Her eyes were no longer the green that he remembered, but they had been gray before, so their changeability was not something unexpected. She was more sophisticated and self-possessed now, to be sure, but then he remembered her tilting her fourteen-year-old chin up with determination, and accentuating her twenty-one-year-old waist with the blue-and-white scarf, and realized that she had probably always had these qualities, but that they were more pronounced now. It was her. It had to be. There was something about the turn of the nose and set of the lips. Besides, no other woman had the ability to steal away his speech and reason and reduce him to a dumb animal capable only of incoherent sound.

For a long time afterwards, he walked down the familiar streets of the City of Kings enjoying the cool night air. It was a good walk, but, even as he climbed up the two flights of stairs to his parents' flat at the Prince's Mansions, he knew that the feeling inside him would remain unsettled until he saw her again.

CHAPTER 12

———◆———

If there was one thing that Emil knew very well, it was women, and Emil knew that Marion Hartley had mentioned that she had tea at the Haddon & Sly Tea Rooms on Tuesdays because she wanted *him* to know that she had tea at the Haddon & Sly Tea Rooms on Tuesdays.

Even though Emil had replayed their meeting enough times in his mind to know that there had been no recognition in Marion's eyes when she had looked at him, he tried to tell himself that Marion had remembered him, which was why she wished to see him without Courteney. He could not satisfactorily convince himself of this, however, and so when Emil decided to go to the Haddon & Sly Tea Rooms that Tuesday afternoon, he had to accept that his reason for doing so was less than honorable. He had to accept that there was a... contentedness about Courteney that he found...grating...and that it was this that explained why he did what he did next.

When Emil arrived at the Haddon & Sly Tea Rooms, he found Marion sitting by herself at a table for two and certainly not waiting for Courteney's mother and six sisters. Perhaps she was waiting for someone and perhaps that someone was him. Sure enough, when Marion saw Emil, she raised an eyebrow and then smiled into her cup of tea, which let Emil know that she had been expecting him.

She was wearing a peach-colored sleeveless dress and had a matching scarf draped over her head and shoulders. The outfit was simple enough, but she was so elegant in it that Emil immediately felt woefully underdressed in his jeans, light-blue shirt and cowboy hat. Not knowing what else to do, he went to sit opposite her. She did not let him speak. Without saying anything herself, she handed him an azure-colored piece of paper and then left with that smile still on her face.

As Emil watched her leave, he admired her body—the column of her neck, the turn of her breasts, the curve of her hips, the tautly moving mounds of her behind—and felt certain that he knew exactly what to do with it. He glanced at the piece of paper in his hands and found written on it, in an impressive left-leaning cursive, an address: No. 1 Pioneer Road.

The yard of No. 1 Pioneer Road contained a struggling garden and a quaint Dutch-colonial house that looked as though it would be more at home in the middle of farmland. In the Dutch-colonial house there were two middle-aged twin sisters who sat—surrounded by books that had the words socialism, communism, and Marxism printed on enough covers and spines to give Emil pause—in a living room that was large but too overcrowded to be accommodating. They were dressed in matching dresses that appeared to have been made from the same fabric as the curtains. Even as the sisters smiled in welcome, their intelligent eyes made Emil so uncomfortable that he sat at the very edge of the seat he had been offered.

"I doubt very much that he is here for our delightful company, Tilda."

"More's the pity, Marge. He can't possibly be here for Rupert. He must be here for the lovely Marion."

"He is about twenty years too late for us, isn't he, Tilda?"

"I'm not so sure, Marge. I may have one more round in me. Be willing to come out of retirement for this one, I would."

From the mirth and mischief gleaming in their eyes, it was very clear that they were toying with him. What if the entire thing was an elaborate joke? What if Courteney and Marion had set him up to humiliate him? Emil stood up and was about to bid the two sisters farewell, when he heard the sound of a car arriving and parking. Suddenly filled with a great expectation, Emil sat back down.

Soon enough, Marion was in the room with them. If she found the situation uncomfortable, she did not let on.

"Tilda. Marge," she said, kissing each sister on both cheeks. "Emil is a friend of Courteney's," Marion stated as she went to stand beside him. She proffered this particular detail as though it was necessary and explained everything, and the two sisters nodded as though they understood perfectly.

Evidently, Emil was the only one who was not altogether sure of what was happening. When he had gone to the Haddon & Sly Tea Rooms earlier that day, he had believed that he knew what he was doing and had thought himself in control, but now he felt out of his depth, as though he had plunged feet first into a never-ending something, a world that was beyond him.

When Marion walked away, he followed her, not because he had any sense of what he was doing, but because he did not know what else to do. She led him to what turned out to be a bedroom at the back of the house. The pastel colors that bathed the room seemed so innocuous that it was only when he saw Marion walk to the white four-poster, queen-sized bed, and casually wrap her peach-colored chiffon scarf around one of the posts that he recollected why he had initially sought her out.

She turned to him and smiled. There was no bashfulness, hesitation or apprehension in any of her movements. She walked toward him until she was close enough to touch and then stood there with the promise of what was to come. She smelled of things he wanted to put in his mouth: vanilla, coconut, and something sweetly and sinfully tropical. He could already taste her.

It could not really be so easy, could it? What they were obviously just about to do should not have been so very possible, should it?

She gazed up at him. Her eyes, still blue, still held no recognition.

"Four years ago, were you at the beach in Durban?" Emil had meant to ask, but when he opened his mouth only two words came out, "Are you...?"

Something dangerous flashed in her eyes, electrifying them—and him.

"Am I...what?"

"Are you a communist?"

Where had that question come from?

Marion was momentarily confused and then she threw her head back and laughed, a wonderful sound from deep within her throat.

The sound enchanted and excited him. He closed the space between them so that their bodies touched.

"Am I a communist? I don't know...I would say, politically, at the moment...I am...open to persuasion."

His mouth went dry as he watched her lips say the words and then he did what he had wanted to do four years ago: he buried his head into the crook of her neck. And she did what he had wanted her to do four years ago: she turned her head and kissed the part of his head that her lips touched.

He heard her say, "In this very moment, does it honestly matter what I am?" And as his lips met hers for the first time, he realized that in that very moment it did not.

As the sun began to set, Emil appreciatively watched Marion put on a stocking and then check to see if its seam was straight. Her tropical scent grew even stronger, intoxicating even, when she reached over and removed the cigarette from between his lips. He watched mesmerized as her lips...her plump and tempting lips...wrapped around the cigarette. Emil found the gesture erotic, as his body made evident. It was her turn to gaze at him appreciatively. She cupped him briefly in her hand and then hesitated before giving him back the cigarette and jumping off the bed.

"You are quite the stud, aren't you?" she said as she put on her dress. "Insatiable...and surprisingly generous...and tender ...but there is also something dangerous lurking there. Something I definitely would not want to find myself on the receiving end of—an anger...a deep anger." She stopped fastening her zipper and studied him with her startlingly azure eyes. "Why the anger, I wonder?"

Thankfully, she was not waiting for him to respond.

"Don't worry. I will let you keep your secrets. And you will let me keep mine," Marion said.

She put on her shoes and then sat on his side of the bed with her back to him. She lifted her glorious, flowing golden-brown hair and said, "Please," as she waited for him to do up the rest of her zipper.

Emil, preferring instead to kiss the inviting column of her neck, did not do as she had asked.

She chuckled deep in her throat before turning to face him. She placed his face between the palms of her hands and kissed him and kissed him and kissed him. That was the moment she did it. That was when she took from him something he had not intended to give. He was surprised at how willingly he gave it to her and at how effortlessly she took it from him.

Breathless, she briefly and lightly touched her forehead to his and then was gone.

CHAPTER 13

————◆————

Emil only picked up the book because Marion had touched it. She had done so in a noticeably distracted manner while in a conversation with an elderly woman, but she had touched it nonetheless. He watched intently as the same fingers that had traveled his body, clasped him to her, dug into his back and buttocks, absent-mindedly flipped through the pages of the book.

He had mistakenly believed that being with Marion once would suffice—that it would be enough to put a sizeable dent in Courteney's contentedness—but once having been with Marion, he found that he wanted to experience being with her again...and again. The memory of Marion had stayed with him for weeks after their assignation. She was definitely no blushing rose or shrinking violet or anything else that well-brought-up women were told they were supposed to be in the bedroom. She was a fiery flame lily and she satisfyingly gave as well as she received. He kept on replaying the scenes of their time together in his mind until he was good for nothing, until he found himself going to the Haddon & Sly Tea Rooms on two consecutive Tuesdays, until he found himself drowning his need for her in endless glasses of whiskey, until he found himself on the third floor of the Cecil Hotel, being told by a compassionate voice, "It's all right, love. Happens to the best of them."

So good for nothing was he that, putting all caution and pride aside, he had attended three meetings of the Capricorn

Africa Society in the hopes that at the end of it all she would be there waiting for Courteney...and that he would see her again...and that she would see him...and want him again.

Courteney, reading the situation accurately, as he always did, said as Emil's eyes traveled the length of the street searching for the old-fashioned Aster, "Marion is not a repeat offender, I'm afraid."

And it was in this very simple way that Emil found out that Courteney knew that he had slept with Marion and that Courteney knew this because Marion herself had told him.

Seeing the expression on Emil's face, Courteney smiled and explained, "Marion and I have an agreement between us." Realizing that his explanation had not made things any clearer, Courteney elaborated, "Our marriage is...open to others. As soon as the two of you met I sensed that something like this might happen. It was in the way you looked at each other— Marion has a certain way about her...and...well, your appetite has a reputation of its own. Some things are just too natural to fight. I warned her about you. I see now that I should have warned you about her." Having thus explained the situation, Courteney shrugged as though that was all there was to the matter.

But, of course, that was not all there was to the matter.

How exactly had she done it? How exactly had she told him? The 'why' was evident enough: she had told Courteney because what they had shared was not special enough to keep secret. Fair enough.

But how had she done it? As soon as she entered the house, while removing her gloves, had she nonchalantly said, "Just been with Emil"? Or at dinner, had she suddenly remembered after she asked him to pass the salt to inform him, "Oh ...by the way, I've been with Emil?" Or had she been sitting on the edge of a tub, watching it fill with delicious-smelling hot water as she trailed her hand through the foam, before she turned to Courteney, who was shaving at the mirror above the basin, and said, "I was with Emil earlier"? Or had she waited until they were both safely tucked in bed, reading books and slowly welcoming sleep, before she glanced over at him and said, as she shut her book and reached for her bedside lamp, "Emil and I have been together"?

However she had told him, she had said what needed to be said and then let her life continue as it would.

After everything that had passed between them, how had he become for her someone so easy to forget?

It seemed like a curiously cruel thing for her to do. Why seek him out only to reject him?

Courteney squeezed Emil's shoulder in commiseration. Why was Courteney always giving him his sympathy, Emil wondered, as he moved away from Courteney's comforting touch. And why was he now, instead of being angry, hurt or disappointed, being so damned understanding? Had Marion told Courteney that he, Emil, had whimpered, called out her name and then cried? Had she turned what had been an overwhelmingly profound moment for him into something pathetic, something that would elicit Courteney's pity?

Courteney reached out to Emil again and, again, Emil moved away from his touch. Undeterred, Courteney continued, "We are entertaining over the weekend. We would both love it if you could join us."

And that was how he had come to find himself sitting in a corner trying not to stare at Marion all night and failing miserably. When he was not watching her, he was replaying the scenes of their time together over and over again in his mind.

He remembered a tongue tasting yielding flesh. He remembered hands clutching tufts of his hair. He remembered the soft flesh of an inner thigh closing around him like a vice.

How could she have shared such intimacy with him and then so easily have returned to the sanctuary and sanctity of her marriage?

Emil watched as Marion, laughing, handed Courteney his Tom Collins, and his heart filled with a new and foreign emotion: envy. That was when he knew, with certainty, that it was already too late for him, he was already too far gone. There was no hope of extricating himself now.

He tried to make his condition easier by lessening some of the power that she had over him. Now that he was observing her objectively, with no prospect of ever being with her again, he saw that she was not pretty—at least not in a conventional sense, which was the only sense that he had understood up until her. Those sparkling azure eyes, that full rosebud mouth that was slightly too big for her face, that touch of olive in her skin, that scattering of freckles on her nose and cheekbones, that thick, cascading golden-brown hair...these things did not make her pretty...did not make her beautiful even...they made her absolutely exquisite. They made Marion Hartley a true revelation.

At the present moment, she was deep in conversation with two gentlemen and Emil wondered if she had slept with them—if they were also offenses that she would not repeat.

She looked at him then for the first time that evening, as though having read his thoughts, and gently touched one of the gentlemen on the elbow as if to say to Emil, "This is the one. But see how I still talk to him? That is because he still has something that interests me and you don't."

She smiled at him then with that very same mouth that had taken him in. He watched as her rosebud of a mouth smiled and smiled and was a villain.

Emil was certain that he had never felt so many contradictory emotions all at once. The idea of Marion excited and frustrated him in equal measure. The reality of her he did not quite know what to do with.

One of the men whispered something in Marion's ear and she laughed, still looking at Emil. Irrationally, Emil convinced himself that they were laughing at him and in that same breath tried to tell himself that Marion was not who he thought she was. Surely the young woman who had smiled at him on the beach in Durban and said, "The day is an absolute delight, is it not?" would not torment him in this way. She would not go out of her way to ensure that all his remaining days were unbearable, would she? Marion was not her. He had made a mistake and was now realizing it too late.

Emil abruptly got up to leave just as someone started hitting the side of a glass. The hum in the room came to a gradual end and all attention was turned toward Courteney.

"Family...friends," Courteney began. "Four years ago I had the great fortune of losing my way on the Labyrinthine Wits Campus and asking this remarkable creature for directions." Courteney gestured toward Marion, who left the two men and went to him. "She evidently did not trust me to find my way because she has been at my side ever since."

There was good-humored laughter in response.

"Two years ago today, we went to a chapel and got ourselves married and from that day to this, I have been the happiest man on earth."

Emil was surprised to find himself a guest at an anniversary party, Courteney's and Marion's no less. Why was it that Courteney always managed to leave out the most important details?

What game were Courteney and Marion playing, Emil wondered, and why had they decided to make him a part of it? If they loved each other so much, then why had they opened up their marriage to other people?

He did not have to stay for this. Emil was already making his way out when he witnessed Marion gently brush away the unruly flop of hair that always found its way onto Courteney's forehead. At that moment, that simple act was the most remarkable thing Emil had ever seen.

Emil did not have to look at Marion's eyes to know that they focused on Courteney with love, but he looked anyway in order to drive the point home. Her face just beamed up at her husband. In that moment she was not an enigma, something that Emil was trying, and failing, to piece together. She was just a married woman in love with her husband. A very ordinary thing to be.

As Emil made his way out of the house, he picked up the book that Marion had touched and as he placed his hand on the door handle, the sound of "Skokiaan" blew out of Louis Armstrong's trumpet from the his Master's Voice gramophone in Courteney's and Marion's living room. Emil hesitated as he listened to the tune. It reminded him of...happiness. When had he ever known such happiness? On the BSAP out-post watching his parents dance? No. That was not it. There must have been another happiness that was now forgotten.

CHAPTER 14

———— • ————

It was only when Emil was five pages into the book that he realized that it was the first book he had ever read that had been written by a black man. He did not know what to think or feel about this and so he closed the book.

His engagement with the book, albeit brief, had been enough to begin to bring Courteney and Marion into focus for him. All the things that he knew about them—the multiracial Capricorn Africa Society, the den of iniquity run by two socialist sisters, the open marriage, the books written by negroes—showed him that Courteney Smythe-Sinclair and Marion Hartley had decided to be a thoroughly modern married couple, with all that that entailed.

Even though Emil understood that things needed to change after the war, he felt that they needed to change at a steady pace and he could not help but feel that Courteney and Marion were rushing the future into existence. Their modernism had birthed a liberalism that wanted to achieve too much too soon and if left to reign would prove disruptive. Emil surprised himself by not only thinking these things but also having an opinion on them. After careful consideration and examination, he felt that he should keep his distance from Courteney and Marion because they seemed already to be influencing his thinking, even if only to make him disagree with them.

Two weeks after the anniversary party, as he was lying in bed at his parents' house nursing a raging hangover after a night out with Rutherford, a last hurrah before Emil left the City of Kings to start his job with the Department of Native Affairs, his mother woke him up and gestured that there was someone on the phone for him. He gestured that he was coming and slowly got out of bed.

His parents had started using an intricately elaborate sign language of their own devising and Emil was taking pains to learn it because at least now all three of them could communicate again.

"Hello?" he said rather gruffly into the receiver, fully expecting Rutherford to be on the other end.

"Emil? It is Marion."

She did not have to offer her name; Emil intimately knew the huskiness of her voice.

He sobered up immediately.

"So have you read it?" she asked, sounding somewhat hopeful.

"Read what?"

"*Up from Slavery*...I saw you take it."

Of course. She was calling about the book. "I started to—"

"Please finish it—I would love to know what you think."

That took him by surprise. Why did she want to know what he thought? Why did she care? Did she not simply see and think of him as a stud?

"I'm trying to convince...Well...it doesn't really matter what I'm trying to do...What matters is that you'll be there. You will be there, won't you?"

"Be where?"

"Our place...in a fortnight...please say you'll be there."

"I..."

"Perfect. So we'll see you then. Goodbye, Emil."

Emil hung up the phone perfectly confused and almost certain that the confusion was not his alone.

From what he could gather, Marion and Courteney wanted him to visit them in a fortnight so that they could discuss the book *Up from Slavery*. He almost laughed at the notion. But, of course, this was the sort of thing they did with their university degrees: they invited people over to discuss books. It seemed completely normal for them to do so. So normal, in fact, that they supposed that it was something that he would do.

Even as Emil packed the book into a suitcase with the rest of the things that he was taking to the Department of Native Affairs, he knew that he was not going to honor the invitation. He packed the book mostly because he did not want his parents to come across it in his room. How would they gesture their way toward having a conversation about the presence, in their home, of a book written by a black man?

It was only when he was in it again, when he felt it envelop him, that he appreciated how much he had truly missed it. The savannah. Familiar. Known. Loved. Where he belonged. He glanced down at the black shadow that he cast on a golden dust road. He reached out and touched the singing elephant grass that was the same color as his hair. He closed his eyes and deeply breathed in the veld and almost wept from the missing of it.

Emil had not returned to the savannah simply to love it again; he had returned to help transform it. After the Second World War, the government was making a determined effort to attract European, especially British, settlement in the colony and, to sweeten the pot, it had promised would-be settlers large tracts of land for commercial farming. The government was convinced that commercial farming was to be the country's future, the engine of its post-war prosperity. To make the government's vision possible, Africans had to be moved away from the arable land that they lived on to arid land where they could subsist but, preferably, not prosper because their labor would be needed on the commercial farms, industries and mines that would be creating the country's fortunes. As a result, the land the Africans were resettled on could not be too expansive and their livestock would need to be culled. And this was where Emil came in. It was Emil's job to travel the grasslands in search of pieces of land upon which to relocate Africans. With his Native Affairs Assistants, he would divvy up the land into allotments and determine how much livestock each section could contain.

Emil worked well with his team of Native Affairs Assistants and his days were filled with surveying the land (his most favorite part) and writing reports (his least favorite part). While his days were blessedly full, his nights were dreadfully empty and it was because of this that he started reading *Up from Slavery*. When he finished reading the book he found that he had done so within Marion's stipulated fortnight and having done so, he saw no reason why he should not go to Courteney's and Marion's place and make an evening of it.

He closed the book and scrutinized the author's photograph on the back cover for a long time, as though trying to bring into focus an at first imperceptible flaw. Booker T. Washington. *What would Master Duthie say if he saw me now?* Emil mused with a smile.

The real question, the important one, was what did *he* have to say? What did he think of it all? He was sure that Courteney and Marion would be curious to know his thoughts on the subject. To this end, Emil decided that it was best to be prepared and so he formulated an opinion. He very much liked Washington's idea of educating the different races for different purposes and honestly felt that this approach to education and creating a citizenry would curtail confusion, give every race a known function, and lead to the smooth and efficient running of the colony. Emil was rather proud of how articulate his opinion was and, when he left for Courteney's and Marion's place, he allowed himself to feel a little confident.

"But that is exactly what we have in this country for the Africans, the Coloureds, and the Asians."

"African and Coloured minds—"

"Oh. Please. Not that again. That is a lie that we have been telling ourselves for far too long. We just want the best for ourselves and we don't want competition."

"But surely you do not mean to suggest that the African brain is as developed—"

"I am not suggesting anything, I am stating fact. The evidence is all around us."

"I don't know where you live, but the evidence all around me shows me that the African mind is primitive."

"I think you are confusing a Negro like our Mr. Washington here with one of our Africans. Mr. Washington is civilized because the Negro in North America has been in contact with western civilization—"

"As a slave! As chattel! As property!"

"With western civilization for four hundred years, whereas civilization is still dawning for our African."

"Where do I even begin to show you how wrong you are?"

"Since I am right, you need not bother."

"Yet again, we have veered woefully off the topic."

"What we need is a meritocracy. A meritocracy will expose the lie that is white superiority."

"Surely for Washington the issue is not one of race, at least not the way we are talking about it. The issue for him is one of racial uplift. He already knows that the Negro is capable. His concern lies elsewhere. How do you get people who were slaves...chattel...property to become viable and valuable to and for themselves? How do you get these people to have self-worth? According to Washington, you strategically educate them so that they become an integral part of the running of the country."

"But they have always already been an integral part of running the country."

They were six of them in all. Courteney, Marion, three men and one woman, and even as he found most of what they said to be beyond him, he was fascinated by their passion for the topic. They argued, got frustrated but not angry; he had never seen people argue in this way before. And the things they said. When did they have the time to think of all these things? How could they be that...invested in an idea—an idea involving black people?

"What do you think?" Courteney asked, as he handed Emil a glass of whiskey.

Emil had absolutely no idea what he thought any more. What Washington had said about the need for technical schools had made sense to Emil when he saw it through Washington's eyes, but now, given the argument he had just heard, he was no longer sure if that was the only way to see things.

Nothing that Emil had learned before had been subject to questioning. Throughout his education he simply accepted and regurgitated what was taught. Even in Master Archie's class, after all the different interpretations that had been encouraged and discussed, there were only a few answers that were considered correct in an exam.

Six pairs of eyes bored into him.

"I don't know what I think," Emil said to Courteney. He was determined not to look at Marion because he did not want to see her reaction to his words.

Emil could see and feel the disappointment of the group. They, of course, always knew exactly what they thought and were always ready to offer it up when the need arose. They read books, and when and where necessary disagreed with what the author had said. Emil had never done that and, until this meeting, had not known that it was something that was possible to do. To disagree with the works of Selous, Haggard, Burroughs, Kipling and Conrad? Not to like them he supposed was possible, yes, but to disagree with them?

"Emil went to school with Africans. He can speak on their mental capacities and capabilities," Marion said, probably trying to save him in some obscure way.

Emil did not feel saved, he felt betrayed. He had told Courteney about the government school for natives in confidence when they were boys together at the Selous School for Boys. It had been Emil's secret. If any of the other boys had found out he would have been teased for being a "kaffirboetie." Over the years, Emil had not ruminated much about his education at the government school for natives. What he had felt, however, was deep shame at having once been thus educated. Now here was Marion imbuing the experience with a significance that he had never given it.

Did Courteney and Marion not have any secrets between them? No secrets whatsoever?

"Don't worry. I will let you keep your secrets. And you will let me keep mine," Marion had said at No. 1 Pioneer Road. What had she meant by that? What exactly did she know about him? What else did she know about him?

Emil suddenly wanted to be far away from where he was, beyond the reach of whatever else Marion knew about him. And he needed to put some distance between himself and these people with their decidedly known opinions. He stood up hastily and upset the chair in his rush to be gone.

"Excuse me...I have another engagement, I'm afraid."

Polite smiles escorted him out of the room.

He did not belong here. Whatever had made him think that he should come?

Marion joined him in the corridor as he was putting on his jacket.

"That wasn't fun for you, was it?" Marion asked rhetorically as she handed him his cowboy hat. "I'm afraid we can be savages sometimes."

She straightened his collar and the gesture took him by surprise. The delicateness of it. The care of it. The closeness of it. The intimacy of the touch.

"Don't mind us. We are just frustrated intellectuals, and we are pitiably enamored with the sound of our own voices." She smiled up at him. "Please do join us next time. We will be better behaved. Or, at least, we will try to be."

What did she want from him?

All she managed to do was confuse him.

Did she not know that?

Or, did she know that? Was she playing with him in some way? Would she, amused by the state she had left him in, go back to her frustrated intellectuals and make some joke about a bush tick?

She was suddenly moving away from him, searching for something. She found it, retrieved it and handed it to him. It was another book.

She touched him lightly on the elbow as she said, "Please do come next time. I promise our gatherings can be extremely enjoyable."

He watched her mouth—that beautiful rosebud of a mouth—say the words and wanted to kiss it. But he knew that the time for that had come and gone. Marion had apparently found another use for him and he was not sure what it was.

The book Marion had given him was written by another black man, W.E.B. Du Bois. Did she only read books written by black men?

To his credit, Emil did make a concerted effort to read the book, *The Souls of Black Folk*. The language was pretty enough, but the content was beyond Emil's grasp. He got lost in the whole metaphor of the veil and could not find his way beyond it.

Emil knew that he would never go back to Courteney's and Marion's gatherings. He was not the sort of man who had intellectual debates; he was the sort of man who was at home alone with his thoughts in the vastness of the veld. For Marion, for a brief moment, he had perhaps tried to be something different, someone else. But the man that he was had been forged a long time ago in the pages of H. Rider Haggard: "I, Emil Coetzee, of Durban, Natal, Gentleman ..."

It was not Marion's fault. She had simply mistaken his taking of *Up from Slavery* as interest in the topic itself, as evidence of something that she would probably call "intellectual curiosity," when really all he had wanted from the book was a closeness to her.

He mailed *The Souls of Black Folk* back to Marion with a note expressing his thanks and his regrets. He would not be able to attend any more gatherings because his job at the Department of Native Affairs was proving to be more demanding than he had imagined it would be and trips to the City of Kings would, of necessity, be infrequent.

In response, a note arrived written on the same azure-colored paper in the same impressive left-leaning cursive that had written the address No. 1 Pioneer Road. The note read,

> *There is a basin in the mind where words float around on*
> *thought and thought on sound and sight. Then there is a*

depth of thought untouched by words and deeper still a gulf
of formless feelings untouched by thought.
—Zora Neale Hurston.

Emil pored over the note for a long time, studying every curve, slant and stroke, before he, with the greatest of care, placed it in his wallet next to the piece of paper that contained the address. When he closed his wallet, he chuckled to himself as he briefly wondered if Zora Neale Hurston was yet another black writer.

Even though he did not know which part of her he was holding on to, Emil could not let Marion go. With distance and time she did not become comprehensible; she, curiously, became more complex. His life was simple. He was a man of a few pleasures and he maneuvered his way through the world in search of them. He had never asked anything more of the world than for it to let him be part of the savannah.

Marion asked questions of the world and when the world could not provide her with answers, she seemed prepared to change it.

Emil and Marion were so very different that there really should not have been an attraction at all. But, from the very beginning, something had drawn her to him and it held him firmly in its sway. It was best to call a thing by its proper name. After having seen her only a handful of times, Emil was in love with Marion. As soon as he had traversed that particular threshold of intimacy, there had been no turning back. All this vacillating between the agony of knowing that what he felt he felt alone and the ecstasy of feeling it at all—this was what love was for him.

Emil knew that Marion had not been changed as he had been changed by their time together—she had happily retreated back to her life, leaving him trapped and alone in the beautiful thing they had created.

CHAPTER 15

———•———

Rutherford was Emil's only source of escape from this part of himself—the part of him that wanted Marion without reason.

Together, Emil and Rutherford went hunting, trekking, hiking, camping and fishing, and, with each outing, Emil's feats became more daring. He wrestled a crocodile. He dived through a waterfall. He had an automobile drive over him. He hunted a lion with an assegai. As Emil did these things, Rutherford joked that Emil had a death wish, but Emil understood that his drive to do the things he did came from another place entirely.

When his image began to appear in the pages of *The Chronicle* and he gained a bit of notoriety, Emil almost convinced himself that he did these things in honor of Frederick Courteney Selous, the man who had followed God's command and shown the world exactly how to gain dominion over the untamed African wilderness. Even so, he knew that a part of him, the irrational part of him, was hoping that Marion would stop whatever she was doing when she came across his image in the paper or heard of his exploits and just look at him or recall their time together. If she did so, she would know that this was his poor attempt to communicate the truth that he could not speak to her.

Marion Hartley had reduced Emil Coetzee to such a pathetic creature that he needed saving from himself and that saving came in the form of Lord and Lady Ashtonbury. Lord and Lady Ashtonbury were to settle on the very land that Emil had grown up on—the BSAP outpost and the surrounding village at the foot of the Matopos Hills. It was Emil's job to resettle the people from the village onto land he had previously surveyed and which he and his superiors thought was sufficient for Africans. It was also Emil's job to supervise the transformation of the outpost and village into hectares of land that the Ashtonburys could turn into a viable commercial farm.

If, upon Emil's return to the BSAP outpost, the Africans of the village recognized him, they did not show it and he preferred it that way because he wanted to be anonymous in his task. Because of this, Emil did not come to know that the Africans did, in fact, recognize him but that they chose not to show it because they had long known that Europeans, especially European children, never returned the same from their travels into the world.

Consequently, there was no communion in the meetings that Emil held with the villagers to prepare them for their resettlement. In these meetings, the village chief, speaking for his people, talked of the land as theirs...as the land of their ancestors...as the land of their children and their children's children. He explained to Emil that the villagers were mere custodians of the land, inheriting it from past generations and holding it in trust for future generations and that, as such, they could not give the land away because they did not have the power to do so.

This type of talk was, naturally, to be expected from the Africans and it was Emil's mandate to inform them that the land—*all* land in the colony—belonged to the government and that it was the government that decided and determined who occupied what piece of land, not the ancestors.

The government understood that there was a high probability that the villagers would prove recalcitrant, and if such turned out to be the case, Emil had been informed that he could and should call on the BSAP for support. Emil was hoping that it would not come to that. He tried to reason with the chief, but the chief spoke again of ancestors. The ancestors were buried in this place. The people could not move away from their ancestral land because that would be tantamount to destroying their own history, and what kind of people would they be without a history? The villagers, emboldened by their chief, rooted themselves even more firmly into the soil, some even going as far as to build concrete structures.

In the end, Emil had no choice but to call in the BSAP.

The villagers were forced onto trucks and only allowed to take what few possessions they could. When they found themselves packed together with their livestock, their grain, their utensils, they must have comprehended then that, to the colonial government, there was little difference between them and the objects they possessed.

The Africans, having collectively come to this realization, were silent through it all.

Long uncomfortable in silences, Emil busied himself putting things that had been left behind in the haste of the moment onto the trucks, things that he felt would be missed later on—a spinning top, a rusty cast-iron pan, a slingshot, a blue suede shoe. It was a kindness on his part and, while he knew that it did not matter in the larger scheme of things and that it was probably not felt as a kindness now, he hoped that it would be felt as such once the Africans had settled on their new land and understood the need for the things they had almost left behind.

The overcrowded and overladen trucks drove off and land that had belonged to a people was suddenly depopulated and all that teeming life and bustling activity was no more. What remained looked as ancient as a ruin.

The bulldozers arrived and soon it was as if no one had ever lived there. An entire past had been removed and the bulldozers had not had a care about what this meant for the future.

As Emil stood in the middle of the new nothingness that had once been an African village, he remembered Master Duthie stressing the point that Africans had a past but not a history, and as he recalled this, he felt an idea begin to form in his mind. He realized that the problem with the African was that there was a lack of permanence in his way of doing things. The African did not build permanent structures: pole and dagha constructions could never withstand the demands of time. The African did not have a writing tradition; all he had was the orality he could carry with him but never leave behind as a record. All that the African possessed were his memories, which were destined to forever fade with time.

Emil began to think that, just because this was how things had always been done, it did not mean that they had to carry on in this fashion. This was the germination of the idea that would make Emil Coetzee a man of history, but as he stood there surveying the ruins of the African village that surrounded him, he had no inkling of what was to come.

CHAPTER 16

————◆————

The City of Kings was halfway in love with Lord and Lady Ashtonbury before they even arrived. Royalty, no matter how far removed, was sure to be a welcome addition to the city's social scene.

And when the Ashtonburys did arrive they did not disappoint. He was charming and she was absolutely wonderful. They took rooms at the Grand Hotel while they waited for their land to be developed. They entertained rarely but accepted almost every invitation, which was the surest way to make them universally loved for being accommodating and agreeable. They were both incorrigible flirts and, thankfully, did not have about them the airs and graces that had been expected and even feared by some. In short, they seemed eager to please and to be pleased. He called her "The Lady," and she called him "The Lord," and no one was so shabby or ungracious as to consider this lord-and-lady business vulgar.

The first introduction Emil had to the Ashtonburys was an invitation to a dinner party he received in the mail. The invitation was written on embossed and monogrammed lilac paper. Even after the many hands it had passed through to reach him, it still smelled faintly of a scent with lavender in it. Lady Ashtonbury.

Since their reputation had preceded them, Emil already felt he knew the Ashtonburys. All the same, with the arrival of the invitation card and its lingering lavender scent, Emil found himself becoming more curious about her...Lady

Ashtonbury.

When the day on the invitation arrived, he put on an ill-fitting tuxedo he had rented for the occasion and allowed himself to entertain the possibility that he would be underwhelmed; she did, after all, strike him as being too good to be true.

Lady Ashtonbury was many things but one thing she was not was too good to be true. When Emil first saw her—sitting on the floor, leaning on her left hand, her right hand holding a champagne glass, her head thrown back in easy laughter, a group of men surrounding her with admiration—she was easily the most (conventionally) beautiful woman he had ever seen.

She, to her credit, did not use her beauty as a weapon the way some women did. Her beauty was a thing that had always belonged to her and she had long grown accustomed to it. In her late thirties, she was still sure that her beauty would always belong to her, so, just at the age when most women were riddled with fear and worry over losing their looks and, subsequently, the interest of men, she instead appeared to take her beauty for granted because she did not believe that something that had always been hers would ever leave her. And, as a result, Lady Ashtonbury was a woman who was at complete ease with herself and Emil found that quality to be more attractive than her beauty. Marion, of course, had that ease too and at a much younger age, which made her even more alluring to Emil.

Emil had taken to doing this, to comparing every woman he met to Marion. He knew it was not a healthy thing to do but found that he could not help it. She had looked deeply into his eyes and then kissed him lightly on the temple before latching on to him.

Marion...

She had made him a man lost to himself.

When Emil noticed that he had spent most of his time at the Ashtonburys' party thinking about Marion, he knew that he was still good for nothing and that there was no need to introduce himself to Lady Ashtonbury. Before he left, though, he did make a point of inviting Lord Ashtonbury to see the property that was being prepared for them.

When Lord Ashtonbury honored the invitation a few days later, he brought Lady Ashtonbury along with him. The Ashtonburys came sooner than Emil had expected them to and found him "gone wandering" as he called it. "Gone wandering" was what Emil did with most of his time now.

He wandered the veld feeling restless. It was a restlessness that trips to Scobie's and the third floor of the Cecil Hotel no longer quelled. The restlessness had something to do with Marion, without a doubt, but he also suspected that it had something to do with the idea that was rattling around in his mind, giving him a strong desire to do something about it. The idea about the impermanent nature of African lives.

Lord Ashtonbury left a note written in bold strokes on a Native Affairs Department writing pad.

Immediately upon his return, Emil found the note waiting for him and dialed the Ashtonburys' telephone number. When the operator connected the call, it was Lady Ashtonbury who answered it.

"We came but missed you. When next can we come?" she asked.

She enunciated the internal rhythm of every word so that it was a pleasure just to hear her speak. Emil almost did not hear the content of what she was saying, so intent was he on the way things sounded.

"Emil?" she made his name sound like something newly

purchased.

Obviously, the Ashtonburys did not have to ask him for permission to come and see their own land, but that was their especial, discreet charm—they treated everyone with respect.

"You can come whenever you please."

"Yes, but when would it please you? We are absolutely at your disposal, you see. And we would so love to finally, properly meet you."

Emil smiled into the receiver, completely won over. "Tomorrow afternoon?"

"It will be a pleasure," Lady Ashtonbury predicted.

And it was.

Emil and the Ashtonburys traveled on horseback over the land and the Ashtonburys were generous enough to love everything they saw and to thank Emil for everything, even that for which he was not directly responsible.

When they came across the government-issued, bungalow-style house with whitewashed walls and no veranda that had been Emil's childhood home, he grasped for the first time the indignity of not even being allowed to have that most colonial of things, a veranda in the savannah. He informed the Ashtonburys that the house would soon be torn down and that the greenhouse Lady Ashtonbury wanted would stand in its place. Emil hoped that they could not hear a part of him break as he told them this.

"Oh. Must it be torn down? It is an absolute marvel—so very...bygone. And you say this is where you grew up?" Lady Ashtonbury asked. Emil chose that moment to look away from the Ashtonburys and into the distance.

"You must have been so very happy here as a little boy," Lady Ashtonbury said.

He had been.

"Oh. They simply cannot tear it down! You will make

sure that they don't, won't you, dear?" Lady Ashtonbury said, getting off her horse for a closer inspection of the house.

"Yes, dear," Lord Ashtonbury said. It was a phrase that Emil knew, upon hearing it, was spoken often from the lips of Lord Ashtonbury.

"The Lord, you see, Emil, grants my every wish," Lady Ashtonbury said, turning from the house to smile at Emil as he laughed obligingly. "You will give me a tour won't you, Emil?"

Most certainly, he would. He showed her the rustic four rooms that had once been his childhood home and, because her interest seemed genuine, he took pride in the bareness that he showed her.

The Ashtonburys visited regularly after that. Their visits usually culminated in a four o'clock tea where brandy was sipped and no sandwiches or biscuits eaten on the very patch of grass, now grown wild, where Emil had sat gazing at his mother and father as they tripped the light fantastic.

Since the Ashtonburys had always come together, when Lady Ashtonbury came alone that first time, Emil really did not think anything of it.

"The Lord has been called to Salisbury. This will be happening more often than not, I'm afraid. Somebody important has taken it into his head to think that the Lord will be instrumental in the implementation of something or other. So, for the foreseeable future, you will only have me for company, I'm afraid. You don't mind terribly, do you?"

Of course Emil did not mind.

Looking back, Emil would often wonder if things would have happened differently between him and Lady Ashtonbury if they had not come across Daisy.

Daisy had not been Daisy then. She had been a khaki

burlap sack that Lady Ashtonbury had pointed to with her usual curiosity as they were riding along the river.

As soon as Emil saw the shape of the burlap sack, the kind that usually contained virgin cotton or cow feed, he strongly suspected that what lay within it was not cotton or cow feed. He jumped off his horse and instinctively asked Lady Ashtonbury to keep her distance as he went to inspect and investigate.

Perhaps the wind had carried his voice in the other direction or perhaps Lady Ashtonbury had been too naïve to suspect what would come next, but, for whatever reason, she was there when Emil opened the burlap sack and found within it the hacked and bloated remains of the African woman he would later learn was called Daisy.

Lady Ashtonbury screamed, covered her mouth and ran off to retch some distance away. Emil went to her to comfort her. As he held her in his arms he told her she would need to go to the government-issued, bungalow-style house with whitewashed walls and no veranda that he had once called home. He would stay behind, radio the BSAP and wait with the remains until they arrived.

She would wait for him there, she informed him. She would not leave until after his return.

She did not have to wait.

She would wait. She wanted to.

The BSAP—two men, one European, one African—arrived eventually. There had been a cattle-rustling incident, which was being attended to by most of their officers, and which explained why only two officers had come to investigate and why they had arrived so late. This occurrence made Emil realize that perhaps it had not been an altogether good idea to do away with the BSAP outpost that he had grown up in.

The two officers introduced themselves as Michael Meredith and Spokes Moloi.

"You know what to do," Meredith told Moloi, who nodded and walked away.

"He's our best man," Meredith told Emil once Moloi was beyond earshot. "Although you will never catch me saying that to his face, you understand. It never helps to have Africans hear praise of themselves. Always gives them ideas above their station."

As Meredith and Emil watched Moloi take photographs of the remains, Meredith prepared to take Emil's statement.

"I was riding along with Lady Ashtonbury, she is the one who—"

"You know Lord and Lady Ashtonbury? I'm stuck out here in the bush—haven't met them but I have heard so much," Meredith excitedly interrupted.

It took quite some time after that for them to get back to the statement.

"What do you think, Moloi?" Meredith asked as all of them carefully carried the burlap sack and loaded it onto the back of the BSAP truck. "Appears to be jealous husband to me."

"I suppose it could be," Moloi said with a shrug and a deeply furrowed brow.

That was when Emil noticed that Moloi had the most spectacular moustache he had ever seen—jet black, manicured to perfection and waxed to fine points at the ends. No one who ever came across that moustache would ever forget it. It was a force to be reckoned with.

"What else could it be but jealous husband?" Meredith asked.

"There is no ring on her finger."

"Africans usually don't have rings on their fingers."

"Ones dressed like she is usually do. Mission educated.

Middle class."

"Dress could have been bought by her lover, given as a present, hence the jealous husband."

Moloi shrugged but furrowed his brow deeper. "Given as a present," was all he said.

After shaking hands with Emil, Meredith and Moloi prepared to drive off.

"Please keep me informed of the investigation, if you don't mind," Emil said.

"If you wish."

"I do."

And he genuinely did. Emil wanted to know how the woman had come to meet such an end. It was the eyes, now dead, that had looked up at him and made him wonder at the life they had witnessed...the life that had been lived.

History: that was what he was interested in. The history of the African woman. Moloi had used the words "mission educated" and "middle class" in describing the woman. For the first time, Emil understood that there was an interiority to African life that, while not apparent to him, existed nonetheless. He was surprised at himself and he did not know if he was surprised at thinking like this about African lives or at never having before thought like this about African lives.

He found Lady Ashtonbury waiting on the patch of grass that masqueraded as a lawn and stood where a veranda should have been. She was holding a glass of brandy that she offered to him with a trembling hand. It soon became obvious that she had already had a few glasses herself.

"How very awful! What a terrible thing to lay one's eyes upon," Lady Ashtonbury said, as she nervously paced back and forth. There was a certain light within her that had been extinguished. An innocence that was to be no more.

Emil felt sad for her and reached out to touch her. He stopped his hand midway between them, suddenly uncertain. He had already comforted her earlier and he did not want to be misunderstood.

But it was already too late. Lady Ashtonbury gazed at his outstretched hand, took it gently in hers, slowly, hesitantly, kissed its open palm and then pressed that open palm against her cheek.

"Lady Ashtonbury—"

"Call me Maryvonne," she whispered as she put her arms around him and placed her head flat against his chest. "Please," she said, gazing up at him. "It is my given name."

"Maryvonne."

The affair began some months later.

Although the Ashtonburys had not been to their land since the discovery of the woman's body, Lady Ashtonbury had telephoned Emil several times. They spoke mostly about the woman who, Emil knew through Spokes Moloi, had been called Daisy.

No one recalled the exact year Daisy had arrived in the village that was several kilometers upriver from where her body was found. She had been brought there by one of the sons of the village who was working in the industries of the City of Kings. It was believed that Daisy and this son of the village had met in the City of Kings, but no one was particularly sure of this. Everyone knew that her real name, the name her parents had given her, the name that her ancestors knew her by, was not Daisy. And yet Daisy, a name she had probably given herself, was the name she had offered freely to the villagers when she first arrived. Not much else was known about her life before she came to the village. Her life after she arrived...well, everyone could tell you about that. Daisy was pretty, but not in the manufactured way city women were, which made some doubt whether or not she genuinely came from the City of Kings. She was a very friendly sort and the villagers soon noticed that she was, perchance, particularly too friendly with one of the teachers at the nearby mission school, with a Greek traveling salesman, and with the shopkeeper at the Idlazonke General Goods and Bottle Store. Despite the fact that she had once received a book from the teacher, always received imbasela from the Greek traveling salesman, and did not seem to pay for any purchase she received from the shopkeeper, none of the villagers saw anything definitive enough to alert the son of the village, who lived eleven months out of every year in the City of Kings. Besides, Daisy and the village's son were not actually married. They were doing what the Matabele called ukutshaya amapoto, which meant that they were playing at being married without really being so, like children. Daisy had lived this life in the village for many years (no one could be sure how many) and then she had suddenly disappeared in the dead of night two weeks before Lady Ashtonbury and Emil had, at the bend of a river, come across her hacked body stuffed into a khaki burlap sack. Some villagers said they had heard the engine of a motor car start and drive away the night Daisy had disappeared. But no one in the village had a car. The rain had fallen for days and nights and, by the time the BSAP made it to the village, washed away all traces of any tracks the car might have left behind. Many believed that a lover—the schoolteacher, the Greek salesman or the shopkeeper—had come to take her away. All the villagers were shocked when Michael Meredith and Spokes Moloi informed them that Daisy's remains had been found in a khaki burlap sack.

What had happened to Daisy was horrific in and of itself,

Emil told Maryvonne, but what made her story truly tragic was the paucity of actual facts about her life. This lack of detail about Daisy's life brought to mind Emil's earlier notions about the lack of permanency in the life of the African, and, as he spoke to Maryvonne, these two ideas in his mind began to converge. The parameters of what Emil wanted to do were fuzzy at first and so he molded them through his conversations with Maryvonne until they had definite outlines. In time it became clear to him that what was needed was a government unit that was dedicated to the African—not the Department of Native Affairs, something more centralized. It would be under the auspices (Emil liked the word) of this unit that the life of every African from the moment of their birth to the moment of their death would be recorded. This way there would be no fear of leaving ancestors behind. Africans would have more than a past, they would have a history—something permanently there. Emil felt that he had it within him to undertake such an enterprise. The very idea made him come alive more than anything else, even the idea of adventure, had ever done. It was as though a cluster of clouds in his mind had suddenly cleared and let the sun shine through. God's visit.

Listening to him, Maryvonne became as passionate about Emil's vision as he was. She promised to help him and soon enough had persuaded Lord Ashtonbury to help Emil as well.

Without even searching for it, he had found the purpose of his life, and after having found it, he could not help but feel that, perhaps, it was his destiny to be one of those great men of history that the Selous School for Boys had promised to produce.

One afternoon, Maryvonne paid Emil a visit at the government-issued, bungalow-style house with whitewashed walls and no veranda that had been Emil's childhood home.

Before long, kissing tentatively, they found themselves in the stark room that had once been his parents' bedroom, and soon enough on the cold concrete floor. At some point, as Emil trailed kisses along the valley of her breasts, Maryvonne turned her face away and focused on the corner of the wall. Her body seemed to have shut down. Confused, Emil prepared to move away, but she, with surprising strength, locked her legs around him and shut her eyes.

"I don't enjoy it...I never do...But I do so want this closeness with you. I want to connect," Maryvonne explained, her face blushing with deep shame.

Emil saw her the way she had appeared when he had first seen her—leaning on her left hand, laughing with her head thrown back, flirting with an entire group of men—and was saddened to discover that her easy laughter had held within it the secret knowledge that made her promise something she knew deep within herself she could not give.

Throughout it all there was never a point when Emil was not aware that Maryvonne deserved better—when he gave her the gift of finding pleasure in her body; when she looked at him with a frown on her brow and wonder in her eyes; when she screamed his name into the barrenness of the room; when they continued to meet thereafter—throughout it all Emil was aware that Maryvonne deserved better. Better than Emil Coetzee, the ne'er-do-well who had been left good for nothing by Marion Hartley.

CHAPTER 17

———•———

Emil was amazed at how everything fell into place after that initial thought—that birthing of an idea. Once he was sure that his idea was not only a good one but a solid one as well, Emil made plans to share it with the one person he knew would challenge his idea until it had merit—Courteney Smythe-Sinclair. And that was how Emil had come to find himself in a very uncomfortable situation.

As he stood, with a thumping heart and sweaty palms, under the archway, waiting to be introduced to address the crowd that had gathered, he realized that this was a bad idea. He had put too much stock in Courteney's opinion and that, evidently, had been a mistake. The ill-fitting suit and tie bought specifically for the occasion should have been the first indicator that he was out of his element, but at the time he had been too busy trying to put the speech together in his head to take much notice of his appearance.

Just because he had once written an essay that had, by some stroke of luck, impressed his teacher and won him entry to the best school in the country, it did not mean that he was made of the stern stuff needed for such occasions. But, whatever his reservations, before he knew it he was standing by the podium and regretting his decision to take seriously Courteney's suggestion that he address the Capricorn Africa Society.

The words came and Emil's voice trembled but traveled. People at the back seemed to be responding to what he was saying and thankfully, soon enough the speech did eventually come to an end. He was glad that throughout the whole ordeal the glare of the overhead lights had been so bright that he could not see any member of the audience clearly, otherwise he would have spent the entire speech addressing Courteney. There was modest applause, which he was grateful for. Then came the questions, for which, he realized too late, he had not prepared.

Mostly the audience members wanted to know what difference there was between what he was proposing and what the Department of Native Affairs did.

"The issue is one of permanence," Emil responded. "This is a time of great change for the African. Suddenly he finds himself able to move physically and socially in ways he has never before been able to. Not only are entire villages being resettled, for the first time in his life, the African can move around as an individual. He can leave his village and settle in the cities or mines..he can choose to go further still, to South Africa, for instance. As he moves, he moves away from the dictates of tradition. He can chart a new course for himself. A young man who leaves the village as Lobengula, for example, can become Sixpence the Teaboy in the city—"

Emil was interrupted by a rather unexpected and generous amount of laughter from the audience.

"The Department of Native Affairs treats the African as a static being," Emil continued when the laughter had died down. "I work for the department and I know that its approach cannot contain the rapidly changing life of the African. Another unit will be needed for that, which is where I come in. The department does wonderful work; I am not criticizing what they do. I am merely seeking to complement it."

The audience gave the impression of having been sufficiently impressed by Emil's responses and, eventually, he was able to walk away from the podium. He felt relieved and oddly elated. It had all gone much better than he had expected. And, to be honest, he had surprised himself by articulating the problem of the African so well.

Courteney was the first there to shake hands with him. A few of the gentlemen, apparently impressed by his desire to give Africans a history, came forward and introduced themselves.

But, of course, it could not *all* go well.

A small man with a stern face came up to him and asked, "Who are you?"

Although Emil was confused by this question, he replied, "Emil Coetzee."

"I know your name, man...but who are you?"

Emil was puzzled. If the man knew his name, what could he possibly be asking?

"Who are your people? Where are you from?"

Instinctively, Emil knew that he could not say, "I am from the Prince's Mansions on the corner of Borrow and Selborne," because the man wanted something more...permanent...than a rented flat in the City of Kings. He wanted a piece of land with the Coetzee name on it. There was no such piece of land, Emil realized with horror.

"Where were you born, man!" the small man said, exasperated.

I, Emil Coetzee, of Durban, Natal, Gentleman...

"Durban," Emil said, aware that this information was not going to help his situation.

The small man smiled gleefully. "Figured as much," he said triumphantly. "Not from here then, are you? You don't understand *our* African at all," he pooh-poohed, before walking away.

"Don't mind him," Courteney said. "Pioneer blood. A bit

of an elitist."

"Oh. I see," Emil said, even though he did not quite see.

Just then, a tall and dignified Coloured man walked up to Emil and Courteney and introduced himself as Ezekiel de Villiers. He shook hands with them before asking Emil, "And where do I fit in all of this, Mr. Coetzee?"

"You?" Emil asked, truly perplexed. He had never seen the man before in his life—how could he possibly factor in to what Emil was proposing?

"The Coloured man," Ezekiel de Villiers explained. "The thing created by the coming together of the advanced and progress-driven European civilization and the primitive and tradition-obsessed African civilization. Where does he stand in all of this?"

Emil was taken aback by the question. He had never given a thought to Coloureds at any point in his life. He had no idea where the Coloured man stood in all of it.

Emil was honest enough to say as much.

"I attend these meetings regularly and there is always a lot of talk about the creation of a multiracial society, one that is built on equality and governed by the representatives of all the races within the country," Eezekiel de Villiers said. "It all sounds very good—honorable, even. But when one examines all the talk, one finds that it is built on a very black-and-white idea of history—on the idea that the races are still, as yet, to come together. The reality is that the races have already come together and created a history. This history is not black or white. It is mixed." Having said what he had come to say, Ezekiel de Villiers shook hands with Emil and Courteney before adding, "Of all the talks I have attended, yours has been the most honest. It takes a very brave man to say the things that he knows need to be said and not the things that he thinks others want to hear. I sincerely thank you for that. I thank you for your bravery."

Emil was genuinely surprised to hear that what he had just performed had been an act of bravery.

As Emil watched Ezekiel de Villiers walk away he felt something needling at him that he could not quite put his finger on. The entire exchange, while pleasant enough, left Emil with a slightly bad taste in his mouth. He turned to Courteney for him to explain Ezekiel de Villiers as he had explained the small man with pioneer blood, but Courteney had obviously been too impressed by Ezekiel de Villiers to think of much else but how impressed he was by him.

At the end of it all, the important thing was that Emil had come, had seen and, even if he had not conquered, had spoken.

At Scobie's the next day, Rutherford threw a copy of *The Chronicle* in front of Emil, before sitting himself on a bar stool. On the front page was printed an image of Emil along with some of the words he had said in his Capricorn Africa Society speech. The media attention was more than he had hoped for and he did not know quite what to do with it; this was a very different thing from making it into the paper because you had allowed a motor car to drive over you.

Emil briefly wondered what Marion thought of it all. "You're quite the stud, aren't you?" she had said, but that had been before she invited him to the gathering. Had she seen this side of him all along, even before he knew it was there?

"I see you happily bought the horseshit that the Capricorn Africa Society is equally happily selling by the ton," Rutherford said.

"The horseshit?"

"Yes, the horseshit. This idea that blacks and whites can live together happily ever after fa-la-la-la-la-la-la-la-la."

"I think a lot of work still needs to be done, to be sure, but

I agree with the Society on a basic level."

"You honestly think munts want to share the running of the country with us?" Rutherford asked, incredulously.

"Yes. And given the right education, geared toward specific skills, after a few decades, they should be able to do so."

"Then you, my friend, don't understand the kaffir...no, forget the kaffir...you don't understand man. If someone came into your home and ran it without your permission, would you work toward running it with him or would you work toward removing him from your home?"

The answer was so clear to Emil that he did not have to voice it.

"The Capricorn Africa Society is made up of Master Duthie's 'gentlemen'—the Master Archies of the world. They do not comprehend the business of empire. Their bleeding hearts are in over their heads. We took this country by force. The only way the African will take it back is by force. Any man who convinces himself otherwise is merely lying to himself."

Rutherford downed the entire contents of his beer mug in one long gulp. "I see so much to love in this country of ours. We have done great work here in a very short space of time and idiots who don't know their arse from their elbow want to make a mess of it all, undo the great work already done."

"I love this country too," Emil said.

"Then why would you want to change it? Your love is very peculiar. It is a love that does not appreciate what a thing is, but, rather, what it could or ought to be. That is not love—that is wanting to love something."

As Emil wandered the veld feeling that old familiar feeling of connectedness, he dared anyone to find what he felt for the land peculiar. His love for this land was as true as any man's. Quite possibly he deserved to get burned for entering affairs that were beyond his scope, but this—he watched his hand weave through the singing elephant grass—this was the realest thing.

"Who are you?" the smallish, elitist man had asked after his speech at the Capricorn Africa Society, and while Courteney had done his best to shield him from the truth, slowly Emil had wised up enough to see how he came across to people. He was a young, rakish, roguish, lock-up-your-daughters sort of chap whose passion for the idea of providing Africans with a history would probably prove fleeting. He was too young and reckless to invest permanently in an idea or anything else for that matter. Emil could not fault the smallish, elitist men of society for thinking little of him and not respecting him—had he not been doing the same as them his entire life? What had he ever tried to do with his name besides prove that he was the grandson of his namesake?

He could get particularly low at such moments and while he rode around the grassland the image that would come to him would be of the government-issued, bungalow-style house with whitewashed walls and no veranda that he had called home. The house of his idyllic childhood. The house that the government had seen fit to let suffer the indignity of not having a veranda. The house that the Coetzees did not own in much the same way that they did not own flat 2A in the Prince's Mansions. Property mattered to the men of the Capricorn Africa Society and the Gentleman's Club. Property meant that one had established oneself permanently. After three generations on this land, the Coetzees had no property and had never taken steps to acquire any.

To make matters worse, for many years his father had been unable to secure a promotion within the BSAP. Courteney had a rich father who owned hectares of farmland in Essexvale that the government relied on. Rutherford had a rich and influential father whose manufacturing industries were the pride of both the City of Kings and the country. No smallish, elitist man had ever asked Courteney or Rutherford, "Who are you?"

What Emil Coetzee would become was anyone's guess.

Courteney, in his way, had tried to help him along by encouraging him to address the Capricorn Africa Society. But while they generally agreed with his idea, the members of the society were too gentlemanly to come out with the truth of what they sincerely felt—that Emil Coetzee was not the man for the job. When they learned that he had been born in South Africa and gone back there after he finished school, they decided to make of this that he was, at heart, a South African.

Africans needed a history. Emil had an idea of how to go about giving them one but, because of his own personal history, the idea would never see the light of day. Emil saw the irony of his situation and felt that it was just too cruel.

Yet, with a great deal of encouragement from Maryvonne, Emil determined that he would achieve his dream. It would just take greater effort on his part. It was a formidable undertaking but he knew that he could do it. Now that he better understood the inner workings of the social and political structure of his country, he understood that he needed someone else...an influential someone else...a man of wealth and property to believe that he was capable.

Engrossed in such considerations, Emil traveled the length and breadth of the Ashtonburys' land, making sure that all was in order. He often found himself wandering into the places of the property that were still wild, which was where he began to feel most alive. He loved the beguilingly serene savannah that could turn savage in the blink of an eye because he never knew what to expect. More than once a rustling had interrupted his thoughts and he had found himself face to face with a rhino, leopard, or a lion. In that moment, when the hunter became the hunted, as his hair stood on end, as adrenaline pumped through his body, he looked the magnificent beast in the eye and felt an exhilaration that was second only to being with a woman. Not just any woman. The woman who knew exactly what she wanted from you... what you wanted from her...and could use this knowledge to destroy you...

Marion.

CHAPTER 18

————◆————

The Ashtonburys proved instrumental to the realization of Emil's dream. They knew and introduced him to all the right people and, now that he was connected to the Ashtonburys, all the right people were open to his idea. Nevertheless, even with the help of the Ashtonburys, it eventually became apparent to Emil that if anything was actually to be done, he had to become as respectable as all the right people. There was only one way that he, Emil Coetzee, confirmed bachelor, born in Durban, and a man without property, could become respectable enough for the City of Kings. He had to find himself a wife.

Soon enough, the wife Emil needed to find came along in the form of eighteen-year-old Kuki Sedgwick. She walked into Emil's life at just the right moment to fulfil his desire. This was to be the only time that Kuki, bless her heart, would so wholly fulfil Emil's desire, but neither of them knew this as they hastened through their courtship, both of them eager, for very different reasons, to be married, which they were within a year of Kuki's walking into Emil's life.

Emil had vaguely been aware of Kuki Sedgwick for the past few years. She was a plain sort of girl who was a little too tall and apologetically compensated for this by slumping her shoulders. For a while she had also been a little "on the plump side" and at parties never put anything in her mouth without glancing at her mother first. She was something of a permanent fixture at gatherings and stood in corners drinking

Shirley Temples and wearing dresses that did not seem to know quite what to do with her body. In spite of this, for all her awkwardness, Kuki was surprisingly popular with the young men—she was, after all, a Sedgwick. Not only was her family wealthy, but they also had running through their veins the blood of proud pioneer stock. So although Kuki was no great beauty, she was what the boys of her youth called a "catch." Luckily for her, Kuki also had something else that made her very attractive: a strong desire to please. She laughed at every joke the young men made and when she laughed so easily, the young men imagined that she would make an uncomplicated and pleasant wife.

Fortuitously, toward the end of Kuki's seventeenth year, her fortunes began to change. She lost her weight, and the bloom that had so far proved elusive finally blossomed. So much so that a few days after her eighteenth birthday, when she made her grand entrance at a party she knew Emil Coetzee would be attending, she had the satisfaction of turning every head in the room, including his. Later she would say to her friends, "Remember the expression on Montgomery Clift's face when he first sees Elizabeth Taylor *in A Place in the Sun*? That is how Emil Coetzee looked at me that evening." Kuki did not care that most of her friends had been terrified by *A Place in the Sun* and saw the film as a cautionary tale. She had been too mesmerized by Montgomery Clift's good looks to take heed of any lesson that the film might have offered. All she cared about in the telling of the story of how Emil had looked at her was that her friends understood that Emil, with his movie-star good looks, had looked at her as though they were part of something that had been produced in a dream factory.

As the evening of their first meeting progressed, it became clear to Emil that she wanted to rouse his attention and so he let her succeed in doing so. When he called the Sedgwicks a few days later, he spoke to a Kuki who had been enchanted by the time they had spent together and was eager to embark on a relationship with him.

Kuki was ten years his junior, so their courtship was not of the sort Emil was accustomed to. It was quaintly chaste. There was much hand holding and quick pecking on the cheek, all meant to sow the seeds of a desire that would magically erupt into blissful compatibility on their wedding night. Added to all this, Kuki had a very definite idea of the type of romance that they should have and did not need his input at all. Emil did not begrudge her the running of their relationship; in fact, he was amused by it. It was, after all, her first romantic affair and she had probably been dreaming of it since childhood.

And, besides, he had Maryvonne.

Kuki had their entire relationship so well planned that during its fifth month she started to drop not-too-subtle hints about marriage: so-and-so she knew from school had just got engaged; a boy who had had quite a "pash" for her had just got married; a distant cousin had eloped. Kuki also hinted, more than once, that the fact that they were born exactly ten years apart, 18 April 1927 and 18 April 1937 respectively, meant that they had been predestined to be together...forever. So when Emil proposed to her on their six-month anniversary, which Kuki felt needed to be celebrated, what surprised Kuki the most was not the proposal but the size of the diamonds. From the way her mouth opened into an "O" that would not close for a very long time, it was obvious that she had been expecting something more modest. Emil was surprised that there were diamonds on the ring at all—it had taken three pay checks and the sale of a few hunting rifles to be able to purchase it at T. Forbes & Sons.

After Emil proposed, it soon became evident to him that

all he had to do for the wedding was to show up wearing a tailored tuxedo. Kuki and her mother, Dorothea, had everything else well in hand. The date was set, the venue chosen, the guest list meticulously determined, the seating chart designed with discriminate care, the best caterer in the City of Kings booked and the five-star, seven-course menu decided.

The year before, 1954, Kuki's heroine, Audrey Hepburn, had married Mel Ferrer (Kuki used the age difference in this union to justify to her family and friends why it was fine for her to marry Emil), which gave Kuki a wealth of ideas for her own wedding. All she had to do was find people in the City of Kings to emulate what she had gleaned of the wedding from fashion magazines and that would make her the happiest bride in the world. Since Kuki's wedding was to be the City of Kings' wedding of 1955, in order to prepare for it, Kuki spent less and less time with her betrothed and did not seem to mind the separation. As did Emil.

The only wrinkle that presented itself during the wedding preparations came in the form of the groomsmen. All Emil had to offer were what Kuki and her mother considered "old men": Lord Ashtonbury, Courteney, and Rutherford. All Kuki's bridesmaids were, of necessity, young women. It was the bride's duty to put her bridesmaids in the way of finding husbands, preferably in the groomsmen. Emil's groomsmen were not only old, but they were all also already married. The Sedgwicks decided that it would be best to have six young men from their set stand behind Emil at the altar. The compromise was that Lord Ashtonbury could stand as best man.

With much fanfare in the City of Kings, the wedding day finally arrived.

The bride was radiant. Many hours had definitely gone into making her so, but she was a magnificent sight to behold.

As Emil watched Kuki walk down the aisle with her father

by her side, something caught in his throat. This young woman was to be the making of him and for that he would always be beholden to her.

It was a wonderful occasion: the bride was resplendent, the groom was dashing, and the guests were awed. Everything was as it should be. The only thing that raised a collective critical eyebrow was that Lady Ashtonbury was conspicuous by her absence.

The honeymoon was to take place at the Victoria and Alfred Hotel in Cape Town, but could only begin after a lengthy first-class train ride from the City of Kings. Along the way there was much hand-holding, talking to other passengers in the dining car, showing off the rings and, when they were alone, doing some proper kissing, but not so much as to rouse the passions. It would not do to consummate their marriage in a train suite, no matter how first-class, deluxe and accommodating it might be. Kuki was very happy with this state of affairs, Emil less so.

When they arrived at the Victoria and Alfred Hotel, the newlyweds found a telegram from Dorothea informing them that Kuki had been chosen as *The Chronicle's* Bride of the Week. Upon hearing this news Kuki was so elated that as soon as they entered the honeymoon suite, steps were taken toward consummation.

At some point, however, things started to go awry. Kuki seemed to understand the need for what they were doing well enough but did not seem to understand that she was supposed to enjoy it. She pushed Emil away at a most inopportune moment, rushed to the bathroom, and locked the door behind her.

She was only willing to do this the way God had intended, she informed him through the bathroom door, her voice teary but assertive.

The way God had intended?

Yes! With her eyes looking up to heaven.

Oh...and...and...her lips would only kiss his lips.

And...and...his lips would only kiss her lips.

The way God had intended?

Yes! She understood that he had a...history...but she, as his wife, expected to be respected throughout the entire process.

Kuki only left the bathroom after Emil had promised that he would respect her body, wishes, and desires.

Kuki was very happy with this state of affairs; Emil less so.

CHAPTER 19

———————◆———————

As soon as Emil saw the present he knew it was from her. Not *them*. Her. It was one gift-wrapped box amongst many others that greeted Emil and Kuki Coetzee upon their return from Cape Town. It was not the biggest box on the table. It was not the smallest either. The size of the present had been chosen with great care. The present was supposed to mean something, but not mean too much. Emil did not have to see her handwriting; the color of the wrapping paper was enough—crimson in a sea of uninspired pastels. It was bold. It was just like the woman herself. Marion Hartley.

As Emil carefully removed the wrapping paper, he noticed that his fingers were trembling. Get a hold of yourself, man...What did he expect? It was a wedding present for both him and Kuki. It was not something to get excited over; he was half-expecting to find something useful—a tool set or a toaster. What he found instead was a glass menagerie of fifteen spectacularly colorful exotic butterflies. Emil delicately ran a finger over each one and marveled at the care that must have been taken to create each butterfly.

The gift was so beautiful and personal that Emil did not quite know what to make of it. Then he noticed the azure note, floating to the floor, and found that he could not breathe.

The note probably had something as innocuous as "Best wishes, Marion Hartley" written on it.

But maybe it did not.

Perhaps this was the thing that would finally reveal to him

what Marion thought and, yes, felt for him. After all these years, Emil still wanted her good opinion. He wanted other things as well but the promise of those could not be contained within a note.

He gently placed the glass menagerie back on the table and bent over to pick up the note, his still-trembling fingers making the entire business a very clumsy affair.

If he had not been so anxious, he would have laughed at himself, and he was a man who almost never laughed at himself. Marion Hartley seemed to have the ability, the power even, to make him explore the different tracks of this thing called manhood in which he suddenly found himself, the terrain of which was not always easy for him to navigate.

Her handwriting, which he had come to know intimately over the years since he carried it with him everywhere he went, was still a gorgeous cursive that defiantly, but elegantly, leaned to the left.

Did she, wherever she was at the moment—passionately arguing a point at one of her meetings or dispassionately putting on her lipstick at No. 1 Pioneer Road as she prepared to leave yet another lover behind—have any idea of the power that she had over him? Then. Now. Always.

The note read,

There are years that ask questions and years that answer.
—Zora Neale Hurston

Emil blinked at the note card. If she had written about butterflies he would have understood—if not the message itself, then the fact that the butterflies were supposed to be a metaphor for marriage. But she had not written about butterflies, she had written about questions and answers.

With the note, Marion was making something legible for

him and he did not know quite what it was.

His fingers still trembling, Emil opened his wallet and placed the note with the other notes that had been written on azure-colored paper with the same left-leaning cursive. Just as he had done with them, he would carry this note with him everywhere.

Emil was well aware that his situation was pathetic; he was also aware that it was very much his own. He would have been embarrassed by his inability to shake her had he not been in the grip of a very powerful thing indeed. At some point during the years of knowing Marion, Emil had become the kind of man who trembles in anticipation of what a woman has written to him. He had been aware of this transformation happening within him, but he did not fully understand it. He did not understand himself. He did not understand why it had to be her for him. Why *this* woman and not another? She was intelligent. She was beautiful. She was exciting. There were other women with these qualities, so why her in particular? Was it all still because of a moment shared years earlier and the promise held in that moment?

In the beginning he had tried valiantly to move on by finding comfort in a new conquest. Next, upon realizing that he could not free himself from her hold, as an antidote he had tried to ridicule Marion in his mind. Here she was, this liberal so eager to be seen to be forward-thinking that she voraciously read the works of black writers. No one in the City of Kings could out-liberal Marion Hartley. Her bleeding heart was firmly beating in the rightest of places. But he could not laugh at her for too long because he remembered well the passion with which she had argued her points. That kind of passion existed not to impress others but, rather, so that its possessor could be at peace within herself.

And now here was something new to contend with, this

crimson gift with its note that held the promise of answered questions.

Knowing that Kuki would be justifiably suspicious if she came home and found just the one present open, Emil, his fingers no longer trembling, opened a few more gifts and discovered two toasters, a silver dinner bell, an ivory-handled letter opener and a complete Wedgwood tea set. Kuki would be ecstatic.

Several times a day, Emil would remove the note from his wallet and reread it very carefully, as if it were a cipher. What was it that she was trying to communicate to him?

In moments of reason, he would remind himself that the note had not been intended for him alone, but, rather, for them: for him and his wife. Marion had probably not expected him to be the one to open the present—what husband did that? Kuki would have been the one to open the present. Kuki would have been the one to read the message and take its words as well wishes for a happy marriage, as most notes that accompanied wedding presents were. The note, from someone Kuki did not know very well, would have been discarded. Chances were very high that he would never see the card, and Marion would have known that.

There had been another gift from the both of them, Courteney and Marion, a very modern-looking kitchen appliance bought from Kuki's wedding registry at Meikles Department Store. That gift, which sent Kuki into raptures because it was what she wanted most, had been simply signed, "from Marion and Courteney," in that left-leaning cursive.

So why then had Marion sent another gift solely from her? Why the gift of butterflies? Why had she written about a promise fulfiled? She must have meant for him to see the note and make something of it. But what was that something that she wanted him to make of it? A poor, wretched creature by now, Emil would, with his forefinger, trace her left-leaning cursive and imagine as possible all kinds of impossible things.

Soon after receiving the gift of butterflies, a most deplorable occurrence transpired. Mr. and Mrs. E. Coetzee had been invited to a party at the home of Courteney and Marion, and Kuki had innocently RSVP'd—informing Emil that they would be attending only after she had put her card in the postbox. Kuki had done nothing wrong; it was part of her job as wife to organize their social life, and Emil resolved that he would spend the entire party making it a point not to stare at Marion and to gaze at Kuki instead.

True to his promise, anyone who saw Emil that evening believed him to be absolutely besotted with his newly wed wife. Since all had gone according to plan, he had been confident that the evening would end well without him embarrassing himself. His confidence had made him feel safe, and perhaps a little too sure of himself, until he entered the bathroom and saw it...hanging carelessly and languidly on the shower rail. *Was this not the guests' bathroom?* Emil thought as his eyes fell upon it, this shimmering and diaphanous thing that beckoned to him...begged him to come and touch it. Why was it here—why had she left it here?

The rational part of him knew that it was just a nightgown that Marion had absentmindedly forgotten in the excitement of putting together a party. But again, where Marion was concerned, rationality did not prevail long for Emil, and he thought that, possibly, she, knowing that he would at some point enter the guests' bathroom, had left it behind so that he could find it and touch it. The shimmering, diaphanous thing continued to beckon to him and, heeding its call, he went to it and touched it...feasted his eyes on it...buried his face in it...

breathed in its scent. It smelled of things he wanted to put in his mouth—vanilla, coconut, and something sweetly and sinfully tropical. Emil almost cried from the sheer joy of it.

And then he watched in stupefaction as he held the nightgown in his hands and rent it apart.

The violence of the act took him completely by surprise. He had been happy—joyous, even—so where had the violence come from?

He dropped it to the floor—this poor nightgown that had been negligently forgotten by its owner only to be violated by a total stranger—and walked away from it.

Suddenly, Emil was afraid. Afraid of himself. Afraid of what he was capable of.

That settled it. He would never see Marion again.

CHAPTER 20

———◆———

All the same, the fact that Emil would never see Marion again did not mean that he would never see Courteney again. The something between them had existed before Marion and would exist beyond her as well. So Emil and Courteney continued to meet in the billiards room of the Gentleman's Club. Since Courteney was a member and Emil was not, Emil sat in the Billiards Room as Courteney's guest.

The Gentleman's Club, with its strictly-no-women-dogs-and-natives-allowed policy, was a place Courteney loved and frequented. The very same Courteney who got red in the face defending the rights of women and the need for equality of the sexes; the very same Courteney who staged critically acclaimed takes on Shakespearean plays—a black Hamlet and white Claudius; a white Othello, coloured Desdemona and black Iago; a female Lear with three sons; a Lady Macbeth poised to be the first queen and a Macbeth whose desire for the throne makes him sabotage her—at the Repertory Theatre and had been lauded by *The Chronicle* as the "voice of our times"; the very same Courteney who believed that racism should be a thing of the past; the very same Courteney who volunteered at the SPCA and publicly called for the better treatment of animals was also the very same Courteney who liked the privilege of drinking a Tom Collins and smoking a cigarette in the Billiards Room of the Gentleman's Club, as he was doing now, and talking business with other European men, all the while knowing that women, dogs, and natives were not allowed in the building.

Liberals, like all humans, did not always know what they were about and could, like all humans, be self-contradictory. Emil was, however, not the sort of man to begrudge another man his inconsistencies.

Seen through another lens, there might not have been anything inconsistent about Courteney's choice of haunt. The Gentleman's Club was probably the safest place for Courteney in the entire City of Kings; it was here that he did not have to fear bumping into Marion and one of her lovers. No matter how open-minded Courteney was, seeing Marion with a lover would surely hurt, Emil was certain of this. Emil looked at the plush environs of the Gentleman's Club, a place where Marion could never be, and contemplated that, conceivably, he could overlook the heftiness of the membership fee and join the Gentleman's Club himself.

Now, with some effort, Emil dragged his thoughts away from Marion and tried to focus on the reason he had asked Courteney to meet with him. The time had come to make his plan to give Africans a history a reality.

"And Lord Ashtonbury is still up for it?" Courteney asked.

Emil nodded.

"Even after the Lady Ashtonbury fiasco?"

Emil flinched at the word "fiasco." Maryvonne deserved better than that.

Lady Ashtonbury had filed for a divorce from Lord Ashtonbury and the ensuing scandal had almost ripped apart the City of Kings.

Despite the fact that both Lord Ashtonbury and Emil had begged Lady Ashtonbury not to go through with the divorce, she had gone through with it. Heartbroken and humiliated, Lord Ashtonbury had no choice but to grant her the divorce and leave her with almost nothing. She left the Ashtonbury Farm and Estate and went to live in a cottage on Tenth Avenue under her maiden name, Maryvonne de Rusbridger. The City of Kings did not know what to do; they wanted to continue loving her, but she was no longer Lady Ashtonbury, and so they had no choice but to effectively shun her.

Emil was making real strides toward setting up his organization and, for this reason, he could not afford to divorce Kuki, not now, and definitely not for Maryvonne de Rusbridger. Besides, he had sincerely tried to dissuade Maryvonne from going through with the divorce, so when she was left ruined by it, he felt that he really could not blame himself entirely.

Lord Ashtonbury and Lady Ashtonbury did not let the reason for their divorce be known publicly and Emil felt deeply indebted to them for that. But of course the City of Kings gossiped and conjectured, and whispers about an affair between Lady Ashtonbury and Emil Coetzee eventually reached everyone's ears, including Kuki's.

"If Lord Ashtonbury supports you, then you are home and dry," Courteney went on. "Everyone will want to be seen to be supporting you as well."

Emil was grateful that Lord Ashtonbury had been a gentleman about the whole Maryvonne affair. He was probably just saving face by continuing his support of Emil's idea, but by taking the high road, he was ensuring that Emil's project received the funding it needed to get started.

"You are a very lucky fellow, I'll grant you," Courteney said with a chuckle. "When you began with Lady Ashtonbury, how did you imagine it would all end?"

Emil shrugged and tried to steer the conversation away from his personal life. "So," he said. "I've been trying to come up with a name. What do you think of 'The Organization for

Native Affairs'?"

"Sounds too much like the Department of Native Affairs. The Africans might get confused. But I like the sound of 'The Organization'," Courteney said as he took a puff of his cigarette and squinted his eyes in concentration. "How about 'The Organization of Domestic Affairs'?"

"Sounds like a women's social club—something Kuki would join."

"Don't be hasty...Let it feel itself out."

Emil nodded non-committally. "Whatever it is called, I am now thinking that there should not be any government involvement."

Courteney stared at Emil for a long time through the smoky haze and then nodded at him respectfully. "I am glad you have arrived at that decision. I sense you are onto something truly important here."

That was when the enormity of what Emil was embarking on hit him. This was a truly audacious endeavor. The Organization of Native Affairs...The Organization of Domestic Affairs...Whatever it was called, this was the very thing that would propel him to greater heights. He could feel it.

"You can start out with a couple of offices in Sinclair Court and take it from there," Courteney said. "I will make sure Pa does not charge you rent for the first three months."

First Lord Ashtonbury. Now Courteney Smythe-Sinclair. Emil could not believe his fortune at having somehow, surely through no merit of his own, garnered the support of two true gentlemen.

He had not meant to hurt Lord Ashtonbury, but he had. He had meant to hurt Courteney, but he had been the one to get hurt. He had treated them both shabbily and, instead of being destroyed by his betrayal, they had shown him that they were better men than he.

Why could he not be like these men: upright and true? Why could he not be a gentleman? What weakness within him made him unable to rise above being just another Emil Coetzee?

Here he was, once again, feeling around the edges of himself...trying...and failing...to see the whole. He was tired of this. How could a man be such an enigma to himself?

"Did you tear Marion's nightgown?"

The question, so innocently asked, took Emil by complete surprise.

Emil could have lied to Courteney, but he did not want to. On the other hand, he could not bring himself to put into words what he had done.

"Why do you keep offering me your friendship?" Emil asked. "With all that you know about me, why do you even bother?"

"All that I know about you? What do I know about you?"

Emil was tired of fumbling around the edges of things.

"You know I slept with your wife. You know I tore her nightgown. You know I am good for nothing...and yet you keep offering me your friendship."

"We were boys together once."

"That cannot excuse everything, make it all forgiven..."

"It doesn't...excuse or forgive anything. It does, on the other hand, make me understand."

"Understand what?"

Courteney was just about to say something and then decided against it. He said, instead, "Marion thinks you hate her —believes that's why you tore the nightgown."

The very idea that he could hate Marion was almost laughable.

"I don't hate Marion."

Courteney, dipping into his ever-flowing stream of

sympathy and understanding, said calmly, "So that's how it is."

Yes. That was how it was.

"I have always supposed that you did not particularly like women. I know that you appreciate them physically. But the voraciousness of your appetite made me believe that you did not care for women on an emotional level. And I've always thought—"

"You can hit me if you want. Lord knows I deserve it," Emil said, not wanting to hear any more of what Courteney thought. The picture that had been painted of him was too pathetic for Emil to bear.

Courteney looked at Emil with all the sadness in the world.

"We were boys together, Emil," was all Courteney said in response.

CHAPTER 21

———◆———

From 1956 to 1960, Emil contentedly spent his days and nights off the beaten track: driving down dust roads and slim strips of tarred road canvassing villages, farming estates, mining compounds, mission stations and townships, talking to Africans and telling them why it was important for them to register with their Native Affairs Commissioners and Location Superintendents, why it was important to report all births and deaths, marriages and divorces, school and work attendance, why adults had to do this not only for themselves and their children, but for all those who had departed whose biographical details they knew.

The Africans asked how the work that The Organization of Domestic Affairs was doing was any different from the work done by the commissioners and superintendents. Emil told them that The Organization was gathering all the information of their lives. Why? Because Africans did not have a history. When they frowned and murmured at this, and they always frowned and murmured at this, Emil told them the story of Daisy. In the beginning he had started with the story of Daisy but she always got lost in the facts. After almost losing an argument over the fact that Africans did not have a history, Emil had twigged to the fact that Africans preferred stories over facts. So he now ended with Daisy's story. It never failed. She, or more accurately her transience, left a lasting impression. The fact that she had died with little to nothing being known about her, and that this lack of information meant that her murderer was never found, brought home to his audience the need for them to have recorded lives.

Emil found that he addressed the Africans with ease. No sweaty palms for him here. He did not have to wear ill-fitting suits to be taken seriously. He could wear his signature khakis and cowboy hat and let the whiteness of his skin do the rest.

Because he was taken seriously by others, he started to take himself seriously as well. Yes, he was the grandson of his namesake, but that was not all he was. He was also a man of vision. He was also a man capable of doing great things, of leaving his mark, of being remembered by history.

The Organization of Domestic Affairs was his destiny. He was in his element, traveling deep into the veld again. And the ease with which he—who was always fumbling, questioning, bungling—filled his role proved that this was what his life had been leading up to all along.

Emil wished that this state of affairs could carry on forever, but, understandably, it could not. Lord Ashtonbury and those wanting to please him had raised enough money for The Organization to have its own building. Construction of The Tower started at the beginning of 1960 and was completed at the end of 1961. Emil was needed to oversee its construction and so had to put his days off the beaten track behind him. The Tower, with its ten floors, bay windows, and modern architectural design, was very impressive and, for a time, one of the attractions of the City of Kings.

The completion of The Tower did not come a moment too soon. The four offices in Sinclair Court that had kindly been provided by Courteney were overflowing with documents. The six members of staff whose job it was to collate the information were soon overwhelmed. The Organization was proving too successful. It had to grow. By 1963 The Organization had fifty office workers and twenty field agents, and all ten floors of The Tower were occupied. Reluctantly, Emil found himself confined to a desk, impossibly busy overseeing the staff and the successful running of The Organization.

He was ensconced in a very impressive-looking room, which he had had absolutely no hand in putting together. It had all been Kuki's doing. She, who understood the importance of appearances, had seen to the furnishing of the room herself. She had chosen the colors, green, red and white, which she called emerald, burgundy and ivory. She had chosen the rich mahogany furniture. She had chosen the paintings and the trophies that were mounted on the teak-paneled walls. Then, with the room furnished to stately elegance, Kuki's interest in The Organization of Domestic Affairs had ended.

The Organization of Domestic Affairs was so efficiently and successfully run that Emil Coetzee, seemingly overnight, became a very important man not only in the City of Kings but in the entire country. He became something of an authority on "The African." He gradually moved to the front page of *The Chronicle*, where he was quoted with reverence. Men who once would have asked him superciliously "Who are you?" now curried his favour and invited him to speak at their societies.

Emil Coetzee, of Durban, Natal, was acutely conscious of his reversal of fortune.

CHAPTER 22

———◆———

In the late summer of 1958, Kuki was very much pregnant and deeply in love with the Everly Brothers. She could be heard from every corner of the house waking up little Susie or saying bye-bye to love. That Kuki was happy in her marriage no one could doubt, although most people were surprised by her happiness, not least of these being Emil. For whereas her marriage had started well with Kuki being named Bride of the Week, Bride of the Month, Bride of the Year, The Country's Bride and Queen of Brides (with whispers of her possibly winning Bride of the Decade and, potentially, even Bride of the Century), by the end of 1956 the marriage had been rocked by the scandal of Lady Ashtonbury's divorce.

Whatever Kuki felt upon hearing the news of the affair can never be known because she never confronted Emil about it and opted, self-preservingly, to go with her parents on a three-month tour of post-war Europe that had very much been inspired by the film *Roman Holiday*. When she returned, she seemed happier than ever to be married and soon made it known to Emil, in no uncertain terms, that she wanted a baby.

While the fact that Kuki had not confronted him about Lady Ashtonbury had, at first, put Emil at ease, he soon came to suspect that there was more to it than Kuki's famously forgiving nature and desire to please.

What kind of wife does not react at all upon hearing of her husband's infidelity?

A wife who loves her husband but does not necessarily

love the man she married.

The realization of this apparently paradoxical state of being came to Emil slowly. Replaying their time together, he saw Kuki enter the room at the dinner where they first met. He saw her seek out his particular attention. He saw their hasty courtship, their lavish wedding and their almost disastrous honeymoon. He saw them moving into the double-story house her parents had bought for them in the new and modern suburb of Brookside, which had been built by post-war prosperity. He saw her furnish rooms the way she had seen in home magazines. In short, Emil saw Kuki living the life she had always dreamed of. In order to live this life, she needed to be married and so she had found herself a husband as soon as possible after finishing school. Any husband really would have done, but Emil was so far removed from her circle of friends as to be exotic. That was why she had chosen him; it was not because he was Emil Coetzee but because he was different from the boys of her youth that her friends were marrying. Emil could not quite bring himself to acknowledge that perhaps Kuki had also married him merely because Audrey Hepburn had chosen to marry a man twelve years her senior.

Emil understood that Kuki had married her idea of a husband and not the messy reality of having an actual man as her husband, and, in time, Emil came to comprehend Kuki's happiness as well. Her parents had a successful marriage and so Kuki fully believed that her marriage would be successful too. She was living a life that felt predestined and therefore she did not have to be original, she did not have to question things, she did not have to react adversely to news of a philandering husband. Let him philander, if he must; she would always be the princess in the castle. Her prince had come along, woken her with a kiss and, having done his duty by her, was now free to go off and do whatever he wanted with whomever he wanted.

Had he not married her solely for the respectability of her last name, Emil might have felt ill-used indeed.

Nevertheless, even this understanding on Emil's part changed over time. While he did not mind Kuki marrying him merely to provide herself with the husband that would make her preordained life complete, he did mind that she never attempted to go off-script from this predetermined life.

It was through Kuki that Emil was able to finally fully appreciate his attraction to Marion. Marion did not simply follow life; she chose it. And her choices were not determined by the latest magazines but by the things she held dear, the things she argued passionately for. During their time together at No. 1 Pioneer Road, Marion had followed the dictates of her body—she had given and received pleasure without caring a jot about what any magazine had ever said about how a woman should act. Marion was just unapologetically herself. And through Kuki, Emil saw Marion in full relief for the first time.

Things might have been tolerable for Emil in his married life had Kuki, at least, tried to know or appreciate him as a person. Here he was, after a long struggle with himself and the City of Kings, finally on the verge of realizing his dream, and Kuki showed absolutely no interest in it. He had tried to tell her about Daisy and how inspirational she had been, but Kuki covered her ears and informed him that she did not like to hear of unpleasant things.

For Kuki, their marriage was a picture-perfect thing meant to be admired by the outside world. Living with Kuki was, Emil thought, like living in a snow globe containing within it a depiction of a happy marriage. No one was allowed to pick up the snow globe, shake it, and temporarily disturb the tranquillity of its contents.

For Emil, such an insulated life felt oppressive. One day, unable to help himself, he picked up the snow globe and gave it a good shake, all the while fighting the strong desire to bash it against the floor. With something in him breaking, Emil told Kuki about how he had married her for her family name, how she had once been so unattractive to him, how she had married not him but an idea of a man, how he wanted to be more than an idea, how he wanted to be something real in her life.

Emil had hoped that, with this confrontation, Kuki would finally grow up and face the life she had—the real life they had made together and not the fantasy she had hoped her married life would be. But Kuki did not do what Emil hoped she would. What Kuki did do was to stop singing around the house. Little Susie had finally woken up.

CHAPTER 23

———•———

The baby was born a boy and Emil wanted him named Frederick after his hero, Frederick Courteney Selous. Kuki wanted the baby named Everleigh—after the Everly Brothers, Emil assumed. When Emil insisted on Frederick, Kuki, after her convalescence at Mater Dei Hospital, went with the baby to her parents' home. Some days later, Kuki's father, Reginald, called Emil and reminded him that Kuki had never asked much from him, which was Reginald's gentlemanly way of saying that Kuki had not made a fuss over Lady Ashtonbury and any other affairs that Emil might still have up his sleeve, so, never having asked much of him, they expected him to grant Kuki this one wish.

A few months later, the boy was baptized Everleigh Reginald Coetzee.

Once again, Kuki's life had gone according to her plan and she began singing around the house again. This time she had found something more lasting to celebrate.

Kuki absolutely adored The Boy Who Was Not Frederick. As soon as he was born, he became the center of her life. She actually said, on more than one occasion, that the reason she had been born was to bring this wonderful being into the world. Emil sometimes wondered if she had married simply so that she could be a mother. As a mother, she arranged her life around the boy and took him with her everywhere she went—to her parents, to Emil's parents, to the Haddon & Sly Tea Room, to the Monte Carlo Theatre, to the Ladies of Distinction Hair Salon, to the meetings of the Pioneer Benevolence Society of the City of Kings, to the Municipal Bathing Pools, to the Centenary Park. She loved nothing more than being stopped on the street so that the boy could be admired by complete strangers. Everyone who saw him agreed that he was a beautiful baby boy.

The only photographs of Emil and Kuki together were the ones taken on their wedding day and at their honeymoon. Before The Boy Who Was Not Frederick was born, these pictures had proudly adorned the mantelpiece in the living room. Kuki and Emil had indeed made a handsome couple. But, after the boy's birth, the mantelpiece underwent a change. Everything that the boy did had to be recorded—his first suckle, his first burp, his first gummy smile, his first funny face, his first cry, his first clasp of his mother's finger—and the evidence enshrined on the mantelpiece. By his second birthday an entire album was dedicated to the boy and he was the star of several 8 mm films: Everleigh's First Steps, Everleigh's First Words, Everleigh's First Birthday Party. There was even a film taken of Emil sleeping on the sofa with the boy sleeping on his chest; Kuki took pride in showing this particular film to guests.

For his part, when the newborn baby boy had first been placed in Emil's arms at Mater Dei Hospital, Emil had experienced a love so profound that it immediately became unspeakable. There were no words that could ever capture what he felt for the child. He was so overwhelmed and overpowered by the intensity of the emotion that it left him perpetually awestruck. How was it even possible that he, Emil Coetzee, could have created something so unbelievably and utterly perfect?

At first the smallness of the boy had worried Emil. What if he could not be gentle enough to handle such a delicate thing with care? As a result, he held the boy rarely and always with apprehension. However, as the boy grew older, Emil became more and more at ease with him. The boy began to resemble him and Emil marveled at the fact that he could ever have been so small himself. That small Emil would have lived in Durban during the years he no longer remembered.

Emil haltingly established something of a relationship with the boy. On long trips, which he came to enjoy, Emil would, from the driver's seat, tell the boy sitting in the back seat with Kuki all the names of the trees and animals they came across and make the boy repeat them after him. Emil liked being a fount of knowledge for his son. When they went walking the streets of the City of Kings or visited the various exhibitions at the agricultural show, Emil would proudly put the boy up on his shoulders so that the whole world could admire him. When Emil had time, he and the boy would play Cowboys and Indians, although it worried him that the boy always wanted to be an Indian.

Yes, the boy belonged mostly to Kuki, but Emil was happy to have been able to carve out a place for himself in the boy's life.

The edges of this father–son relationship began to fray when the boy was about five. The first thread unraveled when the boy, from his privileged perch on Emil's shoulders, asked why Africans were not allowed to walk on the pavements. Emil understood that the boy was too young to understand the policies and laws of segregation so he chose instead to tell the boy of the wonderful work he was doing for the African through The Organization of Domestic Affairs. The second thread unraveled when Emil took the boy hunting for the first time. Upon seeing the slingshot and realizing instinctively what he was supposed to do with it, the boy had refused to get out of the car. The boy told him, as he folded his arms and pouted his lips in resolution, that he did not want to be responsible for the death of anything. Emil told the boy about Frederick Courteney Selous, the great white hunter, after whom he was supposed to have been named, but the boy remained unmoved. The third thread unraveled when Emil read *King Solomon's Mines* to the boy one night and the boy came crying to Kuki that he had had a nightmare not about Gagool with her shrunken monkeyness or about King Twala with his one evil eye, both of which would have been understandable, but about Captain John Good and his removable teeth. As Kuki lifted the boy onto her twin bed, Emil realized simultaneously, with a sinking feeling, that the boy was soft and that he did not know what to do with such a son.

The entire fabric threatened to unravel on one of those weekends that Kuki made long by leaving on a Thursday morning and taking the boy with her to visit her parents. Returning from the Gentleman's Club earlier than intended, Emil found himself home alone on that Saturday night. He poured himself a glass of whiskey and went to stand by the door of the boy's bedroom. The bedroom was painted yellow and filled with an abundance of pastel-colored toys. The boy's cot, even though he had long outgrown it, stood calmly in a corner, stuffed with a surfeit of teddy bears. Emil regarded the teddy bears and, instead of finding fault in their softness, he lamented the absence of the boy who took so much pleasure in them. It would be Father's Day the next day, and here he was, a father without his son because Kuki had decided to celebrate the day with her father.

Emil suddenly felt like a teddy bear that had had all its stuffing removed. On impulse, he downed what had not been his only glass of whiskey of the day and grabbed his car keys, determined to fetch his family.

He had driven halfway to his in-laws' house when he

recollected that they were at the Matopos Dam Hotel—"The Silver Llake in an emerald frame"—and so he turned the car around and headed to the hotel. He drove for what felt like the whole night and arrived at the hotel a little before midnight. With the help of a sleepy concierge, he found his in-laws' chalet and knocked on the door several times before a light came on.

He had enough time, before someone opened the door, to decide whether he was going to spend Father's Day there or drive his family to Brookside in the morning. But when Reginald opened the door and looked both surprised and dismayed to see him, Emil made up his mind on the spot to take his family with him immediately.

"You're drunk, man," Reginald whispered as Emil pushed past him. Reginald's disappointment had turned into disgust, which only served to make Emil even more single-minded.

The rest of the night might have gone differently had Emil not opened one of the bedroom doors and found Kuki and The Boy Who Was Not Frederick sleeping blissfully under a yellow candlewick bedspread. Emil had said more than once that it was time for the boy to learn to sleep alone. It was time that he started learning to be a man. He pulled the boy away from his mother, waking him up. Kuki woke up and, upon seeing her son being pulled away from her, instinctively leapt at Emil as though he were not her husband. The boy, initially shocked into dumbfoundedness, started to cry aloud, like a girl. Kuki clawed at Emil, wanting her son back, demanding to know what exactly he thought he was doing.

"*Think* he is doing?" Reginald jeered. "He is Emil Coetzee. He never thinks of what he is doing. He just does it."

When Emil carried the boy to the front door, he found that Dorothea had locked it and was pressing her body against it.

"Kuki does not ask for much—" Reginald began to say.

"She may not ask for much," Emil said, cutting him off. "But she definitely takes everything." He was not altogether sure what he meant by those words, but he believed them nonetheless.

While Emil held on to the boy, who hiccupped himself back to sleep, Kuki packed their belongings and convinced her parents that it would probably be best if they returned with Emil.

"Drive very carefully, my boy," Reginald said, closing the rear door after ensuring that Kuki and the boy were safely settled in the car. "You have here the two most precious things in the world to me."

"They are precious to me too," Emil said.

"Very fine way you have of showing it, then," Reginald sneered.

As Emil drove away, he wondered why what he felt was seen as tainted somehow.

"All you needed to do was telephone," Kuki said from the back seat. When had anything between them ever been that simple?

They were on the outskirts of the city when something hit the car in the night. It woke up Kuki and the boy. Shocked, Emil stopped the car by the side of the road and stepped out to check the damage. He used the moment he had to himself to steady his nerves. There was not much damage to the car save for a dent on the bumper. On the ground a few meters away, Emil could just make out the outline of the animal that he had hit. Since it made no sound, he assumed it was dead and got back into the car.

"What was that?" Kuki asked.

"I think I hit an impala," Emil said, starting up the engine again.

As he prepared to drive off, Kuki said, "You're not going to just leave it there, are you?"

If Emil had been driving by himself, he would have put the impala in the back of his station wagon, gutted it as soon as he got home, and then taken it to the butcher first thing in the morning and asked him to make some very nice peri-peri biltong out of it. But Emil was not alone; he had a wife who lived in a bubble where bad things did not happen and a son who did not believe in killing things.

"You're not going to leave it? What if it's still alive?" Kuki said.

Emil was almost certain that the animal was not alive and was about to say as much, when he glanced back and saw the boy's eyes staring back at him, filled with hope. He was loath to extinguish the boy's hopefulness and so he got out of the car and went back to check on the animal. It was an impala. A fawn. The size of it explained the minimal damage that it had done to the car. It was still warm...still breathing...still alive. Emil carefully picked up the fawn and carried it to the boot of the station wagon, where he placed it on a quilted picnic blanket.

As Emil got into the car, he heard the boy say, his voice filled with astonishment, "It looks just like Bambi, Ma."

Emil had no idea what a Bambi was, but he blamed it for giving his son false hope.

Kuki did not say anything in response. She just smiled sadly and rubbed the boy's back.

"I can keep her, can't I, Ma? As a pet?" the boy asked, still kneeling on the back seat and staring at the fawn.

"Sit down, love," Kuki said. "Your pa has to drive now."

The animal would probably be dead before they arrived home and that would be the sad end to this sorry business, Emil thought as he started the car.

"You couldn't stop by at the vet, could you, Emil?" Kuki

asked—for the benefit of the boy, Emil assumed.

"No vet open at this hour, I'm afraid," Emil said, playing along.

"But I'm sure that Johnson would see us regardless of the hour. He is a family friend."

With dismay, Emil realized that Kuki was in earnest. In her snow globe, of course, things could not die.

All that Emil could reasonably hope for now was that the animal would pass away peacefully, preferably before they arrived in Brookside.

Instead, as though all the forces of heaven and hell were conspiring against Emil, the animal's hooves started kicking the side of the car's boot. The animal itself was dumb but Emil understood exactly what it was communicating; it was in agony and wanted a way out of the pain. There was only one way out. Emil prayed that these were the impala's last kicks.

From the back seat, the boy began to cry in the way that the animal could not.

And still the impala's hooves kicked the side of the boot.

Emil found himself, in the early hours of Father's Day, driving to Dr. Johnson's house and veterinary practice in the suburbs. It was almost two in the morning when Emil carried the fawn, still alive, but barely, into Dr. Johnson's fluorescent surgery and laid it on the metal slab. A disheveled but accommodating Dr. Johnson took one look at the animal and said what Emil had long known: "Poor thing. Will not make it, I'm afraid."

The boy who, Emil only realized too late, should not have followed him into the room began to gulp loud, wet sobs.

"I can give him an injection. Put him to sleep," Dr. Johnson offered.

For a confused moment, Emil thought that the doctor was referring to the boy and almost agreed to the suggestion before realizing his error.

Emil looked at the fawn lying on the cold silver slab and watched as its trembling body took its last breaths.

Emil knew that its ending would have to be more meaningful than that. He went to his car and retrieved an object from the glove compartment. He reentered the surgery and, without saying a word to anyone, used the knife in his hands to cut out the impala's heart.

Kuki was screaming something about barbarism. The doctor was yelling that it was not necessary. The boy was wailing.

Emil ignored them all and held the warm heart in his bloody hands like an offering. He cut off a piece of the heart and ate it to ensure that the animal would live on in him forever.

PART THREE

———◆———

MANHOOD - HIS HOUR UPON THE STAGE

CHAPTER 24

———◆———

On a beautiful day that promised rain, a beige Zephyr Zodiac began its journey from Tanganyika to the City of Kings. A successful trip would mean that it would arrive in the City of Kings on Christmas Day. The year was 1962. The Zephyr Zodiac valiantly traveled through the vast and varying terrain of southern Africa during brilliantly blessed days and rested in the cover of night. Its integrity was only questioned twice, at Ndola and Livingstone, but it finally made it through Northern Rhodesia and crossed the mighty Zambezi River.

Nothing was particularly remarkable about a Zephyr Zodiac making such a journey and so no one asked it why it was going where it was going. It probably helped that it was beige in color and a little weather-beaten and, therefore, absolutely unassuming.

Its journey was successful and it arrived in the City of Kings on Christmas Day, 1962, as intended.

Those who welcomed it did so with relief. They had been anxious ever since the Zephyr Zodiac had started on its journey. No, to be honest, they had been anxious since Joshua Nkomo and Edward Ndlovu had procured the weapons—grenades, explosives and bombs—in Egypt months before. They had been anxious too as the weapons traveled down the coast of the Indian Ocean toward Dar es Salaam. Their anxiety had given way to terror as the weapons were loaded onto the waiting Zephyr Zodiac in Tanganyika because this marked the point of no return.

It should be noted here that the weapons may have been obtained through more nefarious means, namely by poisoning Congolese rebels and looting their military materiel.

The weapons traveled to the City of Kings in the company of Abraham Dumezweni Nkiwane, Misheck Velaphi Ncube and Kennias Mlalazi. In order to carry out this very important mission, Misheck Velaphi Ncube and Kennias Mlalazi, along with Bobbylock Manyonga, David Mpongo Khumalo and Solomon "Mupfukacha" Mabika had been briefly trained in Egypt. Once they arrived in the City of Kings, the weapons had a story of their own to tell: after a short sojourn at Nkiwane's father's homestead in Lupane, they traveled to the house of Findo Mpofu—who coordinated and commanded the whole operation—in Mzilikazi Township where they rested briefly before carrying on their journey to the Matopos Hills to receive the blessings from the ancestors before they performed the immense task ahead of them—for, you see, these weapons were destined for greatness because they were to bring about the end of British rule. The City of Kings was not their final destination; the weapons were on their way to Salisbury, the capital city. In order for them to reach Salisbury, they had to pass through the hands of Thomas Ngwenya—an integral part of the pipeline—who would then hand them over to Bobbylock Manyonga.

Unfortunately...or fortunately...depending on how you chose to regard it, Bobbylock Manyonga was arrested somewhere between Shabani and Salisbury as he ferried the weapons to what should have been their final destination. While under interrogation, he named names and Thomas Ngwenya found himself in Grey's Prison. The weapons' glorified place in the history books was not to be.

The beige Zephyr Zodiac made yet another trip, this time with Amon Ndukwana Ncube accompanying Misheck

Velaphi Ncube, and, just as it had driven past Wankie, it was intercepted by government operatives and both men were arrested and imprisoned at Grey's Prison.

The two journeys of the beige Zephyr Zodiac and the weapons seemed to anticipate the sharp turn to the right that the country's politics would take. As it turned out, it was not just the weapons that had prepared themselves for this sudden change. In 1962, a few Africans, led by Kennias Mlalazi, had left the country as well: Clark Mpofu, John Mondiya Ndlovu, Amen Chikwakwata, Ellias Ngugama, Gordon Butshe, James Chatagwe, Mbhejelwa Moyo, Phebion Shoniwa and David Mpongo Khumalo left for Northern Rhodesia where they were trained by Ambrose Makiwane. The following year, in 1963, four of these men—Clark Mpofu, Mbhejelwa Moyo, James Chatagwe and Gordon Butshe—left Northern Rhodesia for China. In Dar es Salaam, Tanganyika, their group was joined by Felix Rice, Lloyd Gundu and Charles Dauramanzi. They went through the Soviet Union en route to Peking. If any of these men, born and bred in the savannah, minded traveling through the unforgiving tundra of Siberia, they stoically did not let on. They were simply following in the footsteps of another group that had included Philemon Makonese and had been led by Charles Chikerema the previous year and blazing the trail for another group that would follow and was made up of Stone Nkomazana, John Maluzo Ndlovu, John Mondiya Ndlovu, Benson Maphosa, George Mudukuti and Johnson Ndebele and led by Luke Mhlanga. While these men had headed to China, Sikhwili Moyo (an erstwhile vital conduit in the smuggling of weapons into the country), Thomas Ngwenya (who had escaped from the country while on bail), Zephaniah Sihwa, Edward Mzwazwa Bhebhe, Walter Nqabeni Mthimkhulu and Zebediah Mapfumo Gamanya had headed to Ghana. Another group, which included Misheck Velaphi

Ncube (who had made a rather daring escape from Grey's Prison), Emmerson Mnangagwa and Shadreck Chipanga, had been sent to Egypt for initial training and later dispatched to China in order to gain a more ideological and practical understanding of the Chinese revolutionary experience. Joseph Zwangami Dube went to Cuba for his training.

The purpose of training these men was quite simple: they were to be the saboteurs who would weaken the state and hasten the way to more equitable racial politics within the country. The idea was that they would attack the very things that made the state money: the commercial farms, the mines, and the industries.

To make all this possible, there was a network of contacts throughout the country—Dumiso Dabengwa, Ethan Dube, Enos Chikowore, Akim Ndlovu, Abel Siwela, Cephas Cele, David Lupepe and Khesiwe Malindi—that would provide shelter, food, and the means to carry out these acts of sabotage. Since the would-be saboteurs had to leave and enter the country without being detected, the planning of logistics was essential and was carried out at the Mthembo Garage in Mpopoma Township. Some of these contacts, namely Dumiso Dabengwa, Akim Ndlovu and Abel Siwela, had in 1960 become saboteurs themselves, along with Pilane Ndebele and Bernard Mutuma, and had later been joined in their endeavors by Charles Nyathi, Daut Mabusa, and Roma Nyathi. In a few short years, they had come to understand the importance of organization and formal training.

Having been thus militarily trained, one of the groups stole back into the country in 1963, but one of their party, Shadreck Nkomo, was intercepted and arrested, necessitating that the others flee the country. This did not mean that other acts of sabotage were not attempted. That same year a faulty time bomb was discovered at the highly popular hypermarket, OK Bazaar, in Salisbury. And later, after re-entering the country in August, Johnson Ndebele was blown apart while putting together another time bomb.

Emil had read about the bomb found at the OK Bazaar in Salisbury, but because the bomb had been faulty he had written it off as a hoax. Apparently, the bomb threat had not been a hoax and that was why Rutherford was now sitting in Emil's office. According to Rutherford, some of the Africans who had attended the Capricorn Africa Society meetings and talked of multiracial governance were now calling themselves "nationalists" and calling for black majority rule, when what they truly were were terrorists trying to bring the politics of the country to a head so that there would be a civil war. All of this confirmed what Emil had long suspected: Rutherford was a member of the Central Intelligence Unit. Most of the Bootlickers from the Selous School for Boys were.

Emil studied the overwhelmingly extensive list of African names that Rutherford had handed him. He knew some of the names on the list and tried to fit them into the narrative that Rutherford had just told him. "Of course, we have not made most of this public, you understand?" Rutherford said.

"No need to cause unnecessary worry," Emil responded understandingly.

"No need to have the buggers know how much of a dent they have created in our national security, more like," Rutherford said matter of factly. "Keeps them questioning their own effectiveness. It doesn't take much to create doubt, chaos and confusion in that lot. So for now we prefer to have a silent war, as it were."

His country at war with itself? Emil could not quite see it. For what purpose? To what end? Any rational person would agree that the best thing for the country's future was for all races to come together to run the country. But any rational person could also see that the African had some ways to go before catching up to the standards of western civilization. Emil knew the African and knew that it would take a few decades, two or three at least, for true equality to finally take root. There was no need for war, no need to rush things. What all the good citizens of the country wanted would come to pass...eventually.

Emil examined the overwhelming list of African names again. "A civil war, you say? Why?" he asked.

Rutherford scoffed. "We've been in their house without their permission long enough. They want us out."

"I know some of these men. They are good men."

As he read the expression on Emil's face, Rutherford scoffed again. "Do you remember what we used to call you in school? Emil 'On the Fence' Coetzee."

Emil did not remember having such a nickname and highly doubted that anyone would ever have used it to his face, especially during his later school years. "On the Fence?"

"You couldn't make up your mind whether you wanted to be a gentleman or whether you wanted to be a man"

"I don't know about that. What I do know is that multi-racial governance and racial unity are the only viable future for this country," Emil said, handing the list of names back to Rutherford.

"You sound like one of the wonderful gentlemen of the Capricorn Africa Society. Well...the gentlemen have had a go at it for more than ten years now. Almost botched up the whole business, and have left the mess for us, the men, to clean up. You see, a gentleman thinks he can know the African, but he cannot. An African is a kaffir and a kaffir is irrational. There is no reasoning with these people. Us men, we know that." Rutherford shook his head. "You need to get off that fence, Coetzee. The men, the real men, have taken over now. It would be in your best interests to join them—to join us." Rutherford handed the list back to Emil. "They received their training in Northern Rhodesia, China, Egypt, Cuba and Ghana for a reason. They have been taught, or, should I say, they have been indoctrinated into a communist way of thinking. They are going to do away with capitalism and implement socialism. They are hell-bent on sending us back to the Dark Ages. I don't think these things. I know these things."

Emil just could not see this future that Rutherford was trying to paint for him. Africans were simply not ready to run the country on their own. Surely they must know this. A civil war would not only be devastating—it would be futile.

"What do you want from me?" Emil asked.

Rutherford sat back in his chair and Emil watched as his whole demeanor changed. "In a very short space of time, you have managed to accomplish something truly amazing through The Organization of Domestic Affairs. It was a mammoth task that you set out for yourself and, if I am being honest, I did not trust that you would pull it off. But you did, and I am impressed. We are impressed."

The words did not sound like Rutherford at all and Emil knew that he had delivered them exactly as he had been instructed to deliver them, with an emphasis on the "we." He wondered how many times Rutherford had rehearsed the lines and swallowed his pride before paying him a visit.

"By 'we' do you mean the new government?"

"Yes. We would like to work with you."

"The Organization, although autonomous, already liaises with several government institutions."

"The new government would like to work with you more... directly. The Organization already works with several government institutions; it can become a branch of government."

It was Emil's turn to scoff. Rutherford had assumed that he was the same Emil he used to drink with at Scobie's, but running The Organization had changed Emil. "The Organization is independent of the government for a reason."

"These men," Rutherford said, pointing at the list, "and their numbers will surely grow, mark my words, want only one thing—to bring about the end of this country as we know it. Now you are many things, Coetzee, and one thing you definitely are is a man who is proud of his country and loves it. Just look around you and look at what the European has achieved in a very short time here. Imagine what we could do in the next fifty...hundred...thousand years. They want to put an end to all that progress." Rutherford stood up to leave. "Please just don't sit on the fence about this. Please give it some serious thought. I am sure you will come to see things the way we do." With Rutherford gone, Emil went to stand by the bay windows that looked out at the City of Kings. He surveyed the city's modest concrete sprawl. He had not always loved it, but he definitely loved it now. Nothing more than a dust bowl fifty years ago, it was an absolute marvel to look upon now. It was a modern city with storied buildings, wide tree-lined avenues, fully functioning factories, billowing smokestacks and a robust railway system. What had been made possible within a short span of history was, without a doubt, amazing.

But, unlike Rutherford, when Emil looked at the city, he did not see just the hand of the white man. He saw the black hands that had forged the railway that gave the city its lifelines, the black hands that had laid the brick and mortar that built the very structures that one could look upon with pride, the black hands that carried the messages and tea that allowed the business of the city to run smoothly. There were brown hands as well, specifically trained to assemble and fix the machines that drove the country's progress. There were browner hands still that were part of an essential mercantile class, doling out, at affordable prices, everything that the colony needed to prosper and grow. Rutherford believed that Emil did not see his country clearly when, in reality, the thing was that he saw his country too clearly. The races were working well together...had done so almost since the very beginning. All that was needed was for the different civilizations to be on par with one another and all would be well. If every race stayed in its lane, as it were, there would be absolutely no need for a civil war. They could all move forward into the future together. Unfortunately for Emil Coetzee, others had a very different idea for the future of the country. Men who had previously been focused on changing the country through acts of sabotage had come to understand, after their political parties were officially banned in 1964, that the only way to achieve their goal of majority rule was through outright warfare. And that is how former saboteurs Dumiso Dabengwa, Akim Ndlovu, and Ethan Dube, along with Robson Manyika, Jabulani Ncube, Joseph Nyandoro, Edward Bhebe, Ambrose Mutinhiri, and Gideon Ngoshi found themselves in the Soviet Union, the first to be sent there specifically for military and specialist training. Another group consisting of, amongst others, Tshinga Dube, Roger Matshimiri, and Report Phelekezela Mphoko later joined them. That same year more African men willing to fight for majority rule went to, in addition to the already established training grounds, North Korea, Algeria, and Bulgaria for military training. They now all understood themselves to be preparing for one thing: armed struggle.

Closer to home, in the newly independent Zambia, William Ndangana put together a group of five men. In addition to Ndangana, the group consisted of Victor Mlambo, Amos Kademaunga, James Dhlamini and Master Tresha Mazwani.

Their mission was to infiltrate the eastern part of the country and commit acts of sabotage. On 30 June 1964, the group arrived in Umtali and were met by Joseph Shasha. Another compatriot, Obed Mutezo, had already found a cave for them to operate from. Almost immediately upon arrival the group of five men went to purchase knives and explosive devices. Perhaps, having seen the weapons, the reality of what they were about to do hit Kademaunga and he left the group.

The very next day, the remaining members of the group attacked Nyanyadzi Police Camp. On 2 July, they set up an ambush for a traveling European man on the Chikwizi Bridge, but instead they ended up attacking Lucas Siyomo, an African man, who was traveling with his family. Due to his race, Siyomo and his family were allowed to leave virtually unharmed.

Two days later, on 4 July, Pieter Johannes Andries Oberholzer was not as fortunate as Lucas Siyomo had been. Ambushed while also traveling with his family, Oberholzer was stabbed to death by Ndangana, who spared the lives of Oberholzer's wife and daughter.

The murder of a European man proved to be the group's undoing. With the BSAP hot on their trail, they had no choice but to disperse. Dhlamini and Mlambo were caught, arrested, charged with terrorism and hanged in chillingly quick succession. Mazwani was caught, but spared because he was a minor. Ndangana survived it all and, while this could not be known in 1964, would become a politician of some renown in the early years of the post-independent country.

In the few days that the group had operated they had come to be known as the Crocodile Gang.

When Emil read about Oberholzer's death in *The Chronicle*, he knew to anticipate another visit from Rutherford. And so, when Rutherford sat down before Emil, Emil was ready for him.

"While you were sitting here twiddling your thumbs, the men that you claim to know so well have been trained to use AK-47s, light machine guns, all manner of weapons and ammunition. They know how to stage a coup. They have been taught guerrilla tactics. And now they have killed a white man, one of us," Rutherford said, shifting in his chair. "Now, what I would like to know is what you plan to do about it."

"The government does not need The Organization," Emil said calmly. "The Organization gets its information from Native Affairs departments, location superintendents and mission stations. The first two already belong to the government, and I am sure that the third can be made to comply with the government's wishes. The Organization of Domestic Affairs is a private entity and, as such, cannot involve itself in politics."

Rutherford appeared both angry at Emil and disappointed in him, which he was. "Those savages killed a white man, Coetzee."

"It is a tragedy."

"You're bloody right it is—a tragedy and a travesty. And you're not willing to do anything about it?"

"You want The Organization to do what, exactly? Give you information on people you suspect of being terrorists?"

Rutherford sneered with derision. "I should have known that you would not see the bigger picture. The Organization has the most centralized and comprehensive database of Africans living in the country. Surely even you can see how it could come in useful. Let us say a tea boy, let us call him Sixpence, does not come to work on a Monday morning. We check your database to see what kraal he is from, where he lives in the city, that sort of thing. That is when we contact the Native Affairs departments, location superintendents, and mission stations. Within hours we can know where Sixpence is and where he is not...Coetzee, this is the beginning of war.

We cannot afford to spend days trying to sort out our arse from our elbow. This thing that is already happening needs us to act quickly. So you see, we very much need The Organization to work integrally with us."

Emil knew that Rutherford's naming of the hypothetical tea boy, Sixpence, was not accidental. He was showing him how the system that Emil had articulated to the Capricorn Africa Society years earlier could be used to effectively do the government's work.

"And what will you do once you find Sixpence?"

"The Organization need not concern itself with that... as yet."

The government was asking now, but Emil knew that they would not be asking for long. He truthfully had no choice in the matter; all he could do was play for time.

But, unbeknownst to him, time had already run out because at that very moment Moffat Hadebe was firing the rifle that would mark the beginning of the war.

"You are a right lucky bastard," Rutherford said, taking in Emil's impressive office. The envy was plain to hear in Rutherford's voice. "You stumbled on the very thing that the country needs to successfully fight the terrorists. This will probably be the making of you. You will be the man of the hour. You will become a man of history."

CHAPTER 25

———•———

Emil knew that the government had approached him not only because he was The Head of The Organization of Domestic Affairs, but also because of the way he had handled the Beatrice Beit-Beauford situation.

Beatrice Beit-Beauford was someone whom Emil had felt he already knew long before he met her. She had been a part of Emil and Kuki's relationship from its very beginning, and this was because every idea that entered Kuki's head had to run through what Emil came to call the "B-Check." Before she articulated her own thoughts and feelings, Kuki would start most of her sentences with the words "B says," "B thinks," "B feels," 'B strongly suggests." The B-Check was such a constant in Emil and Kuki's relationship that Emil had strongly suspected that when he asked Kuki to marry him, the "yes" would need to come from Beatrice Beit-Beauford.

Although Kuki said "yes" immediately when Emil asked her to marry him, the B-Check came soon after. As Kuki sat there gazing at the diamonds on her ring, loving Emil for understanding that they were a girl's best friend, she had said, "I really wish B were here. She is the only person who deserves to be my maid of honor. Now I will have to ask Margaret because she is a cousin and all. B does not like rings...does not like the commodification of the marriage union. Actually, B does not care much for the union itself and says that she will never get married. But I don't suppose she really knows what she is talking about. What woman could possibly be happy without being married? And how will she have children? Silly B, always having to think differently from everyone else. But I absolutely love her for being so...contrary. I wonder what she will say of my ring." At that point Kuki's lungs could not take it anymore and she had paused to suck in a breath. Emil took the opportunity to kiss her, chastely, the way she liked, and in so doing silenced all talk of Beatrice.

Emil understood that Kuki and Beatrice had been friends since they had met on their first day at Eveline High School, when and where they had forged a steadfast solidarity against Matron Pulvey's war on privileged girls. Even so, Emil very much doubted that Kuki was an expert on Beatrice Beit-Beauford. The B that Kuki spoke of seemed too...liberal minded to be real. B, according to Kuki, believed in impossible things: abortion and women's rights over their own bodies, same-sex marriage and unions, interracial marriages and unions, the equality of the races, the equality of the sexes, and the most outlandish of all things—a person's right to choose their own gender. This last consideration had allegedly come about after B had read the story of Christine Jorgensen, years before.

Now, Emil did not doubt that B believed herself to believe one or two of these things; what he sincerely doubted was that she believed all these things. Emil suspected that Kuki probably had not caught on to the fact that B had been pulling her leg with some of these ideas. I mean, a person's right to choose their own gender—honestly, how gullible could one person be? Kuki was too innocent and trusting to fully recognize and appreciate irony and deceit.

Such a liberal-minded person as the one that Kuki believed B to be could not possibly exist because, as far as Emil was concerned, Courteney and Marion were as liberal as people could get. They both believed in racial and gender equality. Courteney, for his part, had joined the Capricorn Africa Society, refused for his wife to take his last name and, Emil suspected, reluctantly participated in an open marriage. Marion, for her part, religiously read Negro literature, refused to take her husband's last name and, Emil suspected, very happily participated in an open marriage. They did not have children and, though Emil never asked, it struck him that this was the product of a choice rather than the product of an unspeakably terrible misfortune. There was, according to Emil, no point of liberalism beyond Courteney and Marion.

Besides, Emil had learned all about Bennington Beauford in Master Duthie's History class. Although really a contemporary figure, Bennington Beauford had featured a little too frequently in a section of the syllabus that Master Duthie called "Great Men of Empire."

According to Master Duthie, Bennington Beauford was a hero of empire because he was a man who understood his role in the larger scheme of things. He had single-handedly, after arriving in the colony with no money, created a commercial farm whose successes had enabled the young colony not only to take part in the war effort but also prosper in a volatile global market. Bennington Beauford, born a gentleman, had chosen to be a man who understood what it really took and meant to build an empire. Although he had traveled to the colony in the twentieth century, he had been determined to follow in the footsteps of Frederick Courteney Selous and so, instead of catching a train from Cape Town to the City of Kings, he had trekked through the savannah. He—and Master Duthie loved this detail—had almost died twice on his way to the new colony, when a severe bout of seasickness left him so weak and emaciated that the doctor on board actually pronounced him dead, and when, after a successful recuperation in the Cape Colony, he contracted malaria while traveling over land by ox-drawn carriage. Again, he was so weak and emaciated that those he was traveling with left him in the care of two natives, whose task it was to wait for him to die so that they could bury him in an unmarked grave. Miraculously and fortuitously, Bennington Beauford had kept on surviving as the two natives carried him in a jungle hammock all the way to the new colony.

"He should have been an unmarked grave in the middle of the vast veld but his enterprising spirit would not let him. His soul, which knew of his great future, would not let him. He understood implicitly the kind of man he could be in this country. In this country, mind you, and no other. This country with its virgin land unspoilt and untouched...this country with its virgin land stretched wide open...this country with its virgin land that lay ready for any man of grit and determination to enter it and claim it." At this point, Master Duthie would pause to get ahold of himself, more embarrassed by his turn to the poetic than his turn to the erotic. He would strike the top of his desk with his open palm, effectively bringing back any young man who had ventured to places that Master Duthie had not quite intended. "No reject of empire is our Bennington Beauford, wot! A man's man, that. A man's man. He stands like a colossus over the length and breadth of this country."

Emil had not needed Master Duthie to tell him that Bennington Beauford was a hero. From a young age, Emil knew that most of what he wore and ate had started out as an animal or a plant on the Beauford Farm and Estate. What Master Duthie had given Emil were the details of Bennington Beauford's rags-to-riches story that made him come alive for Emil in a way that other historic and heroic figures could not. Because of this, Emil had supposed that he knew everything there was to know about Bennington Beauford and, because he knew everything there was to know about the father, he had assumed he knew everything there was to know about the daughter, Beatrice Beit-Beauford.

So it is not difficult to imagine Emil's complete surprise when he first saw Beatrice Beit-Beauford alighting from the plane with long, neglected hair, wearing a flowing garment that one could not be sure was a dress, leather slippers, and a straw hat, smoking a wooden pipe and looking, for all intents and purposes, like one of the great unwashed.

If Kuki had not run toward her screaming, "B! It is so good to have you back!" Emil would never have believed that he was in the presence of the wealthiest woman in the entire country.

Since Emil's first impression of Beatrice Beit-Beauford had not been a particularly favorable one, he probably was not too surprised or hurt when she greeted him with, "I begged Kicks not to marry you. I hope, for your sake, that you are no longer a prancing popinjay."

From the very beginning, it was already evident to the both of them that theirs was a relationship that would work best with little love lost.

The year was 1960, and after six years away at Oxford University, Beatrice Beit-Beauford was already something that the country did not yet know existed: a hippie. However, within a very short amount of time, the country came not only to know but also to appreciate, understand...and fear what a hippie was.

That B did not like him very much, Emil did not mind. That Beatrice monopolized Kuki's time, Emil did not mind. That Beatrice Beit-Beauford thought her having "read art at Balliol" (as she put it) until she had received a master's degree (in what Emil knew to be the most useless subject in the world) gave her the right to have a decided opinion on *everything*, Emil did not mind, and Emil often surprised himself by not minding these things.

What Emil did mind was that Beatrice Beit-Beauford put her opinions and ideas into practice. When she went back to live on the Beauford Farm and Estate, she left the running of the farm in the very capable hands of the foreman who had run it ever since her father had died when she was thirteen, and eagerly turned the estate into an artist's colony, which, as the 1960s progressed, became a vibrant commune. Truth be told, Emil, although not altogether broadminded in his way of thinking, would not have minded this had the colony-commune not been multiracial.

Mixing the races now, he believed, was a very dangerous affair. It would give the African ideas above his station, make him feel himself to be the European's equal, which of course he was not yet. What the country desperately needed was order, everything and everyone in their place. The time would come for mixing...if mixing did, indeed, have to take place.

Most open-minded people assumed that Emil's ideas on miscegenation were backward until they heard his reasoning and then they were not so sure. Beatrice Beit-Beauford was not such an open-minded person. She disagreed with him on every point. According to Beatrice Beit-Beauford, there was no truer citizen of the young colony than the Coloured person. Races had always mixed in some form or another. The only reason that racial mixing had become a "problem" and an inconvenient truth of history was because the country was segregationist and racist, and *that* was what really needed to change. It was the government and its policies, and not the people and their ways, that needed to change.

Since there was no reasoning with Beatrice Beit-Beauford, Emil found himself having to rely on the law. Beatrice Beit-Beauford was contravening the country's antimiscegenation laws and segregationist policies, but when Emil tried to get the state to intervene and remove all non-Europeans not employed by the Beauford Farm and Estate from the property, the state was reluctant because the farm was still vital to the economy, and the government did not want to get on the wrong side of the wealthiest woman in the country. So Beatrice Beit-Beauford and her multiracial community were able to live free and prosper.

When Emil tried to stop Kuki from visiting the aberration that the Beauford Farm and Estate had become, and, worse still, taking The Boy Who Was Not Frederick with her, Kuki, calling Emil "unreasonable," went to visit her parents for three days. While Kuki was away, Emil received a phone call from Reginald, reminding Emil that Kuki did not ask for much and that it surely would be in everyone's best interests for Emil to accommodate her. Emil was left with no choice but to let Kuki and The Boy Who Was Not Frederick spend entire weekends at the multiracial Beauford Farm and Estate. For many years later, Emil would wonder if The Boy Who Was Not Frederick became whatever he was because of his early exposure to the hedonistic multiracial colony and commune on the Beauford Farm and Estate.

Not quite happy, but not able to change the situation either, Emil had to live with the chaos that Beatrice Beit-Beauford seemed eager to create both in his home and in his country.

Even as the country's politics swung from the left to the right, Beatrice Beit-Beauford was left to do as she pleased.

Things would have probably carried on in this not-quite-happy state for a very long time had Rutherford not informed Emil that Beatrice Beit-Beauford was giving away her father's well-cultivated wealth to what she called the "nationalists cause." Emil was incensed. Funding the "nationalists cause" would not only help start the war but also prolong it. Surely

Bennington Beauford, the man who had escaped death twice because he knew he was destined to be a great man of history and empire, would not want proceeds from his farm to be put to such use.

As far as Emil could see, Beatrice Beit-Beauford was not merely being foolish, she was being dangerously so. She was embarking on something that would bring the country to its knees and potentially destroy it. Emil knew that Beatrice Beit-Beauford supported the "nationalists" because she believed she was right. And that was really what was wrong with her: she always thought that she was right. Emil had lived long enough to know that the problem was not with her but with youthful zeal and optimism in general; it was an unthinking thing, chock-full of hubris, something to be pitied really if it were not so bloody dangerous. Emil said as much to the state and this time his plea was more successful; it did not take much to convince the government that Beatrice Beit-Beauford's funding to the terrorists needed to be cut.

However, the government continued to ignore the existence of the multiracial colony and, as it turned out, this was something that they would soon come to repent. When Kuki had excitedly driven a reluctant Emil to the Mater Dei Hospital where Beatrice Beit-Beauford had just given birth to twins, neither Kuki nor Emil could, even in their wildest dreams, have anticipated what greeted them in Beatrice's private ward. Swaddled and placed beside a very contented Beatrice Beit-Beauford were two baby boys with light-brown skin and curly black hair.

Not knowing that her mother-in-law had responded in exactly the same way thirty years earlier when a native girl came asking for Walter, Kuki suddenly felt hot, swore to herself that she, the granddaughter of pioneers, would not be so affected by the heat as to faint, made a strangled noise, dropped the fruit basket she had brought, and would have fallen on the floor in a fainted heap had Emil not caught her.

When Beatrice Beit-Beauford happily announced to the world that the father of her sons was an African nationalist, Emil felt vindicated and almost triumphant. Had he warned every one of the danger that was Beatrice Beit-Beauford? Yes. Had anyone listened and taken him seriously? No. And now they knew that they had not listened to him to their own detriment.

The right-wing government was left with no choice but to treat Beatrice Beit-Beauford as the threat that Emil had long said she was. After a legal battle that was made lengthy by the involvement of the international community, the government finally succeeded in removing her, her sons, and her entire multiracial community from the Beauford Farm and Estate, leaving behind only the African farm workers to continue the running of the farm. As an added measure, a European man who had recently immigrated to the country from Australia, was made manager of the farm. Beatrice Beit-Beauford was placed, along with her twin sons, in a quiet suburb of the City of Kings where she was allowed to socialize only with government-vetted and -approved Europeans. No one called this living condition "house arrest" even though two constables of the BSAP guarded her premises around the clock.

Beatrice Beit-Beauford moved to the quiet suburb during the early hours of the morning of 11 November 1965, Armistice Day, and Emil, at Kuki's behest, made it his business to ensure that she was comfortably settled.

Throughout the entire process they did not say much to each other, but as Emil turned to leave, Beatrice Beit-Beauford said to him, "History—this thing that you purport to comprehend and know so well—is on our side. History will remember us and our valiant struggle in this moment. We are fighting the good fight. We are moving forward with the march of time. We will be memorialized. History will not remember you or your kind. You are doomed to be forgotten. History does not reward those who seek to retard its progress."

She sounded as though her "free-thinking" brain had been removed and replaced with a machine spewing out nationalist rhetoric. Emil decided that it was best to leave her in her self-delusion. He could have told her what he had long learned —that history belonged to the victors—but what would have been the point, since she alleged that she was on the side of the victors?

CHAPTER 26

As Emil drove away from Beatrice Beit-Beauford's new home there was a tension in his neck and shoulders, tension that he knew would worsen with his visit to Rutherford's house to discuss the ways in which The Organization and the state would work together to curb the rising tide of terrorism. Because he had been unrelenting in the way he had gone after Beatrice Beit-Beauford, the government believed that Emil would pursue would-be terrorists with as much zeal and, even though he was ambivalent about having The Organization involved in this endeavor, he strongly suspected that the government was right about him in this regard, and this did not sit well with him.

In his previous conversations with Rutherford, Emil had made it very clear that it was important to him that the information that The Organization had be used for pre-emptive measures only, to help catch would-be terrorists before they left the country. Emil did not agree with most of what the government was doing, like offering rewards to people who came forward with the names of terrorists, and had said as much to Rutherford, but Emil got the distinct impression that the new government was not interested in listening to anything it did not want to hear.

Now, in Rutherford's living room, Emil accepted the shot of whiskey Rutherford offered him. It was too early in the day to be drinking, but it was just that kind of day. There was talk that the Prime Minister would, later that day, declare independence from Great Britain. The entire City of Kings was on edge because it knew, even though it would not admit it to itself, that independence from Great Britain would certainly lead to civil war as the African was no longer happy with minority rule. Rutherford poured himself a vodka, immediately downed it, and poured himself another; this was obviously not new territory for him. He sat opposite Emil and smiled. The government was desperate.

"Eunice, is that you?" The voice of Agnes, Rutherford's wife, carried from another part of the house.

Agnes...Emil could not help but smile into his whiskey glass when he thought of her. She had once gathered enough courage to wink at him at a party and now blushed every time she saw him. She was attractive enough, but was too "house-wife" for Emil. She was a pretty parrot with no opinion of her own; he already had Kuki for that.

"What on God's green earth are you wearing?" They heard Agnes ask, followed by a muted response. "I can bloody well see it's a dress!" Agnes continued. "It is a dress I gave you. How on earth do you intend to work in that dress?"

Listening to Agnes, Rutherford's face was twisted in anger, disgust and something else...hatred. It contorted his face and made it an almost ugly thing.

"I beg your pardon?" Agnes's voice had become shrill.

Rutherford pinched the top of his nose, closed his eyes and took a deep breath. He was trying and failing to control himself.

Emil thought he heard his name.

"Well, I never!" Agnes shrilled.

"Would you please excuse me?" Rutherford asked in a barely audible whisper. Grinding his teeth, he stood up and stalked out of the room.

"The sheer effrontery. Always listening, always sneaking

around, always snooping. One cannot have privacy in one's home with you lot," Agnes shouted.

"Dear? Why all the commotion?" Rutherford asked. "I told you I need peace and quiet today. We are discussing some matters of great national importance."

"I know, dear, but Eunice here wants to see Emil Coetzee."

There was a moment of stunned silence.

"And how does Eunice happen to know that Emil Coetzee is here?" In his voice, Emil could hear all that Rutherford had been trying to keep at bay—the anger, the disgust, the hatred.

"Well...well...Who knows with servants? They are resourceful. They have their ways, don't they?"

"*I* wouldn't know—"

The muted voice outside interrupted Rutherford.

"I will thank you very much not to take part in a conversation that you are not a part of," Agnes's voice said.

"And I will thank you very much, Agnes dear, not to discuss matters of national importance with Mrs. Simpson. You know how important this meeting is to me. You know the strings I had to pull to get it to take place here. If your loose lips cost me my promotion..."

Emil took a long swig of his whiskey, placed the drained glass on the side table, and stood up. It was time for him to intervene.

The light coming in through the kitchen door was too bright for Emil and so he removed his sunglasses from his breast pocket and put them on.

"Is everything all right in here?" Emil asked.

"Yes. Yes. Of course, Emil. Just some domestic trouble," Rutherford said.

"He means trouble with our domestic," Agnes cautiously corrected, blushing up at Emil.

"Mister Coetzee, I would like to speak with you, sir," a

female voice said from the other side of the kitchen door. The voice belonged to an African woman. Emil did not remember an African woman ever addressing him directly before. Ever. Even in the days when he went about proselytizing the gospel of The Organization, the Africans who had directly addressed him were all male. The women tended to speak to him through the interpreter or their chief.

Emil was intrigued.

The woman wore a lovely dress with blue-violet flowers on it. The dress was perhaps too lovely for the time of day, but the woman carried it off well. She was beautiful in that effortless way some women are. She had a smooth complexion, even teeth, and a regal bearing. Standing next to her, held by her white-gloved hand, was a little boy who was a little older than The Boy Who Was Not Frederick. The boy, dressed in a little blue suit, looked desperate to impress. His eyes were overwhelmed into a perfect roundness.

"Mister Coetzee is a very, very important and busy man," Agnes said with something proprietary in her voice.

"I know Mister Coetzee is a very important man," the African woman said.

"And how do you know that he is an important man?" Agnes asked. She looked afraid and guilty.

"Because I read the newspaper, madam," the woman said, calm as you please.

Emil was even more intrigued by the woman. He had never imagined an African woman would talk the way she was talking.

"I know you are in charge of Domestic Affairs, Mister Coetzee. I believe you will find what I have to say very important," the woman said.

She spoke well for an African woman. Everything about her denoted pride, even her well-worn white shoes.

"What is this about?" Emil asked, coming closer to the door, addressing her for the first time.

"It is about my husband," the woman said.

Emil chuckled. When he had gone with Courteney's suggestion to call the unit The Organization of Domestic Affairs, he had worried that Africans would misconstrue its nature and purpose.

"I don't handle those kind of 'domestic affairs,'" he informed the woman. "So what's the story here? You found your husband putting it good to some strumpet?" Emil asked, not quite able to help himself.

The woman raised her chin and lowered the bodice of her dress and that is when Emil saw them—several keloidal scars that jaggedly littered the tops of her breasts. Emil understood perfectly why she had come to see him. She had married a monster and all she wanted was for The Organization to help her get rid of him.

"My husband and his friends...they are plotting to overthrow the government. They should be charged with treason," the woman said.

Emil laughed at the preposterousness of the notion. He understood why she felt the need to get rid of her husband. He understood that the BSAP, location superintendents, and the chiefs had probably disappointed her before by being of absolutely no use to her at all in this regard, as both the colonial administration and the traditional leaders believed that a wife's place was beside her husband. He understood that he was her last resort. But really, the whole thing was just too ridiculous. How could a husband whose wife walked around in well-worn white shoes be plotting to overthrow the government? Emil laughed, even though this was not a laughing matter. This was exactly what he had been afraid of ever since the government had come to him with the proposition that he help it. What was to stop people from using The Organization to settle personal vendettas?

The woman had apparently anticipated Emil's laughter and suffered through it with a grace that gradually embarrassed him. He soon was laughing merely to cover up his own embarrassment.

"My husband is Mbongeni Masuku," the woman continued. "And every fortnight he meets with the following men..." Some of the names she mentioned, Emil recalled from the lists that Rutherford often shared with him.

Rutherford must have remembered those names too because when he cleared his throat it sounded as if something hard to swallow was lodged there.

"They are plotting, you say?"

"Yes, they are plotting to fight for independence. I have heard them."

"Why tell me this?"

The truth of the matter finally revealed itself when the woman reached into her purse and pulled out a carefully folded piece of newspaper and just as carefully unfolded it. She gave it to Emil. It was one of those reward notices that the government had insisted on.

"Hell hath no fury," Emil said, handing the newspaper clipping back to her.

"My son wants to be a doctor someday," the woman said with clear determination in her voice. She wanted Emil to know that she was doing this for her son and not for herself. "I am here to make sure he becomes one."

Emil believed her. He really had been foolish to laugh at her earlier. He glanced at the boy, who was not much older than The Boy Who Was Not Frederick. This boy wanted to become a doctor and his mother knew this about him. Emil had no idea what his son wanted to become.

"I'll see what can be done," Emil said as he walked away.

As it turned out, a lot could be done. The information contained within The Tower was truly powerful. Within a few hours, Mbongeni Masuku and his comrades had been picked up. The ease with which it all came together sincerely surprised Emil.

For their part, Mbongeni Masuku and his comrades were not surprised at being picked up. What surprised them was that instead of being taken to the Central Intelligence Unit's headquarters they were taken to The Tower. Being at The Organization of Domestic Affairs, this institution whose sole purpose was to provide Africans with history, seemed to relax them a little. Since they knew they had always had history, they had never taken The Organization seriously and, accordingly, trusted that nothing could go wrong for them there. They would provide the necessary details and be done with it. But, sadly, they were mistaken: everything went horribly wrong for them. They were processed by Emil himself and charged with treason. This turn of events thoroughly confused them. Was The Organization of Domestic Affairs not simply a place that collected information on African lives? There and then, their world was turned upside down.

Mbongeni Masuku was a very elegant and handsome man with a thin moustache and uncompromising eyes. He appeared to be pleasant enough, if a little aloof. For a moment, Emil had a difficult time believing that the man sitting before him had sadistically carved etchings onto his wife's skin and allowed her to walk around in well-worn shoes. Emil glanced at Mbongeni Masuku's shoes: they were black, new, and polished to a brilliant shine and proved to be the missing piece of the puzzle that made the man in front of him make sense. Mbongeni Masuku was an incredibly selfish and cruel man.

"It was actually your wife who alerted us to your activities," Emil said. Emil had expected Mbongeni Masuku's façade of respectability to slip upon hearing this, but it did not. He still looked very polished and handsome when he quietly and softly said, "The bitch." Mbongeni Masuku glared at Emil just long enough to make him uncomfortable, before he added, "They are easy to crush, but you cannot crush them all. This is why you have to pick them very carefully." Having said this, Mbongeni Masuku sat back in his chair and resigned himself to his fate. "Did she do it for the money?" he asked.

Emil nodded. "For your son. She says he wants to be a doctor someday. He looks like a bright enough fellow."

"That is good for him but the boy is not mine," Mbongeni Masuku said and held Emil's gaze again. "He is not my son," he repeated. This was a truth that he wanted Emil Coetzee to know. "You saw the boy—do you think a man like me would have a son like that?"

It occurred to Emil for the first time that the lives of Africans were very complicated. Definitely much more complicated than they appeared to be from the outside. For all he knew, some of the complexities could not be contained in what The Organization was trying to do. Was this what Ezekiel de Villiers had tried to tell Emil that night he addressed the Capricorn Africa Society?

At the end of it all, Mbongeni Masuku and his comrades were removed from The Tower and taken to a maximum-security prison to await their trial and sentencing. Everyone knew that, with the evidence against them, there was only one possible outcome to their treason trial. Everyone knew that as Mbongeni Masuku and his comrades left The Tower, the specter of death hung over them.

CHAPTER 27

———◆———

The ease with which The Organization could be put to use to carry out the government's bidding left a very bad taste in Emil's mouth. In just the first day of working in direct association with the government, Emil had already compromised himself. But was it really any surprise that he had finally got off the fence only to do exactly what the government wanted him to do? They had expected he would. He had suspected he would. It was, after all, an easier thing to do than standing by convictions he was never too sure of anyway.

He scanned the cold and gray concrete room in which he had processed the six men. He had initially intended this basement room as a place to archive the files of children who had died before they could start attending school; that is, before they could start creating a history. Emil realized now that the room would have to be put to other uses. The wooden desk and chairs he had brought in would have to become permanent fixtures. Modifications would have to be made. A water basin would have to be fitted in the corner of the room. Emil looked at the naked light bulb and decided that he would need to get a shade for it before he turned off the light and welcomed the darkness.

As he climbed the stairs to his office, he suddenly felt drained and wanted nothing more than to be at home with Kuki and The Boy Who Was Not Frederick. The Organization of Domestic Affairs was eerily silent; its inhabitants sat by their desks shocked. Were they all, like him, wondering how they had come to be responsible for charging six men with treason?

Emil was preparing to leave the office when his phone rang. He seriously considered not answering it but, naturally, he picked it up. He always picked it up.

It was Rutherford on the other end, sounding a little worse for wear.

"Where've you been? Been calling and calling," Rutherford slurred into the phone.

"Working on the information that the woman who came to see me gave me. We have processed them. Six in all."

"Well, while you were busy chasing after Eunice's husband, the bloody Prime Minister bloody declared independence from bloody Britain."

Emil had completely forgotten about the Prime Minister's announcement.

"I knew you didn't know. Happened at 11 a.m. I said to Agnes, I said, Emil is probably the only bastard in the whole country to not know this is happening. He'll be too wrapped up in his precious Organization. Didn't I say that, Agnes? What? Are you still pouting? It's all your fault that your loose lips have become bust lips." Rutherford chuckled on the other end of the line.

Independence from Britain? What exactly did that mean? The country had, for all intents and purposes, always seemed to Emil to be independent from Britain. Was that not the point of having been a self-governing colony in the first place?

"Yes," Rutherford said, suddenly sounding sober. "This is it, Emil. There is no turning back for us now. This means definite war."

All Emil could see before him was the unnecessary destruction that the civil war would bring. So much would be lost and in the end it would all be for nothing. Their situation had just gone from problematic to pathetic in the blink of an eye.

"I can't believe that you were busy running around doing exactly what my maid told you to do at the very moment the most important decision this country has ever made was being announced. I know you love a skirt and a pretty face, but she's a bloody kaffir, Emil...and my maid. Even you must have your limits. I will say that she did more for that dress than dear Agnes here ever did. But she is definitely no Mrs. Findlay ...remember that swan-like neck—"

"What is it that you want, Rutherford?"

"You're angry. I've made you angry. Sorry, Emil...so sorry... it's just...it's just that you've come to cast a very long shadow and one gets tired, doesn't one, of always being under it."

"See here, Rutherford, I need to—"

"Tell them I knew..."

"Tell whom that you knew what?"

"When they call you, and they will, just tell them I knew ...Tell them that Eunice, my maid, confided in me, and that I called you to help take care of it. If they know that I did not know, forget the promotion—that will be me out of a job."

"I am sure that it will not come to that."

"Please, Emil." The desperation in Rutherford's voice was palpable. "Don't forget that I am the one who got you the job at the Department of Native Affairs in the first place—that's what got the entire ball rolling. Without me there would have been no Ashtonburys...you are who you are today because of me."

"Goodbye, Rutherford," Emil said, before hanging up the phone. As Emil left his office he convinced himself that all he had to do was see his son and the day would lose some of its bite.

When Emil got home, he found that Kuki and The Boy Who Was Not Frederick were still insulated in their snow globe. The Boy Who Was Not Frederick was wearing his mother's red high-heeled shoes, navy-blue scarf and white pearls, and carrying her red clutch handbag. Together they were giggling and singing "I Enjoy Being a Girl."

Emil saw red...a red cloche hat.

He was upon them in a flash. It had been his intention to grab the boy and push him behind him, to protect him from his mother's influence. Lamentably, in his desperation, Emil ended up flinging the boy to the floor.

To his surprise, Kuki turned on him. He had shattered her snow globe and she did not take kindly to that. There was nothing wrong with her precious and beautiful boy playing dress-up, all children played dress-up. There was, rather, everything wrong with Emil.

Emil knew differently; he knew about the red cloche hat and the havoc it could wreak, but obviously he could not tell Kuki about it. So, instead, he told her that The Boy Who Was Not Frederick would go to the Selous School for Boys to learn to be a man.

One did not learn to be a man, Kuki countered, one simply became one.

But that just showed Emil that Kuki knew very little beyond the bubble of her existence.

"What are you so afraid of?" she asked.

"I'm not afraid."

"Yes. You are. Ever since Everleigh was born you have been afraid."

"I am not afraid."

"Look at you breathing fire and brimstone down on us. This is not normal behavior, Emil."

How could it not be normal behavior to want to ensure

that his son did not turn soft in a country of proudly tough and hard men?

Did Kuki even know that the Prime Minister had declared independence? Did she appreciate what this meant for the country? Did she care? When was she going to grow up? When was she going to join him in the real world? He was tired of her not seeing what was in front of her very eyes. Couldn't she see that there was something wrong with The Boy Who Was Not Frederick? He would have to go to the Selous School for Boys so he could be straightened out. He needed to learn how to be the kind of man that his country needed.

"I'm not so sure that the Selous School for Boys is a good school. Look at what it made you into. A man afraid. Afraid of what he does not know. What kind of a man is that to be? Definitely not the kind of man I want my Everleigh to become."

This was a rare Kuki. She often stood up to Emil via her parents. But here she was taking him on directly. She too had seen red when he had flung her precious and beautiful boy onto the floor.

"Not having been given much of a canvas in your life, you now want to limit Everleigh's choices. I will not let you. I will not let you make the boy live by your narrow definitions. I just will not let you," Kuki said, her chin jutting with defiance and determination.

Not having been given much of a canvas in your life? The construction of those words was too perfectly pointed to have been cobbled together in the heat of the moment. These were words that Kuki had long wanted to say; the tilt of her chin and the challenge in her eyes let him know as much.

Emil heard Mbongeni Masuku say, "They are easy to crush, but you cannot crush them all. This is why you have to pick them carefully."

He saw rather than felt his arm rise. Kuki was too astonished to do anything but stare at his hand in shock.

Emil would have struck her if two things had not stopped him. The first was that The Boy Who Was Not Frederick bit him hard on his right calf and, in so doing, brought Emil to his senses. The second was that Emil caught sight of himself in Kuki's display cabinet and was truly horrified by the distorted image of himself he saw reflected there. When exactly had he become something so frightening?

He was still standing there, arm raised, examining his unrecognizable reflection when Kuki pulled the boy away and led him out of the house.

He heard her drive off and realized that he had come very close to being something that he had never thought he would be.

Was it that word "canvas," a word that was not Kuki's at all, a word that obviously belonged to Beatrice Beit-Beauford, the artist, a word that he had long disliked—was it that word that had made him lift up his hand to strike Kuki in the face? Canvas...But, of course, it was not its association with Beatrice Beit-Beauford that had made him respond the way he had. Emil could not help but wonder what exactly it was that Kuki knew about him.

Suddenly there was a silence. Emil heard it loud and clear. He felt the emptiness of the house and the emptiness was familiar...so like the emptiness of the house of his childhood nightmares...the house he was always shocked to discover had a native girl and a baby boy with light-brown skin living in it...the house she said had always belonged to them.

He heard the wheeze before he felt the tightness in his chest. He fell to the floor, struggling to breathe.

As he battled to steady his breathing, he glanced at the display cabinet and, from his vantage point on the floor, what caught his eye was Marion's menagerie of crystal butterflies that had pride of place in Kuki's cabinet.

Here he lay, a man who had become undone by a single word.

CHAPTER 28

———◆———

The Boy Who Was Not Frederick stood before Emil wearing a uniform that appeared to have swallowed him whole. Everything was at least two sizes too big for him: the navy-blue hat and blazer, the light-blue shirt, the gray-blue shorts, the white socks, the black "see your reflection in them" shoes and even the blue-and-gray striped tie.

The Boy Who Was Not Frederick had to tilt his head all the way back to look up at his father and at that moment, gazing down at the boy, Emil felt so much love he did not know what to do with it.

Ever since the boy had bitten him on his right calf and left a permanent scar, Emil had not really known what to say to him. He did not resent the boy's action. In fact, Emil admired it because in that moment of defending his mother, the boy had shown just what he was made of.

As the boy continued to look up at him, waiting, Emil remembered himself in that same uniform...an unhappy boy of nine always dreaming of the elsewhere that had once been home. He sincerely wished the boy's time at Milton would be happier than his had been.

Emil understood, of course, that Kuki had bought the uniform several sizes too big to communicate to him, in no uncertain terms, that her son would be growing into it. That is, to communicate to him that her precious and beautiful boy would never ever attend the Selous School for Boys.

The boy was still looking up at him, still waiting.

Emil tentatively lifted up the navy-blue hat and ruffled the boy's hair. Hair like his, hair the color of the singing elephant grass of the savannah. He clumsily put the hat back on.

"First day of school, eh?"

The boy nodded, still looking up, still waiting.

Emil remembered having entire conversations with his father at this age, but he no longer recalled what the conversations were about. He recollected being perched on his father's shoulders in the Bambata, Nswatugi and Silozwane caves of the Matopos Hills, studying paintings of the hunt. Had he and his father talked about the story of the hunt? Yes...Emil recollected now...that was what they had talked about. But The Boy Who Was Not Frederick was not interested in the hunt.

The boy blinked once, twice, rubbed his nose and... stopped waiting. He looked from his father to his black "see your reflection in them" shoes. He bent down to wipe off a barely perceptible scuff mark.

A moment had presented itself and been lost.

Emil felt that loss.

"Let me look at you," Kuki said as she entered the room, her voice full of an excitement that did not betray the fact that she had spent the entire night crying because her precious and beautiful boy was going out into the world and she did not trust the world to handle him with the care he deserved. She wore a yellow terrycloth nightgown over the blue dress she would wear to drive her son to school. "My beautiful, golden-haired boy," Kuki said, picking him up and hugging him. "Always as perfect as a picture," she said, kissing him. The Boy Who Was Not Frederick smiled and smiled, basking In the perpetual glow of his mother's untainted love.

"I'd love to take pictures," Kuki said, putting her son down with evident reluctance. She fixed his hair and straightened his hat. She leaned down to gaze at him and make sure he was as perfect as she remembered and her son seized that moment to kiss her.

In a month it would be the boy's seventh birthday. Was he still kissing his mother when he was six, Emil wondered. Had he ever initiated a kiss with his mother or had she always been the one to kiss him?

"You are the loveliest little angel in the whole wide world," Kuki said, as she hugged her son again and fought back tears.

Emil picked up his car keys from the countertop.

"I'd love to take pictures of the both of you. Together," Kuki said, not looking at him, preferring instead to look for her camera, which was never too far away, and which she found with a deceptively ebullient "ah-ha!"

Kuki took three pictures of Emil and the boy. In all of them Emil held the boy's hand awkwardly in his. In the first photo the boy was looking up at Emil, but no longer waiting. In the other two photos the boy was looking resolutely at the camera. In one photo he smiled uncertainly, in the other photo he did not smile.

If only the pictures had been taken earlier when the boy had still been waiting, then at least the memory captured would have been one of hope.

As Emil walked out of the front door, he knew that Kuki would take a plethora of photos of the boy who already had ten family albums dedicated almost solely to him. He also knew that in these photos the boy would be smiling and laughing freely because, together, he and his mother would be happy in a way that they had not been able to be just a moment before—when Emil was there.

Emil, with an incessant sadness, started the car.

"I also wore that uniform, once," Emil could have said to the boy. But the sentence came to him too late.

Hope had already been lost.

As Emil drove away, he decided that all need not be lost. He would make it up to the boy. For his seventh birthday, he would buy him that hula hoop that Kuki said he wanted above all else, and all would be right again. He sorely missed carrying the boy on his shoulders for the world to see.

For The Boy Who Was Not Frederick's seventh birthday, Kuki had organized a picnic at the Khami Ruins. Wanting a small, intimate affair, she had decided on a picnic in a remote location and invited only her parents and his. Unfortunately, because he had not been able to resolve a discrepancy as quickly as he had hoped, Emil had left The Tower an hour later than he had intended.

Given everything that was happening at The Organization, Emil was actually looking forward to the gathering. But, as he drove past the industrial sites, he realized that he had left the present for the boy at home. He turned back and headed home, where he found the present waiting for him by the kitchen door: Kuki's doing. Emil picked up the present, a blue hula hoop with a prefabricated blue ribbon stuck on it because Kuki had insisted that the gift should look like the present it was.

Emil looked at the blue hula hoop, a foreign thing in his hands, sure that Frederick Coetzee, at seven, would have wanted and felt he deserved a better gift—a gift more befitting a boy.

Emil had made sure to buy the gift himself and, in buying it, he had made sure that it was blue. Previous gifts had been bought by Kuki because Emil was too busy and because she knew the boy better. The most Emil had previously had to do was sign a card, as stipulated by Kuki, *Everleigh, Love, your Father*. The gift and the card would have been picked by

Kuki, who would also wrap it, usually in paper that had images of angels (what she thought of the boy), bunnies (the boy's favorite animal) or teddy bears (the boy's favorite toy). But, whatever his other inclinations, The Boy Who Was Not Frederick was very astute, and in his sixth year, he had cleverly deduced his mother's hand in the gifts given in his father's name.

Now, with the blue hula hoop safely placed in the back seat of his car, Emil made his way to the picnic at the Khami Ruins two hours later than he had intended.

They—his family—did not see him approach. All mirthful eyes were on the boy as they sat on a picnic blanket amidst the ruins of what had been a fantastic birthday feast. They all laughed uproariously at something the boy had said or done. Then Emil's mother made a gesture to her grandson and the boy gestured back something that made them all laugh again.

They were so truly happy. Without him. Emil felt certain, in that moment, that if he joined them everything would change. The laughter and happiness would leave as they tried to accommodate his presence. He understood then that he was no longer necessary to their happiness. Had he ever been?

He leant the blue hula hoop with the prefabricated blue ribbon stuck on it against a mopane tree and walked away, unseen.

He heard them—his family—laugh merrily behind his back.

However it had been presented, the gift of the blue hula hoop became a much-cherished fixture in the boy's life. He played with it for hours in the Coetzees' large front yard and even took it to school on occasion. Although Emil was happy to see something that he had given the boy become so dear to him, he could not help but worry. He worried that others would see the boy with the blue hula hoop, see his attachment to it and start thinking thoughts. Emil feared that this, coupled with the fact that the boy was small for his age and had a mother who doted on him, would make him an easy target for bullies.

Emil's fears proved to be unfounded because happily, against all odds, the boy made a success of his junior school years. He had the voice of an angel. He swam with the grace of a merman. He was born for the stage. These were the clichés with which *The Chronicle* highlighted the boy's feats in the paper. In time, the boy took his popularity and successes with him to Milton High School, where he grew to be as tall as his father.

Emil knew that the boy was a success because people and *The Chronicle* told him so, and because every surface in the living room that did not have his picture had, instead, a trophy or medal that he had won. While he took a great deal of pride in the boy's success, Emil had personally never been able to attend a gala, play or eisteddfod because he was too busy, with his country at war. So Emil Coetzee watched the spectacular transformation of his son from a boy into a young man from a distance.

Kuki, for her part, more than made up for Emil's absence. She was involved in everything the boy did. The Coetzees employed three servants—a cook, a house boy and a garden boy—but where the boy was concerned, Kuki insisted on doing it all herself. She woke up early to make his packed lunches. She drove him to school with rollers still in her hair. She made his costumes for the plays. She mended his sports kits. She attended every play, performance, match and competition, at home or away. She always sat in the front row and cheered or applauded the loudest. She gladly and indefatigably drove him back from school and his activities. Back home, she cooked his suppers contentedly. She was an active member of the Parents and Teachers Association. She participated in every bake sale and tombola. She was tireless in her love for him. She filled every waking moment of her life with her beautiful and precious boy; she lived and breathed for him. From the day the boy was born in 1959, the City of Kings would have been hard pressed to find a woman happier than Kuki Coetzee.

Before Emil could tell where the years had gone, The Boy Who Was Not Frederick was sixteen and bringing home a pretty girl called Rosamond Pierce to show his parents.

Emil relaxed because he realized that he had been worrying needlessly all these years. Sometimes a hula hoop is just a hula hoop.

He did not think this comforting thought for too long, however, because one day as he was standing in the living room, sipping on a whiskey and casually looking out at Kuki's abundant and effusive roses, he saw them, two boys at play. The Boy Who Was Not Frederick, blue hula hoop in hand, was chasing The Coloured de Villiers Boy. At first Emil did not suspect anything. It was simply boisterous boys' play. But then as he watched them, he noticed that there was something very different and, paradoxically, something very familiar about this chase. Emil got the distinct impression that, although he was running away, The Coloured de Villiers Boy wanted to be caught. So then the chase was not about getting away but actually about the fulfilment of a desire. The Boy Who Was Not Frederick hooked The Coloured de Villiers Boy with the blue hula hoop and together they fell tumbling and laughing into the rose garden. Emil could not see what happened after the fall. All he knew was that their laughter had come to an end.

Emil was very troubled by this. What exactly had he just witnessed? What exactly was he still witnessing as he gazed upon the stillness of the rose bushes? For what felt like an ungodly long time, the boys remained hidden by the rose bushes and did not come up.

Emil could not bring himself to move; he just stood there transfixed.

Just then Rosamond arrived and joined the boys in the rose garden. Even though she must have seen what Emil could not, she offered her hand to The Boy Who Was Not Frederick, who used it to stand up. The boy and the girl kissed while The Coloured de Villiers Boy must have been watching them from within the rose garden.

Emil was very confused. Was this business with Rosamond an elaborate performance meant to throw him off the real scent? Could the boy really be attracted to both girls and boys? Beatrice Beit-Beauford would probably say yes to the latter question. He definitely saw her hand in all of this. She had exposed the boy to God only knew what in that colony-commune of hers. Kuki, always the weaker part of a pair, always happy to be led, had never understood the real danger that Beatrice Beit-Beauford posed.

Emil felt that he had let the boy down. He should have done more to safeguard him and, perhaps, all things consid ered, he should not have bought him the blue hula hoop.

CHAPTER 29

———◆———

By the beginning of 1972, the government could no longer simply talk of "random acts of sabotage" or "light skirmishes with the terrorists;" they had to call the thing what it had truly become—a war. There were enough people dying to warrant the name. But calling it a civil war was out of the question. Calling it a civil war would mean that both sides fighting were equal and had an equally justified call to arms, so the government decided to call it a "bush war." This was a fair enough title since the fighting did mostly take part in the savannah. However, the government tended to like this phrase for its added connotation—this was not a war like the past wars in Europe, where men of equal ability, dignity , and civilization fought each other. This was a war where the European was once again fending off the darkness in Africa. It was not a gentlemen's dispute; it was a fight against the unreason of the African mind. It was a war against savages who could not be man enough to fight a civilized war and had to resort to guerrilla tactics. Calling the war a "bush war" also created the impression that it was more a necessary nuisance than an actual fight for the future of the country.

While the government wanted the situation to seem a necessary nuisance, the truth was that the country's citizens were being killed in disturbingly increasing numbers. To the government's surprise, there apparently was no end to the number of Africans willing to lose their lives in the nationalists' loftier-sounding "liberation struggle".

Since the government knew its African and knew that its average African was happy, it could not imagine that these men, women, boys and girls marching off to war were doing so voluntarily because they felt that white minority rule was oppressing them. So the government chose to believe that these happy Africans were mere pawns in the terrorists' diabolical game.

In order to deter Africans from joining the terrorists and in order to prove to the Europeans that they were winning the war, the government started giving daily situation reports, "sit reps," via the radio, where the loss of African lives was stressed and the increasing body count reported. With the government's gradual "involvement" in the country's only and once-independent television station, they started broadcasting images of dead black bodies, which the white citizens watched as they ate their supper. The government believed that doing so would prove persuasive because the whites would see that they were winning the war. It undoubtedly helped that the situation reports usually ended with the words "no casualties were incurred on our side." Usually...

Another reason the government showed images of dead black bodies was to send a visceral warning to the black people not to die needlessly in a senseless war. Sadly, since most black people in the country could not afford to buy a television set, the efficacy of this means of sending the message could never actually be tested.

Emil was a man apart. He had never wanted the war and had always seen and known its pathetic pointlessness. All the same, seeing and knowing that the war was senseless did not mean that he would just sit back and watch things unfold before him. As a person who was thoroughly opposed to the war in the beginning, once it had begun in earnest he was equally invested in ending it, and ending it successfully would require his direct involvement.

As the war progressed, Emil and The Organization, in hopes of bringing a quick end to it, began to use whatever means were necessary to achieve that goal. In time, The Organization of Domestic Affairs came to be interested not only in preemptive measures, but also in interrogating captured terrorists and the families and friends of suspected terrorists. It was painfully clear to Emil that this turn of events was regrettable, but there was nothing else for it. As he rationalized, it was better to torture and imprison people now than to have them die senselessly in the killing fields—dying not fully understanding either the ideologies they were fighting for or that their guerrilla tactics and communist weaponry were no match for the European's superior manpower.

In all honesty, his thoughts did not always run in this steady stream when it came to the war, especially after he had read or seen a particularly gruesome situation report.

At that point, he thought that the entire business of war could have done with...a lighter touch. It occurred to him that in showing dead black bodies, the government was not just showing the military weakness of the Africans and the might of the Europeans, but also the...brutality of the Europeans, and that in showing its brutality, the government was actually showing its weakness. The government was revealing its own barbarity and savagery for the whole world to see.

On more than one occasion, as he sat in the comfort of his den and watched the situation reports as he ate his supper, Emil recalled Master Archie's words on that fateful September morning in 1939: *"This is the business of empire, make no mistake. What else could possibly come of a few countries carving the rest of the world for themselves? It was inevitable that that rapacious greed would turn inward on itself...I want you to ask yourselves, gentlemen, where the real heart of darkness lies."*

Emil had not absorbed the words then. Emil was beginning to absorb the words now.

Thinking like this sometimes frightened Emil because it was so...unpatriotic. He would examine his thoughts and suspect the influence of Courteney in them. But the truth was that, although Emil and Courteney continued to meet regularly at the Gentleman's Club, where Emil was now also a member, they usually sat together in silence, squinting through the smoky haze of the Billiards Room. They valued the something between them enough not to discuss the political climate of the country. Courteney was no friend of the new government and the new government was no friend of his; it had banned him from producing plays until he could be more "loyal to the true spirit of Shakespeare and the country."

Emil tried to reclaim The Organization's original function by suggesting to the government that it could use the information contained in The Tower to provide the names and histories of the black dead bodies that filled the pages and screens of the country's media. Personalizing and humanizing the enemy would not only give dignity to the dead, but also bring about a quicker end to the war, as Africans would no longer be able to create emotional distance from an anonymous dead black body; once the body was given a name they would have to recognize that it was their sons and daughters dying.

The government refused to do as Emil suggested. Naming the dead black bodies would make it difficult to kill them with the kind of blind gusto that was necessary during a time of war. And once the black bodies were named, white readers, listeners and viewers would not have the emotional distance that made it possible for them to happily and optimistically send their sons off to war. The government understood that it is very difficult to kill someone whose name and history you know. The war had thrived and was continuing to thrive on the fact that decades of segregation had made the Europeans and Africans not know each other very well—if at all.

When Emil could not reconcile things within himself, he would drive to Barbourfields Township, park his car and watch as a nurse, who had once been a maid married to an abusive husband, and her son, who was going to be a doctor someday, went about their daily lives. They demonstrably had a comfortable life and Emil was happy that this was mostly due to him. He always made a point of looking at the nurse's feet and was always happy to find that she was not wearing well-worn white shoes. Whatever else he had done, whatever else he was doing, whatever else he was going to do in the name of The Organization of Domestic Affairs, at least he had done this one thing right.

Not surprisingly, this particular remedy could only be effective up to a certain point. Soon, Emil found himself searching for another means through which to become more ...at ease...in his role. He found it in the Scaremaster 2000, a silver-and-white electronic device the size of a workman's table that had green and red buttons, black flip switches, voltage signs on its console and a bouquet of electrical wires attached to it. It was clunky and cartoonish and looked like it belonged on the set of a B-grade science fiction movie. Even the name sounded as if it had been dreamt up by an uninspired movie director.

Emil had found the Scaremaster 2000 a little too easily in a catalog that was littered with gruesome-looking contraptions. He favoured it as soon as he learned that the machine could be placed in one room and the electric wires applied in another room. He had comforted himself with the knowledge that he would never have to use the higher voltages because Africans were notoriously afraid of electricity—just the sight of the electrical wires would probably put the fear of God in them.

When Emil started using the machine, he learned that what the catalog and the advert in *Soldier of Fortune* magazine had failed to mention was that, while the machine itself was very quiet, those who were attached to the ends of its electrical wires were not. Even when Emil flipped a switch and pressed on the lowest voltage, there would be a scream from the other room. He suspected that the machine had not been calibrated properly. Unable to stand the cries from the other room, Emil briefly entertained the idea of soundproofing the room, but found that he could not because it was those very cries that let him know how high or low to go next.

Emil's feelings about what The Organization had become were so ambivalent that when Spokes Moloi, the man with the magnificently marvelous moustache who had investigated Daisy's murder, came to interview for a job with The Organization, Emil did not give him the job, even though he knew him to be a very intelligent and able man.

While Emil understood and sympathized with Spokes Moloi, who had successfully solved all the murder cases that he had worked on except that of Daisy, and whose inability to solve Daisy's murder had created a frustration with himself and with the BSAP that had made him apply for a position at The Organization, Emil could not bring himself to give Spokes the job.

Desperate, Spokes Moloi told Emil of his other, perhaps truer, reason for seeking a job with The Organization. His mother had recently been resettled, along with the rest of her village, ostensibly for their own protection, in Tribal Trust Land and he had gone to visit her there. On his first night, the sound of a window shattering—one of the four glass windows in the settlement—announced the arrival of a boy. Here Spokes Moloi looked Emil in the eye to make sure that he understood exactly what he meant by "boy," and as he told the rest of the tale his eyes did not look away from Emil's. The boy, wearing heavy army boots and weighed down by an AK-47, had his own story to tell of black bodies—no, not bodies but limbs, severed limbs and torsos with 'Y's dissected into them—floating in the Zambezi River. These floating limbs would not let the boy sleep and he spent that night screaming himself awake and before the sun could rise, he was gone.

"I was a proud member of the African Rifles in the Second World War," Spokes Moloi continued. "I was shipped off to a country I had always thought would forever be just a name in the World Atlas for me and, from there, I was allowed to witness the spectacularly devastating theatre of war. As irony would have it, I was not permitted to carry an actual rifle but I carried most everything else in all manner of weather and through all kinds of terrain. When I came back from the war I realized that my participation in it had not meant what I had thought it would mean or achieved what I had hoped it would achieve. I was disappointed at first, but I have lived long enough to understand that this is the particular truth of war. This thing that we find ourselves in has only recently become a full-on war and the boy is already screaming. It needs to be stopped. I have to help stop it."

As Spokes Moloi sat opposite Emil, Emil saw more in-tegrity in his steepled fingers than in the entire staff of The Organization put together. Emil never wanted those hands to find themselves placing electric prods and wires on a man's genitals. Spokes Moloi was a true gentleman and the business of war had never been the business of gentlemen.

A man like Emil Coetzee, on the other hand, could find his hands doing all manner of things because the truth of the matter, he told himself, was that a man like Emil Coetzee had never really truly ever been good. He had never been a gentleman. There had always been something lurking within him that was capable of violence.

If Emil told himself this "truth" about himself to make what he did easier, then he never allowed himself to acknowledge the lie within the truth.

When a man finds himself suddenly doing the wrong thing, he prefers to believe that he had always been capable of such an act because it saves him from having to truly investigate the when, how and why of his becoming capable.

CHAPTER 30

———◆———

Emil had read a book once, he no longer remembered the title, in which a man had been shot and his blood described as "sweet smelling." In Emil's experience there was nothing sweet about the smell of human blood. Human blood smelled exactly like what it was. Human. Blood. When a man had to be pummeled to a pulp or a woman's skin had to be broken through with the sharp edge of a knife, the smell that rose to Emil's nose was anything but sweet.

Emil's decision to get his hands dirty was not due to the fact that he had lost his faith in the Scaremaster 2000, but due, rather, to the fact that as the war progressed and The Boy Who Was Not Frederick grew older, their letterbox in Brookside would one day receive a call-up notification. Emil did not want the boy to take part in what he still believed was a futile war, so he did whatever was necessary to hasten its end. The business of war was a messy, unpleasant business, he acknowledged, and there was no getting away from its messiness.

In spite of having been told that the call was urgent, Emil took quite some time to get to it. Usually, he ran up the stairs as a means of communicating to anyone he came across that he was in a hurry and could not afford to be disturbed, but this time he walked slowly, hands secure (or hidden) in his pockets, his shoulders burdened by all the weight of the world. When would everyone come to their senses and bring an end to this bloody war that no side was winning?

When he eventually arrived at his office, he was surprised to find the other person still on the line. It was Rutherford.

"We have a situation, Emil."

"When do we not have a situation?"

"A farm in Essexvale was attacked by the terrs. Entire family killed." Something was not connecting for Emil.

"It is the Smythe-Sinclairs, Emil...Courteney's family."

Something was still not connecting for Emil.

"They are all gone, Emil. Every last one."

Emil saw Courteney on that last day at the Selous School for Boys, being cosseted by a bevy of women—his mother and six sisters—so full of life as they gaggled and fussed over him. Surely, they could not all be dead. Rutherford must have had his wires crossed. The Smythe-Sinclairs were suspected sympathizers of the "nationalist" cause. They had always treated their workers well and were a friend to the African. They were well known and well loved in the district. The terrorists surely knew all of this. They would never attack people who were helping them, would they? But then again, who was to say that it was the terrorists who had attacked the Smythe-Sinclair farm? It could very well have been the security forces, such was the nature of war—as Emil had come to learn.

"I thought that...given your friendship with Courteney... it would be best if he heard the news from you."

"Yes...quite...I will head over there now," Emil said and hung up the phone on a lie.

Emil remembered the boy with a cherub's face that Courteney had once been. That boy deserved to be personally told that his entire family had been senselessly and brutally murdered—and the only friend that the world had to offer him at a time like this was Emil Coetzee.

Courteney had always deserved a better friend than Emil

could ever be to him.

What kind of friend covets his friend's wife, for over twenty years?

Emil picked up the receiver, ready to dial the number and deliver the news this way, but then decided against it. He was going to have to be brave enough to tell Courteney the news in person.

He would have to go to Courteney's house. Courteney's and Marion's house. As Emil grabbed his car keys and headed for the door, it occurred to him that he might see Marion again...

What kind of thought was that to have at a time like this?

Emil had seen Marion sporadically, and never intentionally, over the past fifteen years, which took a concerted effort on his part as the City of Kings had a rather incestuous social life.

He tried to anticipate seeing her again. He could not.

She opened the door a little while after he had rung the doorbell. She was wearing a pink dress that she was zipping up; there were three pink rollers stuck in her hair and two different earrings dangling from her earlobes: Marion Hartley in all her glory. She was unmistakably in the middle of preparing to go out.

She stared at him blankly as though trying to precisely place him in her memory.

He probably had long ceased to figure in her life.

"Emil," she said as she finally let him in. "What brings you here?"

The entire room carried a hint of her tropical scent.

"I've come to see Courteney."

"Not here, I'm afraid."

She talked to him as though twenty years earlier she had not sucked his thumb into her mouth.

She peered at her reflection in the mirror in the corridor, removed the three rollers, and decided on the earring in her left earlobe.

"You're off to meet someone?" Emil asked. It sounded more like an accusation than a question.

"No one to meet—just treating myself to a movie."

"Dressed like that?"

"Where do you suspect I am going?"

Emil shrugged as nonchalantly as he could and changed the subject. "Surely Courteney is not at the office on a Saturday?"

"From what I hear you're at The Tower every day of the week."

"Yes, well, that is me...I would have imagined that Courteney has much to keep him home...Unless, of course, you're off to meet someone, and there wouldn't be much reason for him to stay home."

Marion stood there looking at him in a way that he could not readily read. One minute she was blinking at him as though she had never seen him before, the next minute her eyes—those shockingly azure eyes—were fixed on him as though trying to summon up some very particular detail from long ago...from their time together. Emil was fast losing his bearings.

"Where is Courteney?" he asked.

"At the farm."

And suddenly that thing that would not connect was back again.

"Farm? What farm?"

"Family farm in Essexvale. Left yesterday morning."

If only he could connect, Emil thought. He had come here specifically to tell Courteney the news of his family, so what was Courteney doing at the farm? Why would Courteney not let Emil find him?

Something on his face must have betrayed him, something that had not quite registered within Emil himself, because Marion said, her eyes suddenly wide with fear, "Dear God, Emil. Why are you here?"

The fear in Marion's eyes made everything all too real for Emil.

"I have to go now," Emil said, moving toward the door. "I have to find Courteney."

But she would not let him go. She grabbed hold of his hand and made him face her.

"Why are you here, Emil?" Her voice trembled.

Emil was not going to be the one to tell her what had happened on the farm. He would follow his parents' example and be silent; he would not talk to Marion ever again if need be.

"Why are you here, Emil?" This time she screamed the question, her voice tremulous.

He needed to get away from her—as far as he could possibly get from her reality and her truth.

He tried to break free of her grasp but when he looked down at their hands, it was his hand that was holding hers captive.

"You have to tell me," she whispered. Emil shook his head. "Please," she begged.

She did not want to hear the truth. She wanted what he wanted. She wanted it all to be untrue, some awful and terrible mistake, part of a nightmare that would end some time soon.

But it was none of those things.

She crumpled to the floor then. Her hand still in his, she let out a primal, animal, guttural sound from deep within her.

The truth had finally found them.

Emil could not leave her now.

Hours later, they coupled wildly and ferociously on the floor, both wanting to hurt and be hurt—her nails raking his back, her glorious hair fisted tight in his hand, the taste of blood and tears in both their mouths.

They buried Courteney and the rest of the Smythe-Sinclair clan in a family plot at Athlone Cemetery. Emil was strong through most of it: as he listened to Master Archie's eulogy that repeated again and again how Courteney was a unique diamond in the rough, a true gem that would be sorely missed; as he joined the Selous School for Boys choir when they sang "Auld Lang Syne;" as he acted as pallbearer and marched Courteney to his grave. Emil had no intention of being anything but strong...but then five Unfortunates had stood at the grave sites, hats over hearts, and recited the first act of *The Tragedy of Adam Renders*:

"Suddenly an ordinary man could enter history and become a part of it. His name, his family name, would be recorded for posterity. You ventured forth for all the men in your family who had come before you and had labored on other men's lands, sailed on other men's ships and fought in other men's wars...men whose names had been easily forgotten soon after their final death knell had rung...you did it for yourself as well...at least that is how it was with me. I came for the fame. Others came for the fortune. The song was different but the siren was the same."

Emil walked away from the gathering, traveled as far as his legs could carry him, sank onto a dirt heap and, without a care for who saw him, cried long and hard for Courteney Smythe-Sinclair, the one person who had found it in himself to offer Emil true friendship, even though Emil had not deserved it.

They had been boys together...and so much more.

CHAPTER 31

————— ♦ —————

After the funeral, Emil and Marion continued to meet because that was the only way they could keep Courteney alive between them. More than anything, they did not want to feel the weight of loss. They hated their need for each other and their meetings were violent affairs meant to hurt and humiliate, to punish and to cause pain. This was their own private war and they wore their bruises and scars with the sorry pride of veterans.

The truce came in the form of another note from Marion.

This time the note was not a quote from Zora Neale Hurston. It simply read, *"Let's meet. We need to talk. H&S. Friday at 2 p.m."*

There was nothing special about the note itself but he treasured it as he had the previous ones. He opened his wallet and put the note in its rightful place.

She had come early and was sitting at a table for two in the corner of the tea room. He could see her in profile. She had tied her glorious hair in an uncharacteristically severe bun. Her back was straight, her hands clasped in front of her on the table. She was ready for him. But he was not ready for the confrontation that lay ahead; he just wanted to take as long a time as he possibly could to look at her.

She was no longer the lady in red who had enticed him an entire lifetime ago. She was what now...forty-seven? But whatever she had about her, it had grown even more self-assured with age. Her rosebud of a mouth was still slightly too big for her face, still exquisite. She wore a cream-colored dress that heightened the Sophia Loren of her skin.

It was obvious to Emil that she had asked him here because she wanted to end things, and he, knowing this, had come absolutely unprepared.

She turned suddenly and glanced in his direction. She waved at him to get his attention.

To think she actually believed that she could have been sitting there without his noticing her.

He sat down opposite her and she smiled at him.

Then she reached out and tentatively, gently, touched his left temple. "You're going gray," she said. It must have been an impulsive act because the touch ended abruptly and she chastised her hands onto her lap.

It was as if they had not seen each other in years and in a way that was true because for months now, as they staged their war, they had been in the utter darkness of deeply felt despair and pain.

"I had a gray hair—found it last year—have not been able to find it of late," she said as her hands fluttered around her head uncertainly. "God—I miss him," she said suddenly. "And this is how I will be for the rest of my life—missing him. This empty emotion is never going to leave me."

Her hands were back on the table, this time her palms gently sweeping its surface.

She was evidently waiting for him to say something, but what was there that he could possibly say?

Emil spent so much time trying not to think of what had happened to Courteney and feeling angry over the sheer absurdity of it, but his mouth still could not open to say Courteney's name because to open his mouth to say his name would signify the not-being-thereness of Courteney.

CHAPTER THIRTY-ONE

"You miss him too, I know," she said, briefly touching his hand. "You were such good friends."

Emil chuckled mirthlessly. A good friend he definitely had not been—not in a long time, if ever.

"We were not good friends. I am not so sure we were even friends.

"There was a goodness in...in...him that made him indiscriminately reach out to everybody. He reached out to me and I let him. But I was never his friend. Not a true friend, anyway."

"He definitely considered you a friend," Marion said, sounding somewhat hurt.

"I certainly never gave him good reason to think that."

"How could you say that when—"

"When what? When I came looking for you in this very restaurant soon after I first met you? When all I have done for the past twenty years is want you? When I have spent the last months being with you in the very house he lived in? Where in all of that have I been a friend to him? The maggots are not through with him yet and look at me...look at you...look at us."

"You were boys together, Emil."

"Yes, and I grew into the man who slept with his wife."

"Courteney and I had an understanding. We did not see love as a form of possession—we were both free to be with other people."

"He had that understanding with you, not with me. If I had been his friend, his true friend, I would not have done any of it."

She touched his right hand and held it this time. She squeezed it gently, making him look at her. "We are not bad people," she said.

"Speak for yourself."

"I know you."

Emil laughed derisively. Marion probably still thought that

The Organization of Domestic Affairs simply collected information on African lives.

"*He* knew you."

Emil removed his hand from hers. If she knew what that hand was capable of—what it had already done only earlier that day.

"I slept with you that first time because I wanted to hurt him," he said.

"Hurt him?"

"Yes."

"Why?"

"I...don't know why. I find myself in the middle of things sometimes without knowing quite how I got there ..." This was, perhaps, true enough about some situations in his life, but not all, and definitely not where Courteney was concerned. "No, that's not true. I wanted to hurt him for wanting to find goodness in me—for seeing goodness in me when there is none. Sleeping with you was an act of kindness on my part."

"An act of kindness?"

"Yes. It was the surest way I knew to let him know exactly what kind of man I was. I was not the kind of man you befriend."

"What kind of man are you, then?"

"I am a bastard if ever there was one."

"I think that is too easy an answer. You take too much comfort in believing the worst about yourself."

Did he do that? He probably did. He was still an enigma to himself after all these years.

"I know that in our dealings with each other, he did all the giving and I did all the taking," Emil said.

"A real bastard would not even notice that."

Marion reached out to touch him again but he would not let her. "What is it that you're so determinedly trying to punish yourself for? What is it that you cannot forgive?"

Her questions were asking him to do something that he was not prepared to do.

"You want there to be some goodness in me so that you will not feel too guilty about...the...madness we've just put each other through. But I am no good, Marion, and you are very right to want to put an end to things."

"An end to things? I don't want to put an end to things."

This took him completely by surprise. For a few seconds, he was speechless.

"Then...what is it that you want?"

"I want to get to know you—really, properly. I find myself in need of a friend. I think you do too...We need each other, Emil."

Conceivably there were men who could just be friends with women, but Emil was not one of them and so the beginning of the friendship with Marion was difficult. To his amazement, however, in time he came to appreciate just sitting on her veranda, saying little and sipping ice-cold lemonade that she had made and that he enjoyed all the more because he got the distinct impression that Marion did not make many things. They would sit in near silence and share a solemn solitude that they had carefully and caringly carved out for themselves. And, in time again, he came to believe that he could sit on her veranda for days on end with the only pleasure in sight being the pleasure of her company.

But, in addition to being two people who had lost someone that they loved dearly, they were also Emil Coetzee and Marion Hartley and, in time, too, it became clear that this was the beginning of the beguine for them. It was all very well to sit on her veranda and be polite and proper about everything in memory of Courteney, but this crackle in the space between them—this live wire—this was truly them.

They were merely keeping something at bay, something that they had long lost to.

And so, Emil was not entirely surprised when one day Marion opened the door not with the now customary lemonade in her hand but with a frustrated frown on her brow.

"I honestly believed that I could do this. After years of claiming myself to be an independent woman."

She walked away from the open door, leaving him to follow behind. There would obviously not be any sitting on the veranda today.

"I am thoroughly disappointed in myself, I'll have you know," Marion said before she turned to him suddenly and kissed him and kissed him and kissed him, reclaiming the thing he had not freely given years ago.

To his surprise, Emil found that he could not go on without telling her the truth about himself. "Marion, there are things I do...The Organization—"

She took both his hands in hers and kissed the open palms of his hands. "I know," she said. "I know."

She pulled him to her and their lips met with the imprecision of urgency and eagerness. Moments later he was intoxicated. He did not stand a chance. He never really had. She went straight to his head like the smoothest whiskey, and he knew in that moment that he could never be like Courteney. He could never share Marion. His was a very jealous heart. He did not tell her this. He showed her this and she understood him perfectly because as she held him close, she whispered in his ear, "I know...I know."

For the first time in their long knowing of each other they fully understood each other.

And because they understood each other, their relationship was not easy. There were times when Marion would embrace him. There were times when Marion would strike him. There were times when Marion would give him the cold shoulder. There were times when Marion would warmly take him in. There were times when Marion would gently cradle him in her arms as he allowed himself to cry in her presence.

He definitely figured in her life now.

This was familiar territory for Emil where Marion was concerned. He was floating somewhere between agony and ecstasy, never knowing quite what to do, or what next to expect. But he welcomed the feeling of uncertainty because he had felt it from the first moment he laid eyes on her. For him, it was like being in the deepest recesses of the savannah, where the rustle of the elephant grass meant anything could happen. All his senses were heightened; he could see all that was around him with a clarity that astounded him. In Marion he had found his home again.

"I cannot keep ignoring it—pretending not to see, pretending not to know," Marion said one day, as she hit him with a rolled-up copy of *The Chronicle* as soon as he walked through the front door. In it he had said, in response to Beatrice Beit-Beauford, something intolerant about the races mixing. "You say and do things sometimes...I have tried very hard not to love you. I am not even sure why I love you—but having failed not to love you, I have to find a way to love myself again."

Marion was crying.

Emil understood that she was asking him to let her go. But he would do no such thing. He had told her that there was no goodness in him and she had chosen not to believe him. What he had not told her was that a long time ago she had left him good for nothing else but loving and wanting her.

"I know I am far from perfect," he said, going to her. She backed away from him. "I know I am not what you deserve," he said, still approaching her. She backed away from him again and he advanced again. It was like a dance, an ancient dance whose rhythm he knew instinctively. "But this thing between us is the realest thing," he said as their bodies met.

Later, as she lay before him, he sat beside her, marveling at her body which had been filled out by the slight plumpness that came with age. She was softer now. He found that he appreciated this body more than he did the body of her youth. That body had been perfect; this body was beautiful in its imperfections: the gentle mound of her belly, the slight stretch marks on her waist, the dimples on her buttocks, the extra weight of her breasts. He ran a hand over these things, admiring the skin she was contained in. "I love the golden tint of your skin. There is something so exotic about it," he said.

Marion observed him and, for a brief moment, something dangerous, something that could truly hurt him, flashed in her startlingly azure eyes. He loved it, whatever it was.

"You want to know a family secret?" she asked, leaning toward him. "There was a señorita somewhere in the not-so-distant Hartley past—at least that is what we say when we are in polite company." She reached up and brought his head down to hers. "But I strongly suspect something darker. An Arab woman—Shahrazad herself. Spinning her one thousand and one tales." She pressed her forehead to his, her eyes gazing deeply into his. "What do you think of that Mister Emil Coetzee, Mister The Races Shall Not Mix?"

Whatever he thought about it, he soon did not know because she had captured his lower lip in her mouth and lightly bitten it.

Soon after this encounter, another note written on azure-colored paper arrived. The note read,
When God had made The Man, he made him out of stuff

that sung all the time and glittered all over. Then after that some angels got jealous and chopped him into millions of pieces, but still he glittered and hummed. So they beat him down to nothing but sparks but each little spark had a shine and a song. So they covered each one with mud. And the lonesomeness in the sparks make them hunt for one another.
– Zora Neale Hurston

And with this note, Emil finally understood the gift of the butterflies.

CHAPTER 32

———— ◆ ————

It was evident from its very beginning that 1977 would prove to be a most violent year. On 22 January, Jason Ziyaphapha Moyo, a leading nationalist, was killed instantly by a parcel bomb. Barely more than a week later, on 30 January, approximately 500 to 700 students, staff, and teachers from Manama Secondary School were abducted by guerrillas in a bid to force them to join the liberation struggle. On 6 February, a little after 8 p.m. at St. Paul's Mission in Musami, four Jesuits and four Dominican nuns were frogmarched out of the mission, lined up against the church wall, and shot. One of the Jesuits survived. On 3 April 1977, General Peter Walls announced the government's campaign to win the "hearts and minds" of those it no longer called "Africans" but referred to as its "black citizens." During the course of the war, it had occurred to the government that speaking of Africans and Europeans at war with each other in a country that was on the African continent might give the impression that the Europeans were foreigners on the land that they were fighting in and for. The government then chose to conveniently call these two races "blacks" and "whites" respectively, and to consider them as having an equal share in the country.

As it turned out, the "hearts and minds" were to be won forcefully and so several operations to fight guerrillas were launched. The campaign, which was effectively meant to safeguard the civilian population from the guerrillas, did not get off to a great start. On 9 May, in the southeastern part of the country, the security forces carried out a sortie against the guerrillas that resulted in the deaths of thirty-five black civilians and one guerrilla. Operation Aztec on 30 May saw the security forces attack terrorists in Mozambique; the number of casualties incurred on both sides was heavily disputed. On 6 August, guerrillas using thirty kilograms of high explosives bombed a Woolworth's Department Store in Salisbury and killed eleven and wounded over seventy civilians. On 21 August, sixteen black civilians who lived on a commercial farm in the eastern part of the country were killed and their houses burned. At the end of the first quarter of the year, 846 people had been killed; at the end of the second quarter, 521 people had been killed; at the end of the third quarter, 671 people had been killed, all resulting in a total of 2,038 casualties. At the end of the year, between the 23rd and 25th of November to be exact, the security forces decided to cap the year with what they called Operation Dingo, which was essentially a raid on two guerrilla camps in Mozambique: Chimoio and Tembue. According to the situation reports, these raids killed more than 3,000 guerrillas and wounded a further 5,000. Purportedly only two members of the security forces were killed in the operation. Six were wounded.

It always seemed to Kuki, as she listened to and watched the situation reports, that their side was always winning. Thousands of terrorists were dying but only a few members of the security forces had lost their lives in the bush war. She took a lot of comfort in the word "only" and that is why, when she opened the mailbox on that early February morning in 1977, the morning of her beautiful, golden-haired boy's eighteenth birthday, and found a call-up notice for one Everleigh Reginald Coetzee, there was no trepidation in her heart for him. He would go to the bush, fight for his country for a few months, and then return home.

So when she informed her beautiful, golden-haired boy that evening during his birthday dinner that his turn had come to serve his country, she was very surprised when he vehemently said that he would not serve a country that had never served his interests. Furthermore, he would not fight a war that he did not believe in, a war that was trying to preserve things that he was fundamentally opposed to.

Kuki knew that her beautiful, golden-haired boy did not like to kill things, but surely there would not be much killing involved and he wouldn't have to do it if he did not want to. She knew of boys who had gone off to serve and spent their time reading maps, surveying land, and manning supplies stores. She was sure his father and her father, both men of great influence, could see to it that he got one of those positions.

But her beautiful, golden-haired boy would not hear of it. He did not want any part of the war.

Kuki did not understand. For her the war was like most things in life—it was a question of duty, expectation. It had absolutely nothing to do with personal feelings and beliefs. Where would the entire country be if people did only the things that they were happy doing? What kind of history would such an ethos possibly create?

Although he still believed the war to be senseless, Emil agreed with Kuki and told The Boy Who Was Not Frederick that for love of country he would have to serve. The Boy Who Was Not Frederick was a man now and every man knew that life was about sacrifice. By all means, Emil would see to it that The Boy Who Was Now A Man would not see any real action if he did not want to. Perhaps the boy could even join The Organization of Domestic Affairs and work in a purely clerical capacity—as an archivist on the eighth, ninth, or tenth floor, where one had the best views of the city.

At this point The Boy Who Was Now a Man pulled away from the table and away from both his parents, telling them that if he were to serve then he would do so without any favours being enacted on his behalf, thank you very much. He left his parents behind not knowing whether or not to feel satisfied that he had agreed to go off to war.

The birthday cake, with its eighteen brightly lit candles, stood majestic at the center of the dining-room table, untouched.

The day before The Boy Who Was Now A Man was to be deployed, he came home to bid farewell to his parents, who had not seen much of him during his military training. He had preferred to spend his days with Rosamond and Vida, The Coloured de Villiers Boy, and his nights in the comfortable silence of his grandparents' flat at the Prince's Mansions.

Kuki was hurt that her beautiful, golden-haired boy had pulled away from her after an entire life of closeness. She comforted herself by appreciating that this was a difficult time for him and that when it was over they would surely be close again.

For his part, Emil was proud that The Boy Who Was Now A Man had so distinguished himself during training that he had been cherry-picked to join the Selous Scouts. The Selous Scouts were an elite unit named after Emil's hero, Frederick Courteney Selous. Emil had not, as yet, been able to tell The Boy Who Was Now A Man how proud he was because the boy would not make himself available to him. He had come to see them now, on the eve of his deployment, because they were his parents, and no matter how disappointed he was in them, he knew what was their due.

The Boy Who Was Now A Man seemed to have matured

overnight. His body was leaner, his features more pronounced; his military training had made him into a man, a real man. His buzz cut and the grim set of his lips made him appear stern, very much like a war-weary soldier. The softness that had always worried Emil had finally left him. He stood in front of them with tension in his body, no longer at ease in their company.

The sleeves of The Boy Who Was Now A Man's military shirt were rolled up and that was how Emil got to see the tattoo on his upper arm. The tattoo itself was simple enough— the shape of a heart. There was nothing wrong with the heart except what it contained. At the center of the heart was one word: *Vida*. There was definitely something wrong with that.

"You can't go off to war with that on your arm," Emil said.

"Tattoos are allowed. They can help identify you," The Boy Who Was Now A Man said.

"You know that that is not what I am objecting to—I am objecting to Vida. It doesn't exactly sound like a girl's name, does it?"

"It doesn't exactly sound like a boy's name either," Kuki said, eager for this encounter to fare better than their previous one.

"I don't particularly care which gender comes to mind when people see the name Vida. I just care that it belongs to the person that I love."

"You cannot possibly love The Coloured de Villiers Boy," Emil said.

"Why not?"

Even though he understood why the love between The Boy Who Was Now A Man and The Coloured de Villiers Boy was wrong, it soon became apparent to Emil that he did not know how to explain the wrongness of it. So, equivocating, he said evasively, "You cannot possibly know what love is. You are still too young."

The Boy Who Was Now A Man regarded Emil with scepticism before asking, "And you know what it is?"

"What?"

"Love."

"Yes."

The Boy Who Was Now A Man laughed mirthlessly before asking again, "You know what love is?"

Emil did not see why the boy should be so incredulous.

"Do you love me?" the boy asked.

How could the boy possibly ask such a question? Of course he loved him. It was obvious that he loved him.

"Do you love her?" The Boy Who Was Now A Man asked, motioning toward his mother.

"Your father and I definitely love each other," Kuki hastened to answer.

"I have seen *you* loving *him*...but I have not seen *him* loving *you*," The Boy Who Was Now A Man said, as he stared at Emil. "Why have you not been able to love her? Why have you not found it within yourself to love the one person who deserves all the love in the world?"

Emil was at a loss. For over twenty years he and Kuki had had a more or less peaceable coexistence and that was something, was it not? It was not a passionate love, but it was love of a different kind, was it not?

"You know what she does? What she has always done since I can remember? She waits to hear your car in the driveway and then starts to sing. And do you know why she does this? She does this so that you, who have never tried to make her happy, will think that she is happy."

Emil looked at Kuki, but she would not hold his gaze.

"And *you* speak to *me* of love? You have no right. You cannot speak to me of something that you have never been able to show me."

Emil wondered how a father *showed* his love to his son. All he knew was that his love just was. It had always been there.

"You taught me a long, hard lesson. I did not understand it at first, but now I do. You taught me how not to love and you were successful because I now know how not to love you."

Emil would have much preferred it had The Boy Who Was Now A Man struck him instead. Or, better still, cut his heart out.

"No...no...no," Kuki was saying. "That is not true...the two of you love each other. I have got the proof...you love each other." She pointed a trembling finger at a photograph of Emil and The Boy Who Was Not Frederick that had been taken at the Kariba Dam some five years earlier. The boy was proudly holding a huge bream. Both father and son were smiling and happy. Emil, beaming with pride, had his arm casually placed around the boy's shoulders.

After the photo had been taken, the boy had released the bream back into the water because he did not like killing things.

CHAPTER 33

---·---

The letter that Emil received from Everleigh on 3 April 1978 was the first and only letter he would ever receive from his son.

That there was no sender's address was no surprise to Emil as it was a letter written during the most treacherous part of the war, when secrecy was key. Emil also tried not to be surprised by the fact that there was no salutation, but he kept on peering at where it should have been and wondering what it would have been had it been there: Father...Dad..Pa...? What had Everleigh called him? Hard as he tried, Emil could no longer recall what Everleigh had called him, and, even in his imaginings, Emil could not make the missing salutation start with "Dear." He was not dear to Everleigh.

Without its salutation the letter began unceremoniously and read,

We arrived at the village just before dawn. We fired our rifles into the air so as to wake up the villagers. We had them all gather in the middle of the kraal. We asked them why they were aiding the terrorists. We asked them this as though we thought they had a choice in the matter. We asked them this even though we knew they did not have a choice in the matter. We asked them this even though we know that when the terrorists arrive the villagers have to do as ordered otherwise what we were just about to do to them would be done to them at the hands of the terrorists. We gathered all the men and the boys. They were not that many men. Even though we knew that most of the men were away laboring in the mines, factories, and farms that sustain the country's economy and help keep the war going, we told them that we knew that the missing men had joined the terrorists. We put the men and the boys in a grain hut. Just before my commander set fire to the hut, I noticed that there was an old woman in the hut as well. I pulled her out but she went back in. Looking at me with the most pitiful eyes I had ever seen, she shut the door of the hut. She did not want to survive; she was done with being spared and saved only to be left with terrible memories. We set fire to the hut and it quickly caught flame. Maybe it would have been easier to bear had they cried out. But all there was was silence and the smell of burning flesh. From the moment we arrived the villagers had offered no resistance. They had been through it all and seen it all so many times before that now they were just tired of it all. The old woman's eyes follow me everywhere. If it were not for Vida, I wonder if I would care as much as I do. I have always known that somewhere in Vida's past there is a black person. A woman. It is always a woman. I never asked him about her because it seemed an inconvenient and unnecessary detail. In killing those villagers, I have killed a part of Vida and in killing a part of Vida, I have killed a part of myself. You finally got your wish. You have always wanted me to kill something and now I have. I hope you are finally proud of me. I have become the son that you have always wanted.

That was all that the letter said. There was no love, regard, or sincerity to sign it off.

Accompanying the letter was a photograph of Everleigh. His military fatigues were already faded and worn even though he had only been serving for a few months. His face was smeared with greasepaint. His blue eyes were deadly fierce.

Emil examined the letter and the photograph and knew the truth.

When the telephone rang Emil did not have to answer it to know that his son, Everleigh Reginald Coetzee, was dead. He did not have to know the specifics, which were that Everleigh had deliberately stepped on a landmine and blown himself to pieces, to comprehend that Everleigh had preferred death over the haunted future that was to come.

When Marion came to fetch him, Emil had no idea how many days and nights he had spent at the Gentleman's Club; all he knew was that he had found his way to the bottom of many whiskey bottles.

"You think you have all the time in the world and then all of a sudden you don't. Just like that, it is too late," Emil said as he let Marion remove the whiskey glass from his hand.

Marion, without a word, helped him stand up, supported him as he staggered out of the Gentleman's Club, put him in her car and drove him home.

It was Beatrice Beit-Beauford who opened the door to them.

Together, all three of them watched as Kuki came down the stairs stark naked. She had evidently just stepped out of the bath because her body and hair were wet and she smelled strongly of the peaches-and-cream bubble bath she loved. There were clouds of sudsy foam scattered all over her; she was like an ocean walking with its islands.

Kuki walked up to Emil and touched him gently on the cheek. "We did not deserve him, you and I," she said. "You were too strong and I was too weak. He was too beautiful for the world and we did not deserve him."

Kuki opened the front door and walked through it and

into a world that had proved itself too painfully exacting for her to bear.

CHAPTER 34

———◆———

Emil was lying on a bed in what appeared to be a hospital ward. The ward was circular in shape and the beds in the room were also arranged in a circular fashion, with partitions between them. The entire ward was bathed in fluorescent light that fell on the silver and white fixtures and made everything immaculate. The luminescence of everything stung Emil's eyes until he felt tears in them. He could not turn his head too much to the left or to the right—he tried it once and not only was there a sharp pain in his neck, but it also felt as if he had, about his neck, a brace that limited his range of motion.

There was the melodic sound of a bell ringing, and the chimes made Emil relax even though he did not want to. The double doors that were on the other end of the ward, opposite his bed, suddenly swung open and a group of nurses came in. Emil was able to count thirteen nurses in all. They all congregated in the nurses' station in the middle of the ward. Emil strained his neck enough to see that they were a multiracial group and that two of them were male. They conversed amicably as they put on surgical masks and latex gloves.

So the multiracial future that had been promised had arrived, Emil thought as he settled back into his pillow. The future had paradoxically come too soon and arrived too late. He stared up at the fluorescent light above his bed and then shut his eyes tightly so that the kaleidoscope of colors could play on the pitch-black background behind his eyelids.

When he woke up, he felt vastly more comfortable than

before. There was a black female nurse sitting at the slanted desk at the foot of his bed; she was writing something on a very large sheet of graph paper. She glanced up and, when she saw him staring at her, immediately stood up. She came to stand beside him and her eyes smiled down at him. "I'm so glad to see you're up," she said through her surgical mask. He felt her hand gently squeeze his as she examined something above his head. She scrutinized it for quite some time before going back to write on the very large sheet of graph paper.

Emil realized that he was somewhat surprised that she was his nurse. He had assumed that one of the white female nurses would come and attend to him. Was that not how things were supposed to be...even in a multiracial future?

His nurse walked away from the slanted table at the foot of his bed and went to talk to another black nurse at the nurses' station, while Emil surveyed the ward. There were two nurses constantly stationed in the nurses' station, which was a metal enclosure with a circular white desk, four metal bar stools, and three white computers. One of the nurses, the black one talking to Emil's nurse, wore a blue uniform; she was evidently the matron. A young white male nurse sat in front of a computer and almost ceaselessly typed information into it, even as he occasionally said things to the other two nurses in the station that made them laugh. Something about the scene made Emil slightly uncomfortable and so he focused past them on the swinging doors, which he now noticed had the letters ICU stenciled on them.

So, he was in the intensive care unit. That did not bode well for him, Emil realized with a sinking feeling that he tried to ignore.

Emil had put it off long enough, but it was now time to focus on himself and his condition. The first thing he noticed was that his throat felt dry and scratchy. He realized that there was something in his nose and marveled at how he had not felt it all along. He tried to lift his hand to examine what was in his nose, but the effort was beyond him.

His nurse materialized at the head of his bed. "Try not to move too much," she said as she held down his arm. He turned his eyes in her direction and for a moment was mesmerized by the whiteness of her uniform against the brownness of her skin.

She was adjusting the something above his head but looking down at him. Those eyes...he recognized them...where had he seen them before?

"How are you feeling?" she asked.

He wanted to tell her about the scratch in his throat but found that he could not talk.

She gently placed the palm of her left hand on his brow and looked into his eyes. Emil found that he did not mind her closeness at all.

"Do you feel better now?" she asked.

Emil noticed that the scratch in his throat had instantly disappeared. It was as though she had performed an act of magic.

She lifted up and showed him an oblong white tube that had been lying by his side all along. "For the pain," she informed him before demonstrating how he should press the red button at the top of the tube. He did not really pay much attention to what she showed him because he was not feeling any pain.

His nurse went back to the slanted desk and sat before it and busied herself writing on the graph paper in front of her. She glanced at him occasionally, and when she did her eyes smiled at him.

Emil could not shake the feeling that he knew those eyes. He had never really interacted with African women, but he occupied himself now with combing the recesses of his mind for all possible points of interaction. They all led nowhere. His mind, where African women were concerned, was a wide, empty expanse.

The lights slowly dimmed until everything was bathed in an ethereal amber glow that made Emil feel drowsy.

His nurse got up and gently lowered his adjustable bed with a remote-controlled device. "Try to get some sleep," she whispered with smiling eyes and a gentle touch on the shoulder.

He felt himself smile as he drifted off to sleep.

Emil was woken up by penetrating pain that seized his entire body. His senses were more alert than they had ever been and he felt everything. He felt the oxygen mask covering his nose and mouth. Had it been there the entire time? He felt the intravenous needle attached to the back of his hand. He felt the catheter attached to his urethra. He felt the whatever-it-was that seemed to be pierced into his abdomen. He jerked. In an attempt to do what? He did not know. With all his might he tried to lift his right hand so that he could remove the oxygen mask from his nose and mouth and scream his pain.

There was a loud beeping sound and his nurse stood up sharply, almost upsetting the chair behind her. Had she been sleeping? Was she allowed to sleep? Emil doubted it.

Once she was by his side, she picked up the white oblong tube that lay beside him and pumped it several times.

Emil felt stupid for having forgotten that the white oblong tube was there and for having agitated himself to such an extent that his monitor had beeped in alarm. He was in excruciating pain and it was now all congregated in his abdomen. It felt as if he had been shot in the stomach. Is that what had happened? Is that why he was here? Somebody had shot him? The monitor started beeping again. Emil felt his body begin to tremble.

"Everything is all right," his nurse said, placing one hand on his brow while the other adjusted something above his head. "You'll feel better soon," she said. "I promise."

He was feeling better already. His pain gradually subsided.

She placed the white oblong tube in his right hand. "Just a few clicks of the red button whenever you feel the pain will do the trick," she instructed. "Just a few, mind—too many and it will lock itself."

Emil feebly pressed the red button just once to make sure that he could and to show her that he would and then he was drifting away on a feeling as light as air.

When Emil woke up, his nurse had adjusted his bed to a sitting position and morning had broken.

As Emil surveyed the ward, he realized that he was in a more attentive state than before and that his oxygen mask had been removed. For the first time, he took notice of the other occupants. There was a white man with dyed brown hair and a beard in partition number 3 called "Professor" by the nurses. Throughout the day the nurses kept finding contraband food items secreted around the professor's bed, including a packet of biltong and a bottle of brandy already half empty. Whenever something was discovered, the professor would shrug and say that he could not be blamed: his house boy was the one who brought him these things, because he knew him better than anyone and understood exactly what his baas loved best. He had told his house boy, many times, to stop bringing the items, but surely he could not be faulted if his house boy had a will and mind of his own.

In number 4 there was, propped up as Emil was propped up, a frail old white lady. She had obviously always been small, and old age had made her minuscule. The crocheted baby-blue hat she wore had pink-and-yellow flowers on it and looked like something a young girl would happily wear. Her rheumy but alert eyes traveled the room and the nurses occasionally stopped by her bed to talk to her. It was obvious that she loved having visitors. She had a genial smile fixed on her face and her smile became positively genteel when a nurse stopped by. Emil got to see the frail white lady up close when her nurse wheeled her past his bed on their way to the bathroom. Her skin was as brittle as parchment and her veins as thin as gossamer. She was waif-like but she waved like a queen when she traveled past his bed.

A nurse in the next partition, number 6, was saying, "You'll behave yourself today won't you, Jane? Honestly, you're a handful sometimes." Emil thought he heard Jane respond, "A handful? That's what all the men say." Just as Emil was wondering what kind of handful Jane was, the curtain between his bed and hers opened. Jane stood there, black, beautiful, and looking the picture of perfect health. So his neighbor was a young black woman. Emil was trying to find an appropriate emotion to feel about this discovery. When she naughtily smiled at him and said, "You're a handsome man, I'm a pretty lady. I think we can make our time here pass more...pleasantly," Emil was embarrassed to find himself blushing. He did not remember ever having blushed in his entire life. Jane laughed at his heightened color. "Jane, behave yourself," the matron shouted from the nurses' station. "Back into bed with you," Jane's nurse said, leading her back to her bed and closing the partition between the two beds. She looked at Emil apologetically and he looked away.

Number 8 was occupied by a white man whom Emil suspected must have played rugby at some point in his life. He was built like a tank—a solid tank. Emil was able to see him because his nurse had helped him out of his bed and placed him on a chair within Emil's range of sight. The man sat with his back painfully stiff. He seemed to be in constant pain, but he also seemed determined to soldier through his pain. There were old burn scars all over his body—he must have been through a terrible ordeal. Emil felt embarrassed for feeling lucky that whatever had happened to him was apparently not as bad as what had happened to the man. But when Emil's eyes met the man's, the man gave Emil such a pitying look that Emil closed his eyes to shut out the sympathy.

Of course...he was the one with tubes attached to his body. He was the one who occasionally needed help breathing. He was the one who had had something truly bad happen to him. Even though he was not in physical pain, Emil used his right thumb to press the red button of the white oblong tube.

As Emil tried to sleep, the moans from the patient in number 10 started turning into expletives. Emil opened his eyes and glared at the occupant. There was a distinguished-looking white gentleman, propped up in bed the same way Emil was. The man appeared dignified but had the vocabulary of a sailor ...an extensive vocabulary. More than one nurse went to attend to him but he had nothing kind to say to any of them. They were incompetent, he complained, and he was in pain... had been in unbearable pain the entire day...the entire night ...his entire life...and nobody cared.

During all these antics, an Indian man in number 11 sat up, got out of bed, and walked very slowly until he came to stand by the glass wall of his room. He observed all the goings-on with an expression that was hard for Emil to read. His hands were clasped behind his back and he rocked his body gently, rhythmically, back and forth, as though soothing something deep within him.

And then there was him, Emil Coetzee, in number 7. He

had no idea what had happened to him, how he had come to be here, what would happen to him here.

Was this the full stop of his life, or was this merely a comma...a semicolon...an ellipsis? And what awaited him on the other side of any of those possible marks?

Emil must have been dreaming because out of the blue there were Daisy's eyes looking back at him.

"Daisy?" he asked, his mind still foggy with sleep. He was surprised to hear the sound of his own voice. He noticed then that his throat was no longer dry and scratchy. "Daisy?" he repeated, his voice feeble.

The nurse's eyes smiled at him.

He blinked and saw clearly, maybe for the first time since coming here. Those eyes were...Daisy's. That was why they were so very familiar.

"Daisy?" he repeated the question, this time a little more self-assuredly.

Her eyes still smiling, she said something that he could not quite make out. Emil frowned in incomprehension.

She repeated the sound again, slowly this time. Emil's frown deepened.

The creases at the corners of her eyes also deepened, showing that her smile behind the surgical mask had broadened. She left him, went behind the slanted desk, retrieved her navy blue sweater and brought it to him. On the sweater was her name badge: SIBONUBUHLEMTHETHWA

Emil did not even know where to begin.

"Sibonubuhle Mthethwa," she said. "Sibonubuhle."

To Emil she was just making sounds.

"Sibonubuhle."

The only thing that Emil could clearly make out was that the sound had five syllables.

Why did they have to complicate names so much? Why did they have to imbue them with weighty meaning and purpose that the bearer was forever burdened with? Why did they have to make them so difficult for the tongue to maneuver around?

Emil held that, at most, a name should have three syllables and be satisfied.

"Sibonubuhle," she repeated with a smile.

"Si...si...sibho..."

She giggled and shook her head.

"Si...bo...nu...bu...hle...Sibonubuhle."

Emil valiantly bungled through a few more attempts. She laughed at all of them and he found himself smiling, not for the first time since being there.

"What does it mean?" Emil asked, finally giving up.

"We see beauty—or we have seen the beauty."

"How...beautiful," Emil said, feeling slightly foolish for not being able to find another adjective.

It truly was a lovely name.

"Can I call you Beauty?"

She shrugged and then nodded before going to sit behind the slanted desk where she busied herself writing notes. Emil felt that he had disappointed her by not trying harder to say her name and he found that he did not want to disappoint her.

"I can attempt 'Buhle,'" he said, fully aware that he had mangled even just those two syllables.

She gazed up at him and smiled with those eyes that were so much like Daisy's.

Emil looked at his surroundings—the remote-controlled adjustable beds, the computer monitors, the individual morphine pumps, the nurses' station, the multiracial staff and patients—and asked, "Is this the future, Buhle?"

Sibonubuhle frowned and shook her head.

Emil looked pointedly at the multiracial nurses' station and the many gadgets in the ward.

Cottoning on, Sibonubuhle explained, "It is 1979. We have our first black president and a multiracial government."

1979? A black president? A multiracial government? So it was the future. How long had he been here?

"How long have I...? Why am I...? How did I...?" As soon as he started to ask a question, he realized that he did not necessarily want to know the answer.

"From what we gather, you had a severe fall down a flight of stairs, at work," Sibonubuhle said gently.

That sounded so much better than what he had feared. But it was plain from the soothing way that Sibonubuhle had delivered the news that there was more to the story.

And then Emil remembered 1978.

Everleigh had gone off to war and not returned. High-ranking army officials had visited the house in Brookside and, after expressing their deepest condolences, had explained in one voice that they had done the best they could, but that they strongly and firmly suggested a closed coffin for the funeral. Kuki and Emil had watched, clinging to each other, as a coffin with the country's flag draped over it was lowered into the ground of Athlone Cemetery at the same time that a 21-gun salute blasted through the air. They continued clinging to each other as they peered into the gaping hole, disbelieving. Disbelieving that such a deep, dark, and damp wound in the earth's surface could be the final resting place for their one and only son. Hours later, they were still standing there, still clinging to each other, still disbelieving, as they stared at the filled-in hole whose raised soil looked like a keloidal scar—a permanent reminder of pain.

Soon after the funeral, Kuki had left their home in

Brookside and briefly gone to live with Beatrice Beit-Beauford.

By mid year, the war had claimed 2,690 lives, almost half of them belonging to black civilians.

On 3 September 1978, Golide Gumede had shot down the Vickers Viscount passenger plane, killing many passengers, Beatrice Beit-Beauford's twin sons amongst them. Emil had ordered the head of Golide Gumede to be brought to him, at whatever cost, on a silver platter. In retaliation for the downing of the Vickers Viscount, the security forces had, on 19 October 1978, attacked the Mkushi and Freedom military and refugee camps in Zambia, napalming and killing thousands.

Emil had taken to finding his way to the bottom of too many whiskey bottles.

One day after the Gentleman's Club had kindly spat him out into the broad lightness of day, Emil had found himself walking the streets of the City of Kings. The sweat on his palms had become so warm that he had begun to believe that it was blood and shoved his hands deep into his pockets. He could do nothing to stop it as it had begun to soak through the khaki fabric of his trousers. Several people had stolen glances at him and Emil had been convinced that they were peeking at the blood. The city had stopped making sense to him and he had no idea exactly where he was going.

As he crossed a street, he caught sight of a broken and misshapen man on crutches who was shaking a tin can, rattling with coins, on the other side. Emil felt through the blood on his fingers for the coins in his pocket. As he came closer, Emil noticed that the man's body was horribly twisted and that his brown skin was so severely burnt that the area around his eyes and mouth was pink and permanently depigmented. He was such a sad-looking character that Emil decided to give him more than the coins in his pocket and to give him most of the money in his wallet as well. Upon seeing Emil, the man looked horrified and hobbled away as fast as he could on his crutches. Emil called to the man to stop and explained that he wanted to give him money. The man would not stop and made every attempt to move faster. It was only when the man, his back to Emil, desperately folded himself into the doorway of a building that Emil realized, with horror, that he was the reason why the burnt, twisted, and broken man looked the way he did. Emil opened his wallet and threw all the money he had at the feet of the man before quickly walking away.

Emil had lost his taste for meat after that and had secretly stopped eating it. He became friendlier (if that were at all possible) with the whiskey bottle. But, as the year drew to an end, he found himself doing his best to celebrate Christmas with Marion.

"Madam has decided to do it all herself," Marion's cook, looking both forlorn and apologetic, informed him as he opened the front door for Emil.

Emil walked into the kitchen in time to see a ten-kilogram cloth sack of Gloria flour topple off the counter and plop onto the floor, sending a super-fine white dust floating through the air. The entire kitchen looked like a battlefield—cupboards were open with the contents tumbled to the floor, smoke and steam were rising alarmingly from the pots and pans on the antique Jackson electric stove, a boiling kettle was whistling manically, a food mixer was enthusiastically whipping something into shape—and standing in the middle of it all was Marion, the obvious victor. A glazed gammon decorated with singed pineapple rings and charred cherries already stood proud on the kitchen table.

Marion had turned and looked at Emil through the flour dust. Her white apron, which had an elaborate and humorous recipe for crocodile stew printed on it, was soiled by three stains—one red, one yellow, one brown. From the look in her eyes, Emil realized that the confusion he found himself in the middle of was another manifestation of her love for him. It overwhelmed him. So much so that when Marion pronounced triumphantly, "All that is left to do is the salad," Emil responded, without hesitation, "Please, let me."

Emil went to the garden to pick the ingredients for the salad himself. As soon as he pulled the lettuce from the ground, he was struck by the violence of the act, and as he tore and ripped the lettuce leaves, cut the tomatoes and cucumbers, and watched the sap flow onto the cutting board, it occurred to him, for the first time, that sap and blood were exactly the same thing and that when one saw them flow, one should know that an act of violence had occurred. He inspected his hands then and wondered if all they were capable of was destruction.

The last thing Emil remembered about 1978 was leaving his office at The Organization and heading toward the concrete room in the basement. He had tripped while going down a flight of stairs. And who was to say that it had been an accident?

"A black president?" Emil asked rhetorically. "That means that the war is over then?" He was not quite able to keep the hope from his voice.

If the war was over then The Organization of Domestic Affairs could happily become what it had been intended to be.

Sadly, Sibonubuhle shook her head. "The freedom fighters think that the current president is a puppet of the white regime," she said. "The boys are still in the bush, fighting."

Emil noticed that she had not used the words "terrorists" or "guerrillas" for the boys in the bush. He suddenly felt a very sharp physical pain and pushed down on the red button.

CHAPTER 35

———◆———

When news of the cease-fire arrived, on December 21, 1979, Emil Coetzee was washing blood off his hands. He watched the rust-colored water slosh up until it almost filled the white enamel basin and then he turned off the cold-water tap. It did not turn off entirely and water kept drip, drip, dripping into the basin, as though holding on to a memory. The water gurgled down the drain until it was a disappearing swirl. Next, Emil reached for the black plug that was, by some miracle, still attached to the sink. He pulled the plug up by its metal chain and pushed it in before turning on the hot-water tap and letting the scalding water rise halfway up the basin. Without having to look, he reached for the bottle of antiseptic liquid under the sink. As advertised, when he poured a capful of the liquid into the water, it mushroomed into a cloud of purity. He submerged his hands into the water and his broken skin was thankful for all the many stings it felt. Emil was no Pontius Pilate, however, and so, next, he scrubbed his hands with a bar of lye soap until they were raw and red. As he dried them on the once-white cloth in the towel dispenser, he decided that this was to be his last day at The Organization of Domestic Affairs.

Before he left the room, Emil peered at his reflection in the tarnished mirror above the water basin; his glance was brief as it always was now, and for the first time he noticed how tired he looked. He was weary, more weary of the world than any man in his fifties ought to be. After the bombastic hubris of youth and the blundering determination of adulthood there was supposed to be blissful self-assuredness, was there not? Or was that self-assuredness only reserved for a particular kind of man, a man that he had not become?

He looked into his eyes to see what they carried within them. Nothing. Even on a day such as this, his eyes stared back blankly as though long unseeing.

Emil took one last look at the dark, gray, concrete room with its naked lightbulb that hung from the ceiling and bathed the room and its rudimentary furniture in a cold welcome. It was not much to gaze upon, to be sure, but this had been the crucible of his manhood. Emil tried to reconcile himself to this fact before he switched off the light and closed the door firmly behind him, shutting out the sound of the drip, drip, dripping tap.

On this, his last day as The Head of The Organization of Domestic Affairs, Emil Coetzee entered his office and went to sit behind his desk. He picked up a black orb that had, embedded within it, a gorgeous multi-colored glittery twirl that created the sensation of looking into a vortex. He believed that he had received it as a present from Everleigh. He could only believe this and not know it with certainty because he did not remember receiving it, but it was the sort of beautiful thing that his son would give, or, more precisely, would have given when he was younger.

From under the paperweight that he believed, but no longer recalled with certainty, had been a gift from his son, Emil retrieved the only letter that Everleigh had ever written him. He knew the letter by heart and no longer had to physically read it, but he liked the materiality of the now flimsy and fragile paper in his hands—liked the weight, the burden of it. As Emil read the letter, he tried not to look at his hands.

*You finally got your wish. You have always wanted me to
kill something and now I have. I hope you are finally proud
of me. I have become the son that you have always wanted.*

He always read the ending aloud and let the words fill the silence of the office.

Although his hands were trembling when he finished
reading the letter, he managed to carefully fold it and place
it under the paperweight that may or may not have been a
present from his son.

The reading of the letter from Everleigh was the first half
of his morning ritual. For the second half of his morning ritual,
Emil opened the top drawer of his desk and retrieved his wallet. He allowed his hands to become still before he opened
it and took out five notes written in a left-leaning cursive on
azure-colored paper. He placed the notes on top of his desk,
in the order they had been received:

No. 1 Pioneer Road

*There is a basin in the mind where words float around on
thought and thought on sound and sight. Then there is a
depth of thought untouched by words and deeper still a gulf
of formless feelings untouched by thought.*
—Zora Neale Hurston

There are years that ask questions and years that answer.
—Zora Neale Hurston

Let's meet. We need to talk. H&S. Friday at 2 p.m.

*When God had made The Man, he made him out of stuff
that sung all the time and glittered all over. Then after that*

some angels got jealous and chopped him into millions
of pieces, but still he glittered and hummed. So they beat
him down to nothing but sparks but each little spark had
a shine and a song. So they covered each one with mud.
And the lonesomeness in the sparks make them hunt for
one another.

    —Zora Neale Hurston

The man Emil truly was existed at a point somewhere between the letter from his son and the five notes from the
woman that he loved. He wished that he could pinpoint the
exact spot and know himself confidently and completely. He
wanted to be as assured as other men in their fifties must
be, but he was not. He imagined these men beholding their
reflections in mirrors and feeling something specific like
contentment, confidence, or resignation.

On the rare occasions that he looked at himself in the
mirror, Emil never felt anything specific; his inner world was
too unresolved for him to feel settled in it. All his life he had
seemed only to be able to grasp at the edges of things, never
to see or experience the whole, to find himself in the middle of
something that had already begun. He could have very easily
been another kind of man if he had known how to be anything else but himself.

His story, if it were ever told, would have to contain the
lows of the letter and the highs of the notes. It would have to
be told chronologically in a linear fashion, with a definite beginning, middle and end—none of that starting-in-the-middle
or -at-the-end modern nonsense. It would have to be told in
this fashion because that was the only way to make any sense
of the dark, gray, concrete room with its naked lightbulb,
forever drip, drip, dripping tap and the man with blood on his
hands.

CHAPTER 36

When it finally came to an end, the civil war had claimed the lives of more than 20,000 people: over 10,000 guerrillas had been killed within the country's borders; around 8,000 black civilians and 500 white civilians had been killed by security forces and guerrillas alike; and those "onlies" who had given Kuki such peace of mind had finally amounted to over 1,000 security forces killed. These numbers were rather conservative as they did not take into account the innumerable guerrillas, refugees, and civilians killed in the raids on Zambia and Mozambique.

The cease-fire itself was something of an anticlimax. After the actions of a few had claimed the lives of many, at the end of it all what had won the day were not deeds but words. A conference held at Lancaster House in London succeeded where all previous talks had failed and brought about an end to hostilities. The belated success of the talks seemed like a mockery, as did the smiling handshakes and brotherly bonhomie of all the major players in the civil war that the international press was so eager to capture. If it all could always have been so easily resolved, then what had been the bloody point? To add insult to injury, after more than fifteen years of civil war there was no clear victor.

As far as Emil was concerned, the only good to come of the cease-fire was that he and Kuki were finally able to divorce, publicly. During the war, divorce rates had been exceptionally high. So when Kuki filed for a divorce from Emil, the state, via Rutherford, had informed them that morale amongst the white population was especially low and that they were strongly advised, as one of the more eminent and prominent couples in the country, to hold off.

Kuki wanted nothing from her marriage. She had already moved out, leaving everything behind, even her clothes, and taken with her only the many photo albums and 8 mm films containing within them the life of her beautiful, golden-haired boy and some of his most favorite things—the blue hula hoop included.

The war had taken everything worth keeping and fighting for with it and Kuki wanted the future to know that.

Emil surprised himself when he considered immigrating to another country. The notion occurred to him just once, but once was enough. His life had without warning arrived at a cul-de-sac, which, after its forever-forward-moving momentum, came as a complete surprise to him. Surely it all could not always have been leading to a dead end.

Whenever he tried to be hopeful about the future he saw those innumerable black bodies that had been shown during situation reports: crushed skulls, bloated and blackened bodies, severed limbs, the always open and staring black eyes, the pathetic puppets in the bizarre theatre of war. It was, understandably, easier for him to think of these black bodies and not the black bodies that had left The Tower injured, maimed and broken. He knew that all this loss would have to be repaid, in the future. If there was one lesson history taught efficiently, it was that war begat war and memories of loss were long.

Too late, Emil realized that the imperial project only made sense if it succeeded. Master Duthie had forgotten to mention that in his History class, had he not? And where did that leave the men of its history? Where did that leave Emil Coetzee?

Finding himself unexpectedly without a future to look forward to created a state of confusion within Emil. The only thing he knew with certainty was that he would no longer be working for The Organization of Domestic Affairs. The irony of ending his association with The Organization now, when the war was over, was not lost on him.

As he put on his denim shirt, khaki trousers, veldskoene and well-worn cowboy hat, while Marion, lying supine, looked at him appreciatively (which was a nice way for a woman in her fifties to look at a man in his fifties) from the comfort of her bed, Emil knew that the winds of change had rendered men like him relics of a bygone era.

As though reading his mind, Marion said, "Once independence comes, a friend of mine is opening a game ranch. One of those tourist traps. He's looking for a game ranger. I told him that you might be interested."

"A game ranger?"

"You already have the clothes for it," Marion teased.

Marion was offering him a fresh start, a second chance, and Emil wondered if it could be possible for him to find another way of being in this country.

"Promise me you will at least consider it," Marion said, interrupting his thoughts.

In response Emil smiled, sat on the bed and ran his thumb over the rosebud of her mouth.

"Emil—"

He kissed his name on her lips.

For a moment, he allowed himself to imagine and believe in the future she envisioned.

Marion said, "There is no road traveled that one cannot come back from. Remember that. Know that."

He so desperately wanted to believe her.

CHAPTER THIRTY-SIX

"I want to grow old with you and not the memory of you," she said and then she kissed him until he fully understood and appreciated the sincerity of her words.

Marion got out of bed and went to retrieve something from her wardrobe. It was a much-faded and much-loved blue-and-white scarf. She used it to tie back her hair.

Upon seeing it, Emil could barely contain his elation. "I knew it! All these years. I knew it," Emil said, not quite able to resist the urge to go to her and gather her in his arms.

"You knew what?" Marion asked, smiling up at him with confusion.

"I knew it was always you."

"What a terribly wonderful thing to say," Marion said. She put her arms around him, rested her head on his chest and listened to his heart beat. "I do believe you are becoming something of a romantic in your old age, Mister Coetzee."

Emil kissed the top of her head where a dozen gray hairs had sprouted and made a permanent home for themselves.

Maybe...just maybe...his love for her could make a future here possible.

"The divorce has been finalized," Emil said tentatively.

Marion slowly lifted her head and looked at him so that she could be sure that she had fully understood the import of what he had said.

"A life lived together in twilight," Marion said with a smile. "I would really love that."

Emil knew that he would love that life too and smiled back at her—but Marion was no longer smiling. She removed her arms from around his waist and took a step back.

Marion contemplated him for a very long time before going to open an ancient-looking chest in the corner of the room. She took something from it that she clasped closely to her heart like a secret.

"The truth is that...I am the great-granddaughter of Frederick Courteney Selous," Marion said, as she walked toward him.

Emil did not quite comprehend. Why would Marion keep her relationship to a man she knew to be his childhood hero a secret from him? Emil knew that Frederick Courtney Selous had had two sons, Frederick Hatherley Bruce Selous and Harold Sherborn Selous. Hatherley...Hartley. Yes, it made perfect sense now. He had always assumed that the sons had lived their lives in England, but obviously one of them had not.

Marion contemplated him again for a long time, mentally weighing things as yet unknown to him, before handing him the object she had retrieved.

Emil glanced down at the object. It was an old daguerreotype of a tall woman with regal bearing, dressed in Victorian finery. She was a proud and beautiful woman. Even with the imperfect exposure of the image, Emil could tell that the woman's skin was several shades too dark. Although tamed into a bun, her thick hair was visibly a riot of closely coiled black curls. The woman's eyes, even though replicated in black and white, were striking and vibrant. Emil knew those eyes.

"Magdalen Selous. Frederick Courteney Selous's daughter —my grandmother," Marion said. "She was born of a Matabele woman."

Emil now knew the truth and the truth did everything but promise to set him free.

Emil glanced at Magdalen Selous's eyes again.

Emil gazed into Marion's startlingly azure eyes.

He had loved those eyes to near destruction.

He intimately knew all the hues and moods of those eyes. Marion...

She had tried so many times to show him her truth and he

had chosen, every time, to be blind. Eternally blind.

How could he have lived his entire life with eyes that were not for beauty to see?

With trembling hands, he handed the daguerreotype back to her.

"Did Courteney know?"

"Yes. Almost from the very beginning."

Of course.

Emil felt the back of his neck grow very hot and then he was suddenly light-headed. *He had been born in Africa; there was no way the unforgiving heat would affect him*, he thought as he took a step back

What was he doing? Why was he walking away from her?

Emil watched the distance between them grow as Marion stood there with her blue-and-white scarf. Her chin up, her shoulders back, her head held high, she looked proud even though her eyes were crying.

"From that first moment I saw you outside the Gentleman's Club," Marion said, "this is what I was most afraid of."

He was not leaving her, Emil reasoned. It was the heat. He needed to be in a cooler place. All would be right again and he would come back to her. But for now...he just needed to be somewhere else.

Emil drove his bakkie to the furthest and deepest recesses of the savannah. He was not part of a convoy. He did not come across an ambush. He was once again a man in Africa who was free to travel as he pleased and without fear. It was a freedom he had once had and enjoyed. It was a freedom that the war had taken away from him.

Rain clouds gathered as Emil got out of the bakkie. He had not brought a rifle. He had not brought a knife. He had not brought a weapon of any kind or anything to protect himself.

He walked into the singing elephant grass and lost himself in it. He walked until his legs grew tired and his body became fatigued. He walked on, never looking behind him, looking always ahead, ahead to the future—his future.

The rain clouds parted and Emil peered up at the sky in time to see the sun shine through brightly. God's visit. The sun had been there the entire time, hidden by the clouds. Emil squinted up to the sky and then reached his hand up to the sun as though to touch it. The sun disappeared behind the clouds again, but now Emil knew that it was there and felt comforted.

He looked out at the veld and took in its vastness. The wild wind made the elephant grass sing and swoon before it came and kissed his face. He closed his eyes, took a deep breath, and let the beauty of all that was around him enter him. As that beauty traveled through his body, It turned into something else, and he knew that this thing that he felt in every fibre of his being, this wondrous and rarefied thing, this thing called love, was something that he had felt imperfectly for his son, for the woman he loved, for his one true friend, for his parents and for his country, and that he had cherished it all the days of his life.

He opened his eyes and surveyed the veld surrounding him and still he walked on...and on...and on...until something within him gave way and his world tilted, suddenly off kilter, and he sank to his knees as though in silent prayer.

He placed his hands on the ground in front of him and, once on all fours, became convinced that his hands had turned into paws. This time he braved it and looked down at the end of his arms. He was very surprised to find hands. Human hands. His hands.

He looked at his hands in absolute wonder.

Why not an animal?

Why a man?

What made a man a man?

The answer came to Emil as a story that unfurled itself in his mind. He saw his birth in Durban, South Africa, his childhood on the BSAP outpost at the foot of the Matopos Hills, his adolescence at the Selous School for Boys, his adulthood running The Organization of Domestic Affairs. He saw the people who had made up his life: his parents, Johan and Gemma Coetzee; the women he had known and loved (in his way), Marion Hartley, Kuki Sedgwick and Maryvonne de Rusbridger; his son, Everleigh Reginald Coetzee; his friends, Courteney Smythe-Sinclair, Lord Ashtonbury, and Clement Rutherford; his in-laws, Reginald and Dorothea Sedgwick. His story was so detailed that it even incorporated Scott Fitzgerald, Walter Musgrave, Lili and her light-brown baby boy, Mr. Bartleby, Master Archie, Master Duthie, and other teachers from the Selous School for Boys...Spokes Moloi, Michael Meredith, and Daisy...Eunice and Mbongeni Masuku and their son who was going to be a doctor someday...Vida, The Coloured de Villiers Boy, Rosamond Pierce...Sibonubuhle Mthethwa and the patients and nurses at the ICU. It even included the woman he had met on his last day at The Organization, Saskia Hargrave, because she had wanted to write his story.

What makes a man a man is his life's story. In the story of Emil's life there were the things that he wanted to be known and there were the things that he wanted to remain hidden. In his own mind, his story presented itself in an objective but empathetic style that had been kind to him even where he felt a less forgiving lens would have been best. Thankfully, it unfurled itself in a linear chronology with a beginning, middle, and end that made everything neat and tidy with no loose ends.

And yet, certain images lingered:

A wild wind making the elephant grass sing and swoon before it kissed his face.

A foxtrot promenade and the taste of lukewarm lime cordial.

A hurricane lamp glowing on a newly formed friendship.

A warm piece of an animal's heart that forever became a part of him.

A girl with a blue-and-white scarf, skating gracefully on thin ice.

A young woman watching and listening to the green-blue waters of the Indian Ocean.

A woman with a tropical scent kissing him and kissing him and kissing him and taking from him something that he did not mean to give.

A hand trembling with trepidation as it held a newly born baby boy, the most perfect creature in all of God's creation.

And, of course, there were loose ends.

There was the dark, gray, concrete room with its naked lightbulb, forever drip, drip, dripping tap and the man with blood on his hands, and there was the end of the narrative that made sense of these things.

———◆———

First we must study how colonisation works to *decivilize* the coloniser, to *brutalize* him in the true sense of the word, to degrade him, to awaken him to buried instincts, to covetousness, violence, race hatred and moral relativism
    —*Aimé Césaire, "Discourse on Colonialism'*

Second, facts are not created equal: the production of traces is always also the creation of silences
    —*Michel-Rolph Trouillot, Silencing the Past*

To put it differently, any historical narrative is a particular bundle of silences
    —*Michel-Rolph Trouillot, Silencing the Past*

ACKNOWLEDGEMENTS

———◆———

Many thanks to the excellent Jenefer Shute and the brilliant fiction editors at Penguin Random House South Africa—Fourie Botha and Catriona Ross—for making the production of this second novel an education and a joy. Frieda le Roux, for your tireless work and for injecting much-needed humor into the business of being a writer, I thank you.

Another big thank you to Gretchen Van der Byl for, yet again, creating a cover that so perfectly captures the story.

To Tsitsi Dangarembga, Diane de Beer, Jenny Crwys-Williams, Sue Grant-Marshall, Mulalo Nethanani, Kate Sidley and Jennifer Malec, whose championing of *The Theory of Flight* gave me the courage to venture forth again, much appreciation.

For all their support, I'd like to thank Dumiso Dabengwa, Nkul Tleane, Wandile Mabanga, Tara Thirtyacre, Dashen Naicker, Angelina Mlotshwa, Jessica Powers, Vivian Ncube, Pedzi Mavhurere, Janet Dabengwa, Gugulethu Mhlanga and Praxie Dzangare. A special thanks to Jess Auerbach for reading an early version of this novel and giving me her honest feedback.

To my cousins all over the world, I thank you for all the promise held in this generation of the Ndlovu clan, which is what keeps me going.

For all the dreams that were and all the dreams to come, a great many thanks to my remarkable grandparents, Sibabi Charles Ndlovu and Kearabiloe Mokoena-Ndlovu, and my awesome mother, Sarah Nokuthula Ndhlovu.

Last but definitely not least, I owe a great debt of gratitude to Mrs. Joan Madonko for instilling in me a critical love of literature that has served me well on this journey. I cannot thank you enough for your advocacy and for your sterling example. You are much appreciated.

Siphiwe Gloria Ndlovu

Siphiwe Gloria Ndlovu

CPSIA information can be obtained
at www.ICGtesting.com
Printed in the USA
JSHW020352100122
21889JS00001B/1